FURNITURE SLIDERS

FURNITURE SLIDERS

A MAX CALDER SPY-FI MYSTERY

THE BUREAU ARCHIVES TRILOGY
BOOK 1

ALEXANDER BENTLEY

CHARLTON MANOR PUBLISHING

First published in the United States in 2025 by Alexander Bentley and Charlton Manor Publishing
First Alexander Bentley paperback edition 2025
-oOo-
Copyright © Alexander Bentley 2025

Hardback: ISBN 979-8-9986383-5-0
Paperback: ISBN 979-8-9986383-0-5
eBook: ISBN 979-8-9986383-3-6
Kindle Edition: 979-8-9986383-1-2

Library of Congress Control Number: 2025907649

Printed and bound by Kindle Direct Publishing and Ingram Spark

For Lucinda

The fact that you can only do a little is no excuse for doing nothing.

JOHN LE CARRÉ

OFFICE OF
TEMPORAL ANOMALIES
ORDO IN TEMPORE
AND
STRATEGIC
INTELLIGENCE

1947

CHAPTER 1
MISSING MEMORIES

The Mirror doesn't reflect - it remembers. And when it remembers you, it never forgets. I didn't know it at the time, but I was about to find out.

The cloudy, overcast sky hung drearily over New York City like a smothering veil, daring anyone to head out without an umbrella. It hadn't rained in days - unless you counted the nearly endless, incessant drizzle that accompanied the fog most mornings and evenings. I nursed my second whiskey at The Old Crow, a hangover from the old speakeasy days and an ideal bar for me tucked behind a shop on 10th Avenue. Dim, smoky, and filled with jazz on the weekends. I watched the regulars, as I did most days. Hell's Kitchen was a melting pot of various types. The cigarette smoke lingered in the air from one particularly rowdy table. The men here were equal parts tough and typically respectful, being largely retired officers, navy men, or prizefighters. But when the beer and bourbon flowed, they would eventually become more animated.

That was how they spoke now, swinging their mugs here and there, demanding refills, and generally being an annoying bunch. The biggest of the men sat near the window, his arm resting against the sill and his overgrown beard bouncing in a jolly fashion as he laughed. He was recounting how he used to be the most prized fighter of the lot down on the corner of 34th - a story no doubt embellished slightly by the liquor but still grounded in an element of truth.

I stared out the window once more as best I could from my bar seat, glancing up and down the empty street. It was nearing dusk, and the drizzle would soon begin - impaling itself upon the world in that unwanted fashion like a drunkard upon his wife. I handled mine well, but some of these men did not - just like now.

I watched as she entered the bar, the door swinging shut behind her with a rusty squeak. As she walked in, every man's head at the table turned toward her, the big burly man turning slightly redder in the cheeks than he had been already. I couldn't dismiss their sentiment, either. This woman was stunning.

She held a cig in one hand, her dark clothes blending seamlessly into the musky environment of the bar. Her chin was sharp, but her lips were gentle, red, and alluring. She had the face of a woman who knew who she was - confident and unafraid of the men around her.

I grinned to myself as I took a sip of my drink. I liked to make bets with myself, and more often than not, I cashed in on them. Her auburn hair was a distraction for the drunken crew at the table, but not for me.

I could tell from her demeanor that she was accustomed to environments like this - though the red scarf around her neck was of a quality and cleanliness that suggested she was no lady of the night. Rather, her long trench coat hinted at a woman in a particular profession, like the one I had been in many years ago. Or so I thought… I wasn't quite sure. My memories had become fuzzy recently, and I squinted as I watched her. Was she a federal agent? Or simply a local detective? No, she couldn't have been local - her face didn't scream New York, nor did her polite accent as she slid onto a barstool several seats away from mine and ordered a drink.

"Gin and tonic." Her voice was delicate and foreign.

"You speak Spanish?" I asked her, motioning to her face in a jovial fashion.

She turned toward me, her face masked in the shadows as she tilted her head slightly. She was much shorter than I was, probably no more than five and a half feet tall, with green eyes that flashed in the artificial yellow lights as if covered in flecks of gold. She looked me up and down for a moment as if sizing me up against the men around here. Now, here was the test for her - could she tell I was different from these frequent attendees of the drunk and sometimes disorderly kind? Her gloved hands tightened ever so slightly around the glass the bartender had delivered, and I could tell she was thinking of how to address me. She smirked slightly as I watched, her red lips thinning as she spoke.

"Yes, I do. But you should already know that Max." she said. "You might have aged quite a bit, but at least you're still as perceptive as ever."

"And who are you to know who I am?"

She didn't answer my question right away. Instead, she leaned forward, taking another sip of her gin and tonic, her lips pressing against the glass and fogging up the edges as she withdrew her mouth.

"I need a man who can move without being seen, and I know you're that man, Max. You were always the best one of us."

"Best of who?"

"Why don't we talk somewhere else? Somewhere more private, maybe..." She glanced at the men at the table, who were clearly egging on one of the more handsome-looking fellows, jeering at him until he worked up the courage to approach her.

I nodded, and we stood. This woman was fascinating, more so than any of the other regulars - and oddities - I'd observed that week. People-watching was a fascination of mine, and I confess she had me intrigued. So, I followed her out the door, watching the men at the table almost stand to protest before they saw me. They knew who I was, or at least some part of the story. It was 1947 now, and the war had ended. But even so, they knew what had happened during the war before I showed up here, and they had heard the rumors of my involvement with the government during that time. So drunk as they might have been, they left us alone.

We walked down the dusty, shadowy street. Night had settled in - the moon's luminous glow shining through the dirty clouds, casting occasional rays through the gray and monotonous cityscape. It reminded me of a movie I had seen. Of all the gin joints in all the towns in all the world, she walks into mine. That spelt trouble in the movie, and I had that feeling right now.

"Care to tell me who you are and how you know me?"

She turned her head slightly as we walked, the light from the lamps reflecting off her auburn hair. It was frustrating walking here - I couldn't care less if this was some trap or if some enemy I'd made in the past had come back to haunt me. What I did know, however, was that I'd seen this woman before. The more we walked together, the more certain I became, but I still couldn't figure it out. Had she been some old fling from many years ago, when I still worked for the government? I furrowed my brows. Who had I worked for back then, anyway? What was the name of that God-forsaken organization…was it…

"The Bureau. You know me from The Bureau." Her voice sliced through my thoughts like a knife, dispelling the fog that had clouded my mind. I stopped in my tracks. That name did ring a bell - that was the organization I had worked for, wasn't it? So why was I so damn forgetful?

"How do I know you from there? I don't ever remember working with you. Hell, don't even know your name."

"I figured as much, Max. You've forgotten again."

"Forgotten what, exactly?"

She pulled out of her coat an item which she had concealed expertly. I hadn't even noticed it was there - a thin, black folder with several papers inside.

"These will help you remember," she said as she handed me the folder. "Read through these, then you meet me at the Crow tomorrow, one o'clock. Don't be late."

I took the folder, my fingers brushing against her gloved hand as I did. Something about her felt so familiar, yet as I watched her walk away, her face fading into the shadows of the darkening street between the dim lamps, I still couldn't remember her. I flipped open the folder, thumbing through the papers to figure out exactly who this mysterious lady was and why she intrigued me so much.

What was even more interesting was why I didn't feel the need to be on guard around her. I paused, a face on one of the papers staring back at me. This face - I might not have remembered her, but I remembered this man well.

I read the name hastily scribbled beneath his picture, though I already knew too well what it would be - Dr. Emil Krane, one of the many scientists who had worked at the Bureau. It made sense now; that was the name that had been muddling around in my mind this whole time I'd been cooped up in Hell's Kitchen - the Bureau was the organization I had worked for. But why could I remember so little about the organization? Each time I tried, it felt as if I were dunked beneath a murky lake, struggling to make out the fuzzy features swimming lazily below the water's surface.

Krane had worked there. Though I had never known the man closely, I remembered he held a position of high esteem within the organization. But did I know him, anyway? I squinted up at one of the streetlights. Several small moths fluttered lightly around the lamp, fascinated by the existence of the light source they had discovered.

Suddenly, the light from the streetlamp became brighter, shining toward the edges of my vision, light streaking itself into the very corners of my gaze. I blinked and looked away - then blinked again. The light didn't disappear from my vision; it simply remained, emanating itself comfortably into my sight. Suddenly, I felt a blinding pain in the back of my head.

"Damn - " I muttered as I sank to my knees, not of my own accord. "What the hell?"

The light was gone now, and so was the pain. The world whirled around me, dizzying. I felt like a man prescribed glasses who suddenly finds himself without them. Shapes began to form out of the mist. Noise filled my ears, and I felt myself drifting away from the street where I had been standing, as if being sucked into some spatial vortex. I heard voices. I was no coward, but a spine-tingling sensation crept up the back of my neck as an icy cold enveloped me.

———

I watched as the street faded around me, replaced by the blurry images of a cavernous, underground room. A man stood in front of me, his face alight with eager envy, a lust I had never seen before. I heard him speaking, his wild eyes gleaming.

"Log begins. I am recording this on…" He paused, glancing at the watch on his wrist. "I am recording this on September 19th, 1945, at 21:00. Let the record show that the Mirror has created a temporal anomaly - some sort of echo chamber. The thunderstorm seems to have an amplifying effect here…not sure what I'm seeing, yes - yes, it seems like a face.

"I think it's the face of Max Calder. The abnormality - his time displacement seems to be greater than regularly noted. The subject doesn't appear to see me… at least no reactions on the subject's part. I can't tell whether his reference point here is greater or lesser within the framework. Oh, and now he's fading…"

His voice trailed off, and I felt myself whirling, spinning as if I were a speck of dirt cast down the drain of a gigantic tub. My vision began to fade. But it wasn't over.

CHAPTER 2
THRESHER TO THEO

The wind cut through Rosyth Naval Dockyard like a rusty razor blade, brutalizing any object - living or otherwise - that stood in its way. Beyond the perimeter of the base, the sea rolled incessantly like some living, breathing beast. It rumbled, angry with the world, ready to throw off any sailor or navigator brave enough to attempt to conquer it. Lightning cracked, and thunder roared viciously, echoing across the landscape.

Deep underground, inside the bunker where wind, rain, and lightning didn't bother them, six men and one woman gathered in a room that should never have existed.

Steel walls lined with lead surrounded them. There was only one entrance, reinforced countless times with more metal than the weight of a small elephant. A single viewing pane was smeared with ash, its edges rimmed with frost.

At the very center of the room, slightly raised, was the pedestal for what these men were tasked with attempting to understand, comprehend, and decipher.

It stood nearly eight feet tall, shaped like a standing mirror. Its surface was glassy, and though it looked like a mirror, rarely did it reflect anything at all. That was what made these scientists so dedicated to the mirror, which is why their superiors had assigned them to this project. But it had no fancy name or beautiful term to endear it. Instead, these men - and the one woman - just called it the Mirror.

They stood in front of it, watching intently. The lead engineer, whom I recognized as none other than Krane himself, clasped his hands behind his back. His face was half-lit by the arc lamp which hung low, swaying occasionally as if pulled by some unknown force. One of the men behind him held a recorder into which Krane spoke.

"March 3rd, 1943, at 23:32. Our initial test of the Mirror will now commence. I will relay my findings as this experiment progresses."

He motioned toward one of the men who stood next to him - a slightly balding man wearing a white lab coat who stood by the console. The console was how these men operated the Mirror, at least from what I could tell - a jumble of wires trailed from it, connecting to a cylindrical device at the very end of a three-foot-tall pole.

"Yes, Dr. Krane?"

"Pulse it. Hold the window. No more than three seconds."

The man's fingers moved swiftly over the console, and the device pulsated, its energy wavering. The small cylinder began to glow softly, emitting a gentle hum. The light above flickered, and static hissed from the monitor speakers. Gradually, the noises began to fade, as if hiding from the presence of something unknown that frightened them.

The surface of the Mirror cracked open. It didn't look like a regular crack - all jivy, dancing in the dim light; it resembled a spatial tear or rip. It was like watching a map fold into itself in a perfect crack formation, almost indescribable. I watched, my mind confused; I wasn't quite sure where I was or who I had been the moment before, and the men before me didn't appear to recognize that I was watching.

Instead, we all stared into the Mirror as the low hum from it grew, the tear widening. The air around it started to warp and bend, slowly at first. Several of the men backed away, their faces alight with terror, blood draining from their already pale skin, the only symptom of what they saw in front of them.

Dr. Krane, however, remained standing. He watched, his eyes focused on the very center of the device. It whirred even faster. Several of the men around him screamed, clasping their hands in front of their eyes as if to shield themselves from the device.

"God damn it! Damn it all, it won't stop!" One man dug his fingers into his eye sockets until they almost began to bleed.

Krane, however, stood motionless. His face illuminated by a fervor that I had never seen before - a desire that could only be matched by a man not only dedicated to his wife but obsessed - obsessed enough to kill.

Who really knows how much time passed as the pulse continued? Objects near the Mirror began to slide, almost as if they were smoothly moving toward the device. Yet, when I focused on each object, it remained fixed in its place. It was an illusion, but also reality - my mind buckled as I tried to comprehend what was happening.

Finally, Krane spoke.

"Shut it down."

The command went unanswered by the man at the console. He stood there, his balding head gleaming in the light of the Mirror, smiling wider and wider as he watched it.

Noticing his colleague's state, Krane walked toward the console himself. He shoved the man aside, his fingers deftly gliding over the surface of the buttons to shut down the pulsating cylinder.

The crack in the Mirror disappeared, and the room fell silent.

"W-what... where am I?" one of the men asked, his eyes blank and white. He appeared older now, his face more wrinkled than before. But Krane ignored him, only speaking into the recorder.

"The test of the Mirror has commenced. Several key factors to note: a smell of iron in the air, which will require additional research. The quantum link between our console and the Mirror has been established. Additional tests will be easier. Entanglement appears to be sufficient to control the device in its intermediary stages, though additional runs will be needed to determine the causality of this effect. Project Black Thresher, however, seems to be a success. End log."

I finally snapped out of my stupor, grimacing as I looked around. Where the hell was I? The world before me, which had been as vivid and real as if I had really been there, seemed to dissipate like mist in the wind.

———

I was standing in the street again, the darkness fading, replaced with a rising sun in the far distance, above the tops of the buildings down the street. What the hell had I just witnessed?

Shaking my head, I walked down the street, stumbling several times as I regained my footing. I was still holding that folder, soaked with dew but still legible, which I hurriedly stuffed beneath my coat. I reached into my pocket, feeling around until I felt the reassuring grip on the watch I had kept on me for years. I pulled it out to check the time: just past 0600 hours, meaning I must have been there for at least the majority of the night. It had been late when we'd left The Old Crow, but not that late. I was hungry. I deposited my watch back into my pocket, shaking my hand a bit - I was stiff.

Looking up and down the street again, I noticed a few passersby, but not too many. At least one of them should have seen a man standing there for so long, yet nobody seemed perturbed by my appearance or sudden action. Eventually, I stopped at the side of a busier street and tossed a few coins to the disheveled man behind the hot dog stand.

"Yeh can get two for that, 'n a drink," he said.

"Alright," I responded, nodding. "Give me that, then. I'm starving."

"Yeh got it, ace." He fished two hot dogs out of his cart, slapped them together, grabbed a bottle of Coke, and handed me my food.

I nodded curtly and continued down the street, my mind wandering. I'd have to take a closer look at the file again, but I wasn't ready to do that here - not after what had happened. It was a freakish situation, to say the least, but I now acutely remembered those memories as if I had recalled them often - only forgotten until my latest lapse jogged my mind. I began to remember even more about Krane and the organization I had worked for.

Though it was still foggy, little glimpses of that project - and the other projects we had all been tasked with containing - slipped into my mind. Project Black Thresher, especially, had a familiar ring to it. I didn't remember much, but I knew that it had been the epitome of what the Bureau had been formed to deal with.

From what I recalled, the Bureau dealt with much of the advanced weaponry that government spies had begun to discover during the latter years of World War II. Before I had been approached by them, I had worked in the Secret Intelligence Service - MI6 - that much I remembered. I vaguely began to recall the shadowy man who had approached me one day. Though I couldn't see his face in my mind's eye, his words rang clear.

"Max Calder," he had said, his voice deep and warm, tainted with what I now know had been a small touch of admiration. "We think your talents would suit our new organization."

When he had explained the general role I would have with the Bureau, of course, I accepted. I'd always been interested in these sorts of roles - fascinated by blueprints, ciphers, and, most importantly, the people who created them. I had jumped at the chance to dive into that damn field and done so headfirst, just as I was doing now.

As I thought, I expertly retraced my steps toward The Old Crow - slowly meandering while I pondered, but never losing my direction. It was a few hours before she had asked me to meet her, but I had these folders to go over. I pressed open the door, the hinges creaking as I did, and walked down the center of the dimly lit room to my regular spot at the bar.

"The usual," I said, nodding to the bartender.

He curtly handed me my drink, a brief nod accompanying the whiskey he slid toward me. It was well known by now that I was not particularly talkative, so he left me alone, unlike the other regulars who frequented the bar. A few sips later and with a cig lit, I flipped the folder open once again. It had begun to rain heavily outside, the first time in ages. As I listened to the rain hitting the pavement like gunfire, I stared at the words on the page.

Emil Krane. The papers behind this one detailed his work over the years, along with mentions of Black Thresher, though many of these were heavily redacted. What I did read, however, was shocking enough. According to these documents, Krane had disappeared after 1945 in some experimental incident, a scientific blunder that left dozens dead. It involved Black Thresher, but any information beyond that had been censored.

What the documents revealed, however, was that Krane himself had now resurfaced - alive. According to these papers, he was working with the Soviets. As I read, I could hear the regulars chatting behind me. I always kept one ear open, and as such, I noticed the moment the atmosphere shifted. The voices paused slightly, becoming uncomfortable. The rain grew slightly louder, and the creak of the door heralded a new visitor. I heard heels stepping lightly on the old floor of the Crow. I smiled slightly, waiting. A few moments later, I felt her slide into the seat next to me.

"Hello again, Max."

"Can I get a name now? If you're someone I've known before, I haven't remembered yet."

"You can't remember yet?" she asked, her voice alluring like smoke curling from a cigarette burned to the tip. "Usually, it doesn't take you this long… I'd guess you're getting worse."

"Well?"

"You've known me as Artemis."

"What are we doing here with this file, Artemis?"

"That's a good question. If you've read the files, you'll know that Dr. Krane is working for the Soviets now. He previously worked for us, our organization, after defecting from the Nazis. But now, he's turned up with some extremely powerful backers, and our intelligence suggests he's had these men protecting him… funding him for a while."

I nodded. "Where is he?"

"Vienna."

Of course, he would be in Vienna. That city was familiar to me, though I didn't remember the specifics of what I had done there. Where the lines between East and West blurred like a motorcar behind a blanket of rain, where spies traded secrets for cigarettes and corpses for a bit more. That damn city was notorious in our circles, a place that seemingly had no end of back alleyways, dark secrets, and scandalous affairs. When you wanted to disappear, you headed to Vienna… and when those searching wanted to find you, they sent people like me.

"Why am I involved? This some sort of job for me?"

"How much do you remember about the Bureau, Max?"

"Not much. Just that I used to work for them. Did they do something to me to mess up my head before I left?"

"You never really left, Max," she replied, a quick flash of something in her eyes making them sad. "You disappeared. For a long while, we thought you were dead."

"Dead?"

"In those documents I've given you, you read about the incident that caused Krane to go AWOL? It happened on September

19th, 1945. Krane was working on a project called the Mirror, but he got too cocky - pulsed it too hard - and shattered it. Dozens of men died that day, and everything went haywire. You were there, on base at Rosyth, and disappeared like a goddamn ghost. Our intelligence listed you as a casualty until a few months ago."

I listened intently, but my mind was racing. September 19th, 1945 - I recognized that date from what I had seen last night as I was reading the documents. That was the date Krane had mentioned, the date he had seen my face appear and then fade away again.

"Alright, sweetheart. So, what exactly does the Mirror do?"

"Not too sure. I left the Bureau about a year after the Rosyth incident, but from what I can gather through my network, it was a device designed to create temporal displacements and manipulate the fabric of time."

"You serious?"

"There were rumors that the Mirror let you see through time, but it was much more than that. It could even let you alter time before it was destroyed. It could let agents - like you and me - slip through time for short periods without altering the timeline itself. At least, that was what we initially thought."

"I'm guessing that's not what happened."

She ran her fingers through her auburn hair before speaking. "Not only that, no. See, people like you and I - the device did something to us. It's how we got our nickname…sliders."

Sliders. That term rang a bell in my head. I'd heard it before. I sat still for a second, gathering my thoughts.

"You still haven't answered my question," I said, tapping the folder she'd given me. "What's my role in this? What do you want from me?"

"The Bureau contacted me a month back…took me that long to track you down. They want us to take care of Krane. He's gone rogue, and it's possible he could build some of the same tech for the Soviets. We can't let that happen."

"And you think I'm your guy?"

She smiled slowly and turned to face me, her eyes flitting over my face. "I think you're the man who's left…and besides, once you start remembering, you'll recall your previous experiences with the Mirror."

"This means I have to go back. I don't know how much I want to remember."

"Do you really have a choice, Max? You know how I said you'd forgotten? That's what happens when you spend too much time close to the Mirror - near it, working with it, going through it. The Soviets can't get that tech."

I sighed and set down my empty whiskey glass. "OK. I'm in."

She nodded. "I'll be in contact and give you all the information we have on Krane's whereabouts. Oh, and one more thing - they're watching."

"Who?"

"Everyone, anyone - even the reflections. Just watch your back."

With that, she stood, walking lightly toward the door. She pushed it open, turned the corner, and vanished into the pouring rain. I finished my drink, crushed my cig, and stood to leave as well. I didn't remember much, but I wagered that I was about to find out more.

The next few days were a blurry set of recurring dreams, fading memories, and memories replacing themselves anew in my mind. I had nothing much to do until she contacted me - Artemis, that was - and so I spent my time gathering intel and meeting old friends. The memories that had begun to spring back into my mind were ones of my past life, my work as an intelligence officer, and, later, a Bureau spy.

The first man I contacted was Theo Withers, an old British pal of mine I'd known during my time at the Bureau. I'd met him on countless occasions to exchange information. He worked for the British Special Operations Executive, and our organizations had maintained a friendly relationship during the war.

So I dialed his number from a hotel room I was holed up in. I took Artemis's advice and was more than cautious with where I stayed and always watched my back. But this, I figured, was too important to pass up on. While I waited for her to reach back out, I needed information, and Withers was the kind of man who always had information. I waited as the line rang and was all too pleased when I heard his jovial voice on the other end.

"'Ello?"

"This Theo?"

"An' who's asking?"

"It's Calder."

"Holy mother of - you must be joking! Is that really Raven in the land of the living? Intel sources said you died in some rogue operation gone wrong, n' I'll confess, I'm glad they was wrong."

I chuckled. The man was clearly happy enough to hear my voice - so much so he used my code name. I hadn't heard that name in ages; I preferred using aliases rather than code names, and it brought a flood of memories rushing back to me.

"Well, I'm not out of the game yet. Still not sure on all the details myself, but it's good enough that I'm here. Listen, Theo, I need some information."

"And here I thought you just wanted to catch up. Still playing spy, eh?"

"Yeah, more or less. Listen, what do you know about a device called the Mirror?"

"Eh? First I'm hearing of it. What's it do, reflect things?" He laughed, clearly unaffected by the term.

"Never mind," I replied. "What about a female spy - code name Artemis?"

"Oh, her now - now I do know enough about her...though I'd guess you know more than I do."

"Pretend I don't."

"Huh. Alright, if you say so. Her real name is Alicia - don't know her last or much more about her. She's as good as they come. Worked with the same organization you do. A few years back, she went rogue, disappeared from the organization, an' all but took up odd jobs for the next year or so. I've only heard whispers about her, but she's a brilliant spy. Why, you tracking her now? Friends to enemies…or maybe something more than friends?"

He chuckled, clearly amused by his own joke. I shook my head, annoyed but relieved at the same time - this was the same man I had known during the war. Theo hadn't changed at all.

"Thanks. And listen, Theo. You still have some contacts in Vienna, yeah?"

"What of it?"

"I may need your help; I have a job in Vienna."

"Ah, ya' old bastard. I'll do what I can. Always glad to help a friend, Raven." He laughed again, and I could tell he was all too pleased with his jabs.

"I'll be in touch."

CHAPTER 3
ALICIA RAYES

Her name was Alicia Inés Rayes. That was her real name, not a code name. She didn't care much if you knew her name, either. If she trusted you enough to know her real name, she knew you well enough that she was confident she could kill you if things went sour. It was a bitter, jaded way of looking at life, but she didn't care. She'd grown up in a bitter, jaded way - only taught empathy by her mother, but taught to distrust by life itself and everyone else.

Of course, her life hadn't always been that way. Back when she was growing up, she had run through the streets of Montevideo without a care in the world. Born in the battered, busy heart of Montevideo's Barrio Sur in 1917, Alicia was the child of two people who would have never normally crossed paths. It was possible that her life had been tumultuous from birth, though she didn't realize it until much later.

Her mother was hauntingly beautiful, like the ghost of a woman of royal blood - a Spanish exile, an anarchist by philosophy, a poet by trade, and a brilliant woman despite her proclivity for the simpler things in life. Maria Rayes loved to read, spoke more languages than she likely ever let on, and loved Montevideo as if she'd been born there. It was a city that was constantly evolving, constantly growing, and the source of many intellectuals from the surrounding countryside, something that Maria valued above all else. Alicia's first memories were those of her mother - a sweet, gentle touch, reading poetry together on the terrace, and tracing her fingers through her mother's auburn hair.

Alicia's father, on the other hand, was a different kind of ghost. A naval engineer for the Uruguayan government, he was a man who kept to himself more than he probably realized. As Alicia would later learn, he was a man with many connections, some of which had become his undoing. Although her mother was a scientist in her own right, her father was a man of method and the proper rulebooks. He knew how to design an intricate engine that worked, no matter the purpose or goal. At least, that was how Alicia remembered him - she remembered the times he had taught her Morse code, showed her how to tie knots, and carefully explained how the blueprints he drew would come to life as a ship months later.

But she only remembered him a little. Her father had vanished twelve years to the day after she had been born. Even though he had been a strict man who preferred not to speak when he thought, and preferred to think before he spoke, she had missed him often since. Despite only being present during her most formative years, he had been half of the puzzle needed to gift her the intellect she needed.

Her mother had given her beauty, while her father had given her a jaded worldview. Together, they had given her the ability to plan ahead, speak in half-truths, and convince those she spoke to that she spoke in full.

Though she'd never attended a formal school, her mother had taken it upon herself to teach Alicia everything, not just the basics of academics.

"Today, Alicia, you'll read Acté of Corinth by Dumas and explain to me what Lysander and Aristonicus represent within the literature."

"Yes, mother," she would respond, quickly grabbing the book and running to sit in her favorite chair, a faded armchair by the window that had been her father's perch of choice.

She'd sit there for hours, poring over the pages of the latest assignment her mother had given her while her mother cooked, cleaned, or read books herself. The two of them had little income, but the money from her father's navy pension, combined with her mother's new frugal ways, was enough for them to get by without any supplements.

Later, she would return to her mother, book in hand and eyes aglow, announcing that she was ready for a new assignment. This routine continued every school day, but as Alicia grew older, her distaste for the comfort and paternalistic life began to weigh down on her. It was then, of course, that her father's genetics began to take over. The stubbornness, the hard-headed nature, and the obsession with government affairs began to clash more with her mother's creative and visionary outlook on life, and the two of them grew slightly more distant.

It wasn't a distance of love or a lack of admiration on Alicia's part; they remained close whenever they spoke. It was, however, a general distaste for the simple life of Montevideo that eventually left Alicia with no other choice but to leave.

She had approached her mother one night, shortly after her eighteenth birthday, nervously tapping her hands on the table where her mother sat. Maria glanced up, smiled faintly, and motioned for Alicia to speak.

"Mother, I've made a decision finally."

Maria nodded, her face as blank as it could be, but there was a sadness in her eyes. "You'll go to New York?"

"I will. I wish I could stay, Mother - and I'll write whenever I can, but there's just nothing left here for me."

"I know. I still wish you wouldn't, but I can't stop you. Just… be careful. People out there are not like the ones here - they are cruel."

"I will."

By the end of 1935, she'd cast off the shackles of a life of thought and forged new documents, fully aware it was against her mother's wishes. She had left Uruguay, traveling to New York - the land with as many secrets as immigrants. Of course, that was what Alicia loved about the place. It was a bustling, growing city, populated by people of every type and from every corner of the world.

It was there, in the center of New York, that Artemis had found her first real job. She'd read the papers every day, checking listings for work, attending interviews whenever possible - until she finally landed a job that, unbeknownst to her, would eventually change her life.

"Ahh, Alicia, is it?" The man, Mr. Simmons, peered over his glasses, his balding head gleaming in the dim light of his office. "Well, you're not bad lookin', but that won't help you in this industry. Can you speak?"

"I learn fast," she responded, and she saw the man's face shift slightly. It was in that moment she knew she had secured the job. She began the next day under the alias Elena Vázquez, as Simmons had suggested. Their work was dangerous - the Second Sino-Japanese War had just begun, and the radio station that employed her acted as much as a machine of propaganda as it did a news agency. She quickly found this out, and even though it was never admitted to the public, each message she delivered was carefully crafted by shadowy figures - powerful men aiming to control public opinion on events before they even unfolded. For Alicia, this was the dream. She was eager for more, for something that actually mattered, and it was clear that Simmons and his fellow journalists, along with their backers, were hell-bent on such a mission.

The men and women who listened loved her, but none of them realized her true nature. To the eager listeners of the radio, she was known as Elena. To the allies and enemies across North and South America, her voice was synonymous with clarity. It was her rich and alluring voice that carried the messages these powerful men wanted to share, and because of this, she learned how to weaponize the truth to an extent she had never believed possible. She often found herself thinking back to those times her father had explained how his blueprints didn't just guide the machines he built but society as a whole. She couldn't help but think that she was doing the same now - carefully crafting a blueprint on which society operated.

She advanced quickly, learning new techniques and mannerisms, while slowly taking on more roles within the realm of audio. Unbeknownst to her, her talents were quickly recognized by those who watched, and even those who listened. Her flawless Spanish, French, and English, her way with words, and her ability to lie caught the interest of some of society's more powerful men, who quickly caught onto her tremendously rare abilities. She was smart - they knew as much - and she was valuable far beyond her current role in radio communications.

It was 1939 when they approached her. As she waited for a cab, ready to return to her small apartment in lower Manhattan, a voice suddenly spoke up beside her, as if the man standing there had materialized out of thin air. He was a short fellow yet he commanded a presence that instantly caught her attention.

"'Ello, Alicia."

"Do I know you?"

"Not yet, but I know you. I work for a certain organization very interested in your talents."

"What talents?"

"None that you know of yet, certainly, but you've caught my eye as a very unique person."

"Apologies," she had responded, "but I don't even know who you are or who you work for. Why should I be listening to you?"

"Well, I work for a government - the government, rather. As for my name, well, you might learn that later if you're good. For now, you can call me Intrepid. But if I know you well enough, you'd be thrilled to work more closely with the men in power, wouldn't you?"

"What do you mean?"

The man dug into his pocket and pulled out a cigar before continuing. "Well, Alicia, I've listened to your radio show. Directed some of it, even. I'm one of those men. And you, well, you don't strike me as the type of woman who limits her ambitions to such mundane tasks as you've committed yourself to."

"So, what are you offering?"

"I'm offering a job - one that puts your talent of bending the truth to far better use than some off-the-beat radio show. Espionage, Alicia. And you'll be the best - I can promise you that. I'll be back for your decision."

Without further discussion, the man she would later come to know as William Stephenson, the man she only knew then as Intrepid, sauntered away.

Initially, she had delayed. Though she felt a longing in the pit of her stomach, she had been cautious, researching and learning as much as she could. Intrepid, however, was patient - he alone had the power to decide whether she became a spy or not, and he was convinced of her talents.

It was the summer of 1940 when she finally accepted his offer and was whisked away to Camp X in Canada. Her job at the radio station was scrapped, her alias was killed off in a freak car accident, and the only woman outside of the government who knew Alicia was alive was her mother - at Alicia's request, of course. Intrepid had been hesitant to oblige at first, but the man was somewhat obsessed with the woman he believed to be a once-in-a-generation talent within the business where he was one of the most influential figures.

So, she attended Camp X. It was the place to be if you were a spy or if you wanted to become one. Just outside of Whitby, Ontario, the camp was officially known as Special Training School 103. But to Alicia, it was known as something else - the brainchild of none other than Intrepid himself, who taught subjects of the utmost importance.

She'd arrived on a warm summer day, the sun shining in the Canadian wilderness. Located at the edge of Lake Ontario on the northwestern shore, Camp X was nothing special in terms of location or appearance. She'd unloaded her single suitcase, rummaging around as she organized her things, wondering if she'd made a mistake coming here.

As she soon found out in the coming days, however, attending Camp X was the best decision she'd ever made. This was a camp that finally allowed her to find her purpose. As a new agent in training, she learned every skill imaginable, and her clever mind picked up on these new techniques and information instantly. From silent killing to sabotage, she was instructed by many excellent spies, military commanders, and tacticians - and, of course, Intrepid himself.

It was during his classes that she paid the most attention, listening carefully to every word spoken and memorizing it, practicing every technique, and adhering to every bit of advice. It's said that great minds recognize each other, and there is no doubt that later in her life, Alicia's biggest influence would remain this man. After all, he was one of the greatest spies of all time, and she understood this perfectly well.

She remained one of the most talented students - her calm demeanor under fire while training and almost inhuman instincts earned her the codename Artemis. It was given by Intrepid himself one day after training.

"I think I've finally figured out a code name for you, Alicia," he said, munching on a sandwich as he sat on the central lawn next to her and several other students.

"What's that?"

"Artemis."

"Why?"

"Why not? It fits perfectly. Artemis was the Greek huntress, the goddess of the moon, and the guardian of secrets. It suits you well, doesn't it?"

"I'm not so sure," she responded, lying back on the warm grass and staring up at the sky. "But if you think so, I think it works."

And the code name had stuck, though she was no guardian of secrets - she was a collector of them. Training passed quickly, and Artemis failed no classes. After she aced the school and learned everything Intrepid could teach her and then some, she was recruited quickly into the special unit that only the highest echelons of the government knew about, running operations from Lisbon to Berlin. Casablanca, Marseille, London, Montevideo - you name the city, and she'd most likely been there on a mission.

She traveled the globe at the behest of none other than Intrepid himself, for whom she had worked at the time. However, at the request of several particularly powerful men in the British government, she was transferred out from under the command of Intrepid and placed in a new and upcoming organization focused on revolutionary technologies. Perhaps Intrepid had spoken too highly of her, or perhaps she had simply caught the attention of Elspeth Moreau herself.

Though Artemis did not know the reason, she quickly found herself excited about the new prospects that this organization held. The war dealt with espionage, but Artemis had gained an almost unhealthy obsession with knowledge and the pursuit of new skills from her mother. Although she had no personal say in it, she relished the chance to be part of a new organization such as the one she joined, which would later become known colloquially as the Bureau.

As 1942 had set in and her missions had grown ever more critical to the survival of not just the governments she represented, but the timeline as a whole, she'd met him. She knew it as soon as they'd met - there was something unique about the man. He didn't have that obvious flair of genius that men such as Intrepid had, and yet he continually managed to outsmart even the greatest enemies of their time. They had both been tracking the same scientist back then, and they'd met up while on the case. Of course, the two distrusted each other at first. It was only natural in their field of work, despite being part of the same organization.

"Bureau too? Why'd they assign you, doll?" he said in a rather condescending way, looking down at her. He towered over her, a full head taller.

"Maybe you hadn't noticed, but there hasn't been any progress made here as of yet," she'd retorted, and the two had gone back to evaluating each other in silence.

"Well," he finally shrugged, "It's not your fault. I'll ask Hawthorne what the hell he was thinking when we're done with this mission. Name's Calder."

She hesitated, but finally answered. "My name is Artemis."

"Using code names, are we?" he grinned, lighting a cigarette and offering her one as he walked over to the window of the safe house where they were stationed, looking down at the street below. "Fine by me - in that case, you can call me Raven."

CHAPTER 4
BIER AND BISHOP

The phone rang suddenly, startling me from my stupor. I had been holed up in my hotel room for nearly a week now, simply waiting for her next move. During this time, I had been researching the best I could, but there was a limit to how much I could achieve when I had to be so cautious. According to Artemis, Krane's backers were some powerful men, and I couldn't risk them getting wind of my movements. So my research was limited - reading the magazines and news-papers, a few books I'd paid for the delivery boy to drop by my room, and the occasional premeditated and rehearsed phone call. It wasn't much, but it was the best I had.

I sprang up from my bed and checked the time - it was just after 0300. I realized I had been dozing in and out of a dream state before the ringing. I picked up the phone and held it to my ear.

"Ello?"

"Max."

It was Artemis, and her voice sounded urgent. I quickly grabbed a notepad and pen before responding. "What is it?"

"You need to travel to Vienna and get there yesterday. There's not much time left."

"What's going on?"

"From what we can tell, Krane is working on recreating his initial experiments with the Mirror - maybe even recreating the device itself. There have been strange things going on in Vienna: time displacements, events of individuals aging past the regular rate, and other weird occurrences."

"Then give me the information I'll need."

"That's another thing, Max. There's a high chance your hotel is being monitored and your phone is bugged. All I can give you is an address. Get there, and you'll know what to do."

"Alright," I sighed. I'd figured as much - it was no surprise that if Artemis and the Bureau had managed to find me, Krane's backers wouldn't be too far behind.

"Schwechater Bier."

I heard the line beep, and I put the phone down. I carefully sidled up to the window, pulling barely an inch of the curtain forward to see outside. My lights were off, and it was nighttime, so I didn't fear anyone seeing in at this hour. Still, it was better to be safe than sorry. A few cars were parked along the street, but otherwise, it was desolate. I wasn't going to be caught with my pants down, however, so quickly began to pack. I had instantly recognized the word - Schwechater Bier was a brand of beer produced in Schwechat, a city only a few miles outside of Vienna.

I figured that was what she had meant. Artemis most likely knew that I was quite an experienced drinker, and such names would quickly strike a tone in my head. However, it also meant that, on the off chance someone was listening to our line, she was confident that they wouldn't be able to figure out the extra "element" to it that I was sure she'd planned. It would never have been that simple, nor that straightforward. Still, I'd have to figure out that little puzzle she had given me on the way; it seemed as if Krane was already making his move.

I grabbed my briefcase, which contained all my worldly possessions, opened the door to my hotel room, and headed out into the foggy night for Vienna. The journey would take at least ten days, but I was prepared.

I had more than enough money to buy a ticket, and ocean liners were leaving New York for the European coast almost every day. I waited by the docks, watching as the sunlight slowly illuminated the sky. The yard soon opened, and the hustle and bustle of the day grew louder as I waited. Men walked to and fro, working and chatting as if their lives would go on uninterrupted. I hoped they were right.

When the office opened, I was already at the door, ready to buy a ticket. It didn't take long, either - I still had my FBI license that the Bureau had provided me with, and a quick flash of that badge in the face of the stuttering attendant convinced him that yes, there were cabins still available on the SS Île de France, which would be sailing later that day. I paid my fees, lingered for a few hours, and finally boarded the ship as it prepared to depart.

———

The journey went by fast. Three days in, I had spent most of my time exercising on the ship's deck or holed up in my room thinking - or, of course, drinking whiskey at the bar more nights than not. My room was located at the far end of one of the passages, a delightful spot for privacy. Even better, many of the rooms next to mine were empty.

A map and guidebook of Vienna was supplied by one of the willing passengers I'd struck up a conversation with, and I finally began to understand what Artemis had meant. Flipping through the guidebook, I scoured the pubs and taverns, looking for any mention of Schwechater Bier. Soon enough, I found it. On one page of the book, a particular sentence caught my eye: Loos American Bar, "Famous for its international beer list," and, a little further in the paragraph, "Schwechater on tap." It was noted as the first cocktail bar in Vienna opened in 1908 and was apparently frequented by the likes of Orson Welles, Benjamin Britten and Cab Calloway.

I wasn't entirely sure - Schwechater was fairly common, but many bars had closed after the depression and the war. Still, it was worth a shot. Artemis should have known I'd catch the hint - order the brand, see what happens. I scribbled down the address in my notepad and prepared for my arrival in Europe. It was classic tradecraft.

Of course, I'd have to be careful - if any of Krane's men were tailing me, I'd need to dispose of them beforehand. Luckily, that opportunity came sooner rather than later. On the fourth night at sea, I was making my way back to my cabin from the bar when I noticed something. A burly man - tall, foreign, and with a five o'clock shadow - had been making conversation with another man at the bar. But as I stood up, he did too, positioning himself in front of me as I walked down the passage leading to my cabin.

It wouldn't have been abnormal for a man like this, especially in a drunken state, to do such a thing - yet I felt wary. I hadn't seen him before, which meant he must have been staying else-where on the ship. So why was he walking ahead of me in the direction of my room?

I slowed down slightly, watching him. The man didn't glance back, but I knew he could hear my footsteps. If he were after me, and this wasn't a coincidence, then - I halted. I saw him cock his head for a fraction of a second, then faltered and whirled around, fumbling as he reached for his pocket. That was all I needed to see. With a swift knee to his solar plexus, as he finally turned to face me, the man crumpled, his breath knocked out of him. The knife he had pulled from his pocket clattered to the floor.

Before he could regain his footing, I swiftly grasped the knife and pressed it against his throat.

"Why are you tailing me?"

He struggled, but my grip was firm. I watched as he coughed, regaining enough air to finally speak.

"You are making… a mistake."

"What mistake? If you know who I am, you know I won't hesitate to kill you, so don't try any bullshit with me."

His voice was thick with a Russian accent. "You sound American. You make trouble. You go to Vienna, they kill you there."

I smirked. He knew he didn't have to play games with me or beat around the bush, which meant that Krane and his allies already knew I was heading to Vienna. I had hoped to get the drop on them, but I knew this would happen. The man struggled slightly, pressing his neck against the knife.

"It will be dangerous for you, comrade. You - "

Thud. With a heavy strike, my fist struck the side of his jaw, and I felt his strength leave his body. It wouldn't do to dispose of him here, with the cleaning crew frequenting the hallways for their routine maintenance. Instead, I dragged his body carefully down the hallway, sliding his unconscious form into my room. Here, I could dispose of him quietly.

————

A day later, I landed in Le Havre, France. It didn't take more than a few hours to navigate to Paris, and hardly less than a day later, I found myself in Vienna after traveling through Switzerland by train. The journey took less time than I thought. Travel in Europe was obviously getting better.

The city was like a wounded aristocrat - still dressed in fine clothes but limping through the wreckage. Half of it lay in rubble, with bombed-out buildings, skeletal spires, and crumbling facades looming over displaced persons, widows, and shell-shocked veterans. Grand palaces and cathedrals, their once-majestic domes and stained glass shattered, stood like ghosts of imperial glory.

The black market thrived - cigarettes, coffee, stockings, morphine, even bread could either save you or get you shot, depending on who you handed it to. The currency was unstable, food was rationed, and warmth in winter was a luxury paid for in firewood or favors. Despite it all, Vienna in 1947 still held its strange allure. Candlelit cafés with cracked windows still served strong coffee and played Schubert or jazz on dusty phonographs. Men in frayed trench coats watched from doorways, and women with overly red lipstick laughed too loudly in the wrong corners of the city. Everyone had secrets. Everyone had a story.

Vienna was a haven for spies, both amateur and professional. The Soviets watched the Americans, the Americans watched the Soviets, the British kept lists, and the French drank more than enough red wine as they waited. There were double agents, rogue scientists, and former Nazis trying to disappear into the fog. People changed names as easily as they changed coats. A whispered tip could buy your life - or cost it.

The Central Railway Station was a melancholy crossroads, embodying a time when Europe was still trying to pick up the pieces of its shattered past. It still retained its grandeur, though it was now weathered and scarred by the ravages of war. The trains, with their worn exteriors and intermittent schedules, represented a fragmented system that had yet to fully heal. The quiet metallic screech of brakes, the rhythmic sound of trains pulling out, and the hurried footsteps of passengers moving through the terminal seemed to mirror the uncertainty of the time - an era suspended between the horrors of the war and the emerging Cold War.

There was a notable presence of military personnel from the occupying powers. Soviet, American, British, and French soldiers were common sights, stationed at key points throughout the station. Some wore military uniforms, while others were in civilian clothes, indicating the transition between war and peace. The political tension between the occupying powers was evident.

I understood why Krane and his backers had chosen Vienna as their base of operations. It was located solidly on the line right outside the Iron Curtain, and there was no limit to the accessibility it offered, either.

I believed I would find him here. But first, I needed to reach out to the source Artemis had given me, and I also had to contact Theo. It would be wise to change my outfit, considering the men who had been tracking me had undoubtedly reported all my movements to the Soviets.

After picking up a new set of clothes that seemed to fit in with the locals - a pair of jovial glasses, a striped shirt, and some khaki pants - I made my way to the Loos American Bar. It was late, with the sun casting a golden-red glow as it sank beneath the horizon. I figured this would be the perfect time to arrive. After generously tipping my taxi driver, I wandered into Loos. It was a cozy bar with ornate wooden ceilings, warm lighting, and a magnificent offering of drinks. Mirrors made it look bigger than it was. Making my way to the counter, I sat at one of the stools. The bar was fairly empty now, but it didn't surprise me - the depression had hit everyone hard, and the war had made things even worse. There would likely be no men here other than the kind who had more than enough to afford it, and the kind that cared far too little whether they could afford it or not.

One would be drowning his sorrow away, while the other would be squandering his money. Both were dangerous in their own way - the rich man would have connections, and the poor man would not care what connections you had.

But for me, this bar held a different quality.

"Was willst denn zum Trinken?"

The bartender had sidled up, his face smooth. Clearly, my disguise had worked a bit too well. As I'd been taught, disguises weren't only about clothing; they were about how a man carried himself. A man can make himself seem smaller, more frail, and as if he doesn't wish to live this life - or he can present himself as bold, imposing, and strong, with a limp in one leg that suggests a man of frayed countenance and bold history. At this point in my life, blending in with the people around me - adopting their general demeanor and making it my own - was second nature.

"Ah, I don't speak German - only English and French."

He cocked his head slightly and squinted his eyes, as if reassessing my nature. "My apologies, sir. What can I get you to drink?"

"Schwechater Bier."

He paused, then nodded curtly. "You'll be wanting to sit at the table near the rear, then. I'll bring Bishop."

Bishop. I should have known it would be Bishop. Though I'd never liked him, really, the man was absolutely a talented addition to any mission, and he had connections to the Bureau - he was a subcontractor, the kind of man who did the dirty work the organization didn't want connected to it.

Bishop was the code name chosen by this particular man, a former priest turned assassin, who carried a rosary full of cyanide beads. Soon enough, he seated himself beside me, his face just as I remembered it from one of the previous missions we'd worked together, though his teeth were slightly more yellowed.

His old face was wrinkled, and his hands calloused, but his attire was much the same as always. He wore a thin chain around his neck, to which a cross was attached. Beneath his coat, he wore a preacher's garb, and he held in his hands a rosary he carried almost everywhere. The reason? According to the men he preached to, it was because he was still a man of God, but I knew better. I knew each bead contained a heavy dose of cyanide, enough to kill a bull elephant if left long enough.

He smiled at me and extended his hand in greeting.

"If it isn't Max Calder - back from the dead so soon? Did you meet my Lord while you were there?"

"Cut the crap," I said, grinning. "We both know you're as much a man of the Lord as a street entertainer is a faithful wife."

He chuckled. "Alicia's been in contact with me. She told me all I need to know, an' I've got some plans already drawn up."

"Artemis?"

"Yeah, if that's what she's going by these days."

"It is," I nodded. Now that he'd mentioned it, that name sounded familiar - I'd known it before but must have forgotten.

"Well then, shall we get to work?"

"You going to fill me in on your plan?"

"Oh, you'll figure it out on the way," he said. "You've always been a smart enough guy."

"On one condition - I want Theo to come along as well."

"Theo Withers?"

"Yes, the one and only," I replied.

A slight flicker of annoyance crossed his face, but he nodded. "If you trust him, that's good enough for me."

"Let me make the call, then."

———

A few hours later, the three of us stood over a table in some shoddy, dimly lit kitchen where Bishop had stored his wares. The amount of killing goods here was impressive - an assortment of knives, poisons, guns, and even a crossbow. As much as I preferred a more tactful method of espionage to Bishop's style, I couldn't help but be impressed by his resources. The man was a Vienna local, that was for sure. Spread out on the table in front of us was a diagram, along with many hastily written notes scrawled across every available space.

"And here's the plan," Bishop said, his voice lower than usual. "It's an easy enough one, as long as you're both man enough to move around some furniture."

"Man enough, ya sod?" Theo laughed, but I could tell he didn't get along with Bishop already. "Hardly a question - I could pick up a couch meself if you give me a second to heave it on my back."

"Well, it should be easy enough then," Bishop continued. "From my intel, Krane is working in the basement of the

Kunsthistorisches Museum. The building was partly destroyed during the war, and they're currently in the process of rebuilding and refurnishing it. I have connections, so I've got us an in with a team that's moving furniture that day. O'course, we'll deviate when we have a second, slip out, and head into the basement.

"No doubt Krane's heavily protected - I doubt even the city officials know he's there - but that's why we'll need to lay low until we get close enough to either incapacitate his guards or slip past them. Here's where the play gets fun, gentlemen, because according to a man I trust, Grigory Kulik is in charge of protecting Krane from you, Max."

"Kulik?" I raised my eyebrows, impressed. "I know he had a falling out with the Soviets a few years back, but is he still a Colonel-General?"

"No. Stalin stripped him of his high-ranking position. Demoted him. He disappeared into obscurity after he messed up in Operation Barbarossa. Was blamed for Russian defeats. He's back but in private practice with his own army," responded Bishop. "So...unless you boys want to be target practice for that man and his soldiers, you'd better start practicing moving some furniture."

"An' to think I left me work gloves back in London," Theo muttered wryly. "After this, there's no keeping me here in Vienna - it'll be good to go back to my homeland after these damn years bunkered down 'ere."

"If you pansies survive this," Bishop grinned, his yellow teeth shining in the lamplight. "I hope you're built for a Vienna assassination."

I cracked my knuckles and stretched. "I'll blow Vienna sky high if I have to."

CHAPTER 5
EMIL KRANE

Dr. Emil Krane stood in the cold basement, his face illuminated by the dim lamp on the table. The air was heavy with the musty scent of old stones, dead bugs, and dust. His hands shook as he ran them over the pages of his notes spread across the feverish scribbles of equations and diagrams that had filled his mind for the past four years, if that was indeed how long it had been. It was hard to tell.

In another life, he might have felt proud of his work, of the breakthroughs in physics and the world-changing potential of what he had created. But now, in this place, as the bitter winds of the Austrian landscape curled their fingers through the cracks of the basement, the only sentiment he held was resentment - that, and an occasional flicker of desperation.

They had him holed up here, beneath the Kunsthistorisches, with a promise they would keep him safe - safe, as long as he completed the work he had promised.

It had started innocently enough in the early days of 1942. The war had been at its peak for a while now, and every brilliant scientific mind available was recruited by the military. Those in charge sought individuals who could change the tide of the war, one way or another. The most effective opportunity, of course, was the changes that genius could bring.

Genius, Krane thought to himself - that was how he had often been described. He was a brilliant physicist, recruited for his expertise in high-energy radiation. At the time, he'd been working for the Third Reich at the Wenceslaus mine, which was part of a chain of Nazi facilities called Der Reise in the Polish Owl Mountains. It was there, alongside several notable physicists and scientists, that they were developing the Wunderwaffe - the so-called wonder weapons that would guarantee the Nazi military victory.

One project that Krane and his compatriots had begun to craft, although still in the conceptual stage, was known as Die Glocke - the Bell. Rumors and wild speculation abounded as to what was really going on in the depths of those mountains. Many of the men who were aware of it suggested that it was built on alien technology, was some sort of anti-gravity device, or even a gigantic bomb. But the truth was far much simpler - Die Glocke was purported to be a time machine. British agents were never able to establish any real facts except that it incorporated a new material that the Germans, such as Krane, called Xerum 525, which glowed blue and was responsible for incredibly high levels of radiation.

But Krane himself had been unsatisfied with the development of the Bell and had clashed with the other scientists working on the project. Although he and the other men had initially incorporated the concept of a time machine, this was quickly scrapped for a more simplistic project, and Krane himself grew angry. He had hoped beyond all hope that they would have followed through with their quest to create a device capable of manipulating time itself, which he believed was possible.

Ultimately, when his superiors sided with the other scientists working on the project and demanded that the aspects involving time travel be dropped in favor of more mundane solutions,

Krane had had enough. He was so disillusioned and had so many ideological disputes that he secretly planned to disappear into the Polish underground while stealing some of the technology that had been developed before the initial project was scrapped.

After defecting from the Germans, the British military sought him like a dog after a rabbit. Once they realized he'd vanished, their intelligence services sought him to the ends of the earth with help from the Poles. They hounded him endlessly for months until he was convinced to join their secretive operations, creating technological advancements that wouldn't just turn the tide of the war but rewrite its story completely.

Krane slammed his fists against the table in frustration. He'd been so close to perfection, and now - well, he had to start all over again. He looked up at the wall in front of him but didn't see the old bricks or the minuscule stream of water that threaded its way through the wall from some broken pipe. Instead, he saw it: the Mirror.

He had been introduced to the Mirror Project through the organization that recruited him - the Bureau. It was a project that was merely a concept at the time he had joined, one that would have never been progressed if it hadn't been for him. Krane, of course, thought the idea was simple enough - harness the potential to manipulate the timeline, and the war could be won. He should still have it now - he should still be able to hold it, to touch its metallic surface, to pulse it.

Anger flowed through him as he remembered. He had come up with the name, too, conceiving this beautiful thing in the artificial light of his lab. Men had been assigned to work under him, and the object had finally been constructed. He had named it the Mirror.

It was a beauty - an enormous, metallic device with strange, flickering patterns of light coursing through it. And, of course, there was the reflection itself - that didn't reflect, but contorted and changed.

At first glance, the version he had created in 1943 seemed like an antique. While it was nearly eight feet tall, some of the earlier and later versions he had built had been smaller. Krane remembered every detail. It stained his mind, filling his dreams with a craving that wouldn't extinguish, even in the depths of nightmares.

It was framed in tarnished brass, with intricate art deco scrollwork - the kind you might find in a dusty corner of an old train station or the forgotten wing of some museum. These designs were chosen by Krane himself. The Mirror's surface, however, was where the details were. It was liquid gallium and galinstan, held in place by a delicately designed magnetic suspension - a suspension they could pulse. From a distance, when it was offline, the device shimmered with an eerie light, sometimes catching reflections and at other times absorbing them completely.

But when it was active - ah, when it was active! Krane chuckled quietly as he remembered and smashed his knuckles against the table until they bled. He could feel that magnetic, electric pulse through the air in every fiber of his being. The surface would ripple as he stared into it, distorting reality in waves. The air around it grew heavy, full of static, like a storm waiting for the first strike of lightning.

———

Inside the frame, Krane had carefully crafted the most elegant of hidden technology: miniature quantum compute arrays of immense power that did not need to be at absolute zero, stabilizers forged from alloys found in downed meteors, and a gyroloop core built from cold-forged tungsten. It was decades ahead of its time.

This was what Krane had always told them when they asked. The same was true for The Architect, the only man who grasped what the Mirror truly was. He was the only man, aside from

Krane, who realized the truth of what the Mirror was evolving into. However, he had wanted to stop it. Krane had told them the tech wasn't invented; it was discovered, as if someone else had left the blueprints behind, cemented in his mind since before he was born. But then they had begun to test it.

The first breach occurred when the military used the Mirror to send a test subject - a soldier - through the device. The breach had been inevitable. Krane had seen the signs; he knew what would happen. He had read the data, seen the anomalies in the Mirror's behavior, and predicted what would happen. But he did not tell the men he worked with or those he worked for.

It was a test like many before, but the project's latest phase had officially been launched. Test Subject Delta, a volunteer chosen for his lack of importance to the cause, would enter the Mirror. It was designed as a way for agents to slip through time without altering the greater timeline, and if this test was a success, it would mean that the project had the potential to change the world.

When a soldier went through the Mirror's gateway, there was relatively little telling what would happen, other than the fact that time would be displaced in some manner. And so, the test began.

Krane had entered the Mirror chamber alongside several military officers, their faces masked with excitement - and The Architect, whose face was etched with cautious optimism. Everyone present would witness the first man sent through the device - a brave, or perhaps naive, man. Private Edward Calloway stepped forward, fully suited in his military garb, gazing up at the Mirror. His eyes were wide with anticipation, his expression innocent.

The Mirror pulsed slowly at first, warming up, its glass-like surface flickering ever more brightly. It was as if the Mirror itself could feel, even sense, what was about to happen. A flash of blinding light surged through it, and the pulses intensified. The air around Calloway began to warp, bend, and shiver as the surface of the Mirror cracked open, revealing a great darkness expanding from within, with a multitude of cracks - multi-faced and seemingly never-ending.

The officers around Krane and The Architect fell to the ground, shielding their eyes. Only the two of them remained standing, their faces illuminated by the vision of what they had created.

In an instant, a man emerged from the center of the Mirror, screaming in agony as he pulled his aged body from within it. The Calloway who stood in front of the Mirror now quivered as he was faced with another Calloway - a much older version of himself, yet unmistakably him.

The older Calloway was staggering back from the device, his eyes wild, his chest heaving. His skin was pale and wrinkled, and his hands trembled. He darted his eyes around the room, looking this way and that way, until his face finally fell on the younger Calloway. He lunged toward him, grasping him around the midsection and pulling him wildly toward the Mirror.

The two struggled as they watched.

"Shut it down," a deep, soft voice commanded, cutting through and instructing the men who pulsed the Mirror to cease the experiment.

At that moment, Krane felt a bitter resentment toward The Architect, an anger that he would end the experiment so soon.

Before the pulses could cease, the older Calloway pulled the younger into the Mirror, and emerging a second later was only one version of Calloway.

This version, as they would soon realize, was both Calloway - and somehow, not him. The soldier had returned, but not as the same man. His mind was shattered, his memories different, and his body older.

As they would later call it, the first "slide" had taken place that day. From then on, Krane himself would experience strange flashes of light, other men stalking his peripheral vision, disjointed memories, and…other things.

But as strange and horrifying as that first event had been, Krane had lapped it up like a dog starved of love finally finding itself surrounded by those who would acknowledge it. Of course, that event hadn't been without controversy. The conversation he had with The Architect back then, after the first slide, still rang fresh in his mind.

"We need to - to test it more," Krane had stuttered, his fingers tracing a familiar path over the frame.

"Emil, we have to be very careful when we do. You know the risks of this better than even I do, so are there risks?"

"There's always risk," Krane had spat back. "But you know as well as I do that the Mirror is…it's more than we could have ever asked for."

"I'm not so sure…time has to be respected to remain coherent, Emil."

"Why respect something that can be broken, bent, and then reshaped? I can… we can do anything we want to it."

"And is that good?"

Krane had shaken his head, his eyes darting nervously. "What is good, exactly?"

"I'm not sure - sometimes I fail to grasp it. But if time is broken, that is bad. I know that much."

"And…I'm not so sure of that."

"Well, be that as it may, I am still in charge of this project, Doctor. I need your assurance that if we pulse it - continue to pulse it and test it - there won't be repercussions beyond the acceptable."

"Of course…of course."

But Krane had known, even back then, that this was a lie. The experiments had continued, but Krane made very sure not to take things too far. Instead, he carefully controlled each slide, ensuring that the results weren't too harsh for The Architect's careful gaze to find fault with.

The more Krane worked with the Mirror, the more it began to consume him. He began to question whether or not the Mirror should really be controlled by that organization, by The Architect and his rules. After all, why should Krane not be the one in control of the Mirror if it was this powerful - this unique?

It wasn't just Subject Delta who was affected. The entire team of scientists and any agents who were sent through to Slide found themselves changing.

The Architect's warnings went ignored - the military saw the results and ordered the experiment to continue. They were all too eager to press forward. If the Mirror was such a powerful weapon, it could end the war. The military wrongly imagined a field with dozens of Lancaster bombers easily seen by the enemy that were not really there. Or a full army brigade invisible in what looked like an empty village. To them the Mirror could be a magnificent source of misinformation. It could be the greatest weapon known to man. However, by the end of the war, the Mirror had begun to fracture time on a far larger scale than anyone could have imagined.

Krane himself disappeared in 1945 - the year of the Rosyth Naval Dockyard incident, which he had orchestrated. It was only a temporary setback. Like a ghost, people thought he had died as many others had in that incident. But like a ghost, he had remained - as did the Mirror, though everyone else thought it was destroyed. But Krane knew that what once existed, at such a fundamental quantum level, would continue to exist. He just had to recreate it.

———

In Paris, Krane began to work in secret. He soon contacted the men who had once been his allies - allies before the breach had begun and the cold war was in full effect - begging them for funding. And funding he had found.

In 1946, he moved to Vienna at the behest of Grigory Kulik, one of his old colleagues and fellow enthusiasts of Krane's ideology. It would mean working with the Soviets, but Krane no longer cared. In his mind, anyone who prevented the Mirror from bending time was now the enemy.

Now, here he was - in 1947, working alone in a cramped basement lab for the Soviets and their ilk. The little hair he had left was graying, and his eyes were hollow. Krane himself was haunted by visions, yet more determined than ever to see his beautiful creation light up the world again. The Mirror itself had gifted him with these visions, he thought - haunted by other realities, where other versions of him had made different choices. In his deepest stupor, he'd occasionally see a reality where the Mirror had been allowed to operate unchecked, where he, Dr. Emil Krane, had everything he wished for. If only he could reach that reality.

For now, he stared at the scribbled notes, focusing on the one name in his papers that seemed to appear in every reality - Max Calder. He had seen that man on the night he'd overloaded the sensors, pulsing the Mirror beyond its limits. Why was Calder so intricately tied to this project? What made him unique?

And of course, then there was what Grigory had told him a few days earlier. The Bureau was aware that he was alive and working in Vienna - and they had sent men to find him... likely to kill him.

The Bureau was already closing in, and his connections were thinning. If this new prototype didn't show results soon, Kulik might no longer be the powerful ally he once was.

Krane adjusted his glasses, pushing them up on his nose. He sniffled a bit, wiping his bleeding knuckles with a handkerchief. The Allies were after him... the Soviets thought they had him... and Calder - well, Calder was a monkey wrench in his plans.

But he wasn't going to give up. Not now.

CHAPTER 6
FURNITURE FAKERY

needed to get away from Bishop's hangout for a while. So I took a walk down the street, my face flickering in the passing shadows and the soft yellow light that occasionally shone down from the streetlamps. My cigarette smoke curled upward, wafting lazily into the air. A few days had passed since Bishop first let us in on the plan - the day he'd managed to get us an "in" was Tuesday, and so now, well, that would be in the morning, wouldn't it?

I glanced up at the heavy clouds obscuring the moon's light. Occasionally, I'd see a beam or two, but it was relatively dark otherwise, save for the artificial light of Vienna's streets. We'd been holed up at Bishop's place the whole time, eager to get moving and rehearsing the plan nearly constantly, yet all too aware that the whole city had eyes. I'd only snuck out now because I was confident in my ability to lay low, even while walking the back streets of the city.

Of course, it wasn't always foolproof, so I watched carefully as I walked, making note of any men who strolled the streets at the same time as I. If there were any foreign agents, Soviets or otherwise, I could always dispose of them if they caught wind of my movements. Still, I vastly preferred to remain under the radar. I would never hear the end of it from Withers if I were caught out while he and Bishop were holed up at our home base.

When I suddenly heard the faint clicking of boots up ahead, I froze in my tracks, melting into the shadows of the nearest alleyway in an instant. I peered out from the darkness, my hand resting carefully against one of the cold brick walls to steady myself. There, past me, a man walked - his face shrouded in shadow, his hands stuffed in his trench coat pockets. He wore a hat similar to mine, and I saw smoke exhaled from his obscured lips, no doubt from a freshly lit cigarette.

I furrowed my brows - this man looked familiar, but I couldn't quite place him. As he walked, however, he suddenly turned his head toward the alley where I stood. I knew he wouldn't have been able to see me in the dark, as his eyes would be adjusted to the soft yellow light of the streetlamps, but that wasn't what made my stomach drop or left a jolting electricity running throughout my body, making my skin crawl.

For just a split second, the man's face seemed to resemble my own - his rough, haggard exterior, the deep scar on his jaw, and the ice-gray piercing eyes I'd only ever seen when I looked into a mirror. But that split second was all I got to look at him, as the man had already turned his vision to a sign a few yards ahead and moved on.

I stood in a stupor for a moment, uncertain - had it been a trick of the light? Was Vienna getting to me? Or was this some damn trick by the Soviets? In an instant, I had made up my mind. Moving stealthily, like a leopard on the prowl, I made my way to the edge of the alley and peered past the corner. I looked down the street where the man had walked. But I didn't see him - it was as if he had moved as swiftly as I had, melting into the shadows of another side street.

I shook my head. Whatever I had seen must have been a trick of the light... or a trick of my mind. I had already learned from Artemis - no, Alicia - that whatever the Mirror had done to us sliders was likely messing with our minds, pulling our strings...

making us forget things, forget people. Maybe it even made us hallucinate, too.

I slipped back down the alley, making my way expertly back to the safe house. As I entered, I saw him sitting in the dim light of the table lamp, his arms crossed and a scowl on his face, accompanied by an annoyed grin. Theo was clearly irked I had snuck out.

"Nice one, Max," he said in an exasperated tone.

"Couldn't sleep. You rather me wake you up with the smell of smoke?"

"Still got that bloody habit?" He pulled out a cig of his own, lit it, and inhaled. "It's bad for you, ya know. Smoking kills."

I scoffed and settled back into a chair, waiting for the morning to come. Soon, Bishop joined us, his clothes different from the regular garb he wore - more rough, civilian-oriented, and indicative of a poor, working-class man.

He motioned toward the two of us. "Already up?"

"You're late," Theo chuckled.

"You're not changed."

"It'll only take a minute. Settle down, have a smoke."

I, of course, was already wearing the civilian's garb I had picked up a while ago and watched as a few minutes later, Theo stood, returning only after retrofitting his outfit with some new additions.

"Pick your poison, gentlemen," Bishop said, motioning toward his array of weapons and other choice instruments. "Remember, they've got an army here - so pack lightly, but pack plenty."

"I've already got mine." I motioned toward my side piece, a Colt M1911, lying in front of me.

Theo rummaged through the items for a second, pulling out a switchblade or three from the pile before returning to the table. His preferred instrument, I knew, was the knife - quieter kills and no ammunition issues.

A few hours later, the three of us stood in front of the

Kunsthistorisches Museum. It was a towering building with beautiful architecture and relatively intact from the war, though here and there, men worked eagerly to repair any damaged elements that needed restoration before they could reach their true beauty once more. A large, beefy man walked up to us, his bulging stomach instantly indicating to me that he was a man of authority, not of the workforce.

"Name's Horst," he bellowed at me as he shook my hand. "You fellas are here to supplement my moving crew, yes?"

"We're the ones," I replied.

"Well then, nothing's stopping you! Heard you agreed to the terms as well. Needless to say, you won't get paid an Austrian Shilling if you break anything - this place is more expensive than my backside!"

I nodded, and with a few more careful instructions, Horst let us head on our way. The job went rather well. I was used to exercise and relished the chance to move more than I had in the past few weeks. As we worked, I carefully noted the position of the guards - there was no mistaking them; these were Soviet men. You could tell from their stance and body language. They stood strategically positioned near every corner and door, watching silently as we worked alongside the other Austrian men. Officially, they were there to supervise the movement of delicate artwork and paintings back into the building. Unofficially, they were there to make sure I wouldn't be able to reach Krane.

I had carefully covered up my scar and any identifiable features with dirt, making sure that I had the appearance of a working man who bathed rarely and cursed often. With a slight stoop toward one shoulder and an almost unnoticeable limp, I was unrecognizable to any man who hadn't seen me before or been intricately familiar with my appearance.

Back and forth, we moved the furniture according to the foreman's instructions - a bulky fellow who did his share of the work as well. I checked my watch. It was just past 1145 hours, and we had just enough information to begin. Like clockwork, I moved down one of the corridors, and as I passed, I saw Bishop strike up a conversation with one of the guards. As I walked out of sight, I heard a thump, and I knew the guard would be on the ground by now, dead. He would be dragged away silently, stuffed into one of the closets we'd passed during our traverses of the museum. I knew Withers would take care of another two, and I had to take care of three more - then, there would be no one who could sound the alarm. I snuck behind one of the statues that had recently been moved back into place, directly behind one of the guards who stood watch. This man, I knew, was one of the most important. I could tell by the badges he wore on his chest and the way he stood that he was a higher-ranking official than the rest, so I figured I'd take him down first.

I sprang up suddenly, wrapping one arm around his neck and covering his mouth with my hand, cutting off his air supply as I wrestled him to the ground. The man was strong, but he was caught off guard, and around 15 seconds later, I felt him go limp in my arms. I continued to hold on, making sure he wouldn't wake up. Then, I shoved his body roughly behind the statue and stood warily, scanning my surroundings.

All was quiet, and my next task was to take out the two remaining guards. I was rusty after all that time spent in Hell's Kitchen.

"Damn," I muttered as I popped my knuckles, walking along the corridor. My arms felt a bit sore, and I knew that even my exercise during the trip wasn't enough to fully restore me to my prime. Still, it would be enough to run such an easy mission.

The next two guards were even easier - I had stolen the bayonet off of the first one's Mosin-Nagant and quickly used it to dispatch them. Now, it was time to make my way back to Theo, and together, we would head to the basement level and locate Krane.

As I rounded the corner, however, I suddenly saw a body on the floor that wasn't supposed to be there. In front of me, sprawled face down, lay Theo Withers, one hand around his neck and the other holding a switchblade. The body of the guard he had dispatched lay behind him, bleeding from the neck.

I recoiled in shock. "What the hell?"

Glancing around quickly to make sure there was nobody nearby, I grabbed his shoulder and flipped him over so I could get a good look at his face - it was Theo, all right, his eyes lifeless and his body limp. He had no wounds except for a small cut on his left cheek, no doubt from a struggle with his killer.

But his mouth - I suddenly felt a chill run through my body as I registered the foam near the edges of his lips and the drained appearance of his face.

I recognized these symptoms. This wasn't the work of a gun or a knife - this was the work of cyanide.

Cyanide could mean one of two things: either Bishop was compromised, or someone wanted it to look like it. Either way, I couldn't take the risk of finding out right now - I had a more important job to do.

Just then, I heard shouting - Russian voices coming from the corridor behind me, from the direction where Bishop was supposed to be doing his dirty work. That alone was enough to confirm, more or less, that Bishop had been the man responsible for this work. I melted into the shadowy passage behind me, leaving Withers' body lying dead on the ground. I felt a tinge of remorse that he'd had to die like that. There would no doubt be no burial arranged for him, either. But now wasn't the time to feel any sort of emotion. I was on the job.

I made my way down stairwell after stairwell, hopping over the edges as I timed my descent so as to avoid making any noise. Whether I'd find a trap waiting for me down here - maybe even Bishop - was a question that remained unanswered, but I couldn't afford to back out of the mission now. I anticipated that if it were Bishop, he would have expected me to have discovered Theo's body by now. If that were the case, there was no way he would have let me get this far.

The Bishop I knew - or thought I knew - would have lain in

wait near Theo's body to finish me off once and for all. As formerly religious men somehow seem to go, he relished the kill, being a jealous murderer with a passion to always finish the job he started. So why hadn't he been there? And more importantly, wouldn't he have indicated to Kulik that they needed reinforcements outside the door to the basement?

I had finally made my way down, avoiding the main corridors whenever possible, and now faced the last flight of stairs. There were no lights here, which I vastly preferred, so I slid into the shadows like a snake slithering its way into the underbrush, my senses heightened and my body low to the ground.

Every time I stepped down the ancient, cracking concrete stairs, my body tensed, yet I was also filled with some strange sense of anticipation. As much as I'd never admit it to myself, I had missed this…these life-or-death situations that left one man dead and another alive - the ultimate game of cat and mouse.

Illuminated by an eerily dim light from two lanterns hanging above the door, I finally saw them. There were two men there, neither wearing Russian uniforms at all but instead dressed in civilian clothes, the likes of which I would have chosen to blend in. One wore a scarf, though it was oddly positioned as if he wasn't accustomed to such gear. They hadn't noticed me - it would be nearly impossible to do so - but I was ever more cautious as I approached them. Whoever these men were, they were no ordinary soldiers. Most likely, they were NKVD agents placed specifically by Kulik himself. Though the NKVD itself had fallen into disarray less than a year ago, it seemed like Kulik still retained power over many of the elite ex-NKVD members. I figured - now that I most likely had the entirety of Kulik's military force on my tail — that there would be no harm in being a little noisy.

Pulling out my trusty M1911, I sidled my way along, body pressed against the wall. I was a crack shot with the pistol, but even so, this dimly lit corridor made it so I would leave nothing to chance. Scarcely three yards away, I took aim.

The shot rang out like a whip crack. I felt the recoil hit my arm like a hammer, and the man crumpled to the ground. I'd hit the perfect spot - that place above the nose and between the eyes that I'd always learned meant death. He didn't think any longer. His body simply collapsed to the ground, lifeless. The other man was quick - he didn't react to his comrade's death, but in the very instant he heard the gunshot, he began to reach for his own weapon. I fired again, and this time the bullet went wide, hitting him in the shoulder.

"Suka - " he began to curse and fired a shot in my direction, but I was already on top of him. Leaping to one side, I bashed the hilt of my gun against his face and felt the cold steel connect with the soft, fleshy resistance of the man's body. With a thud, he fell backward against the wall, cracking his head open on the concrete below him. This man, too, was dead.

Only when I stood did I realize the numb, stinging pain that began to travel throughout my arm. I glanced down - the bullet he had fired had grazed my left arm, tearing at my flesh. I was bleeding. From what I could tell with my limited medical training, it wasn't a threatening injury. Instead, I tore off a small piece of cloth from the man's scarf and wrapped it tightly around my wound. The wound stung, but it only heightened my senses, flooding my body with adrenaline. This was good.

Pocketing my M1911, I grabbed one of the dead men's pistols - a Russian-built PM - and kicked open the basement door. I saw drawings, diagrams, notes, and a partly built frame - unfinished but clearly built for the singular purpose I had been informed of. Another Mirror. There, in front of me, stood a man against the far wall, his frail form clearly unsuited to the cold weather of Vienna. I recognized him instantly. Krane. He looked shocked for a second, then his countenance cleared as he stared at my face and then broke into a sneer.

"It's - they really sent you, did they, Max?" His voice was cold and jeering, though I could hear a wavering fear in it that I couldn't quite place.

I waved my gun at him, motioning for him to move across the room. "Krane. Can't say I ever knew you well enough to be on a first-name basis."

"Oh, haven't you? I suppose you haven't, no - but I have."

"What's that supposed to mean?"

"Neither here nor there - you just wouldn't understand, Max. You here to kill me?"

"Yeah, sounds about right."

"I'm not sure you can," he said, his voice growing bolder. "But I suppose you'd like to try."

At that moment, I suddenly heard clamoring outside and the heavy footsteps of men descending the basement stairs. Krane made a hasty movement toward one of the side walls where a giant metal bookcase stood, as if trying to escape, but tripped over one of the smaller devices he'd been building - a bundle of cords and wires - and fell to the ground with a whimper.

I leaped into action. A second later, I was on top of Krane, my hand over his mouth. Pulling a drug-soaked handkerchief out of my pocket that Bishop had passed me earlier that day, I held it firmly over his face until he was forced to breathe in. I could feel his body go limp, but this wasn't good. I didn't have enough time to make a clean kill and get away with my life, especially fighting back through the hordes of men I was certain were rushing down the stairs.

The split second I had to decide felt like an hour - my mind raced, going over the possibilities. I glanced at the door. Maybe I could use Krane as a hostage and work my way out. But no, they had no guarantee he was alive...not in this state, at least - and even if they did, there was no promise they had orders to keep him alive no matter what. But then - why had Krane been rushing toward the bookcase, anyway?

From the noise nearing the door, the men were scarcely fifteen seconds away now. My eyes darted up and down the shelf, examining every part of it - it was a plain old, metal book-case, a bit rusty, with no uncommon features - but behind it, on the wall, in the dim light, I saw the shadow of a door. It was clearly built to be inconspicuous, blending in with the wall and with little to no frame, but it was there.

I wasted no time. Springing up from my position, I threw the bookcase aside. It was heavy and sturdy, but with enough force, it was easily movable. I grabbed onto Krane's lab coat, pulling him roughly after me as I swung the door open and stuffed him through it before closing the door again. Was this some hidden passageway? It was undoubtedly an escape route planned by the Emperor, who had commissioned this old building in the first place, or by his designers. I reckoned that it was some sort of contingency plan in case there ever were to be a revolt, and the Emperor needed a place to hide.

But Krane had known about it, which meant that the men after me likely knew about it as well. The pitch-black corridor in front of me was roughly hewn from the rock - bumpy and unfinished. Grabbing Krane's unconscious body, I heaved him onto my shoulder and began to jog along, keeping my head low to avoid bumping it on the roof. The musty smell of old, dead air and the sound of dripping water intensified as I ran. A minute or so later, I heard a loud banging and shouting behind me. The tunnel had curved now, so I was out of sight of the men pursuing me. As long as they had no lights to guide themselves, the chase would be reasonably fair.

I kept running until I felt the ground beneath me slowly begin to rise. It leveled out here and there, and eventually, I tripped, cursing as I fell. It was pitch black, but I instinctively put my hand out in front of me to protect my face. My left arm was searing now, agonizing pain splitting from the fresh wound I had only temporarily dealt with. Nevertheless, I forced my fingers to feel the ground in front of me. It was a familiar pattern, something I had expected - the rough, rocky ground had come to an end, and in front of me, cut out of the stone, were stairs. Grabbing Krane's body, which I had let fall when I fell, I began to ascend carefully, one foot in front of the other, with my left arm outstretched above me.

Eventually, I felt my fingers meet a rough and wooden surface. As I felt around, I finally brushed my fingers against the latch, and a split second later, a blisteringly bright light beamed down into my face.

It took my eyes a second or two to adjust, but as I squinted, my vision adjusted, and I began to take in my surroundings. An old, tall wooden building, dilapidated with more boards missing than not, seemingly swaying with the breeze, stood above me. Through the cracks, I could see the buildings of Vienna surrounding me - this old, abandoned building stood near the edge of the city, seemingly on an abandoned lot. The lot was covered with overgrown bushes and weeds, large boulders, and occasional trees scattered here and there.

But there was no time to think or admire the foresight of whoever had designed this place. Instead, pulling Krane after me, I climbed the final steps out of the trapdoor and shut it solidly behind me. Using my wounded arm, I grabbed a few of the largest boulders I could find and piled them over the trapdoor until it was almost completely covered.

"Eat shit," I muttered toward the men pursuing me, though I knew none were close enough to hear me.

Krane was still solidly unconscious, and it would look bizarre dragging him around the bustling city of Vienna in broad daylight. Instead, I decided to stash him in some nearby bushes. I assumed the men would have trouble breaking their way out of the trapdoor, at least for now, but I still needed to get Krane back to our designated safe house. I had been told it was a safe house assigned by Alicia and the Bureau for our escape. Then again, I wasn't sure if it would be all that safe, considering that Bishop was likely compromised. But I was out of my depth, and so I scanned the city streets near me. My eyes finally fell on an older model of car parked alongside one of the streets. Sidling up to it,

I tried each handle, feeling the metallic click pushing back at me as I tried - it was locked.

"Damn," I muttered as I glanced around, my eyes scanning this way and that until they landed on a thin piece of metal lying on the ground. I quickly snatched it up and, making sure nobody was watching, expertly angled it into the crack of the window until I felt the locking mechanism slip. With a tiny click, it was open.

Before I finished my car project, I heaved myself back toward where I'd stashed Krane, my arm burning like the devil as I did. I pulled his limp body from the bushes, dusted off his lab coat - scoffing to myself as I did so - and hauled him to the car. After dumping his body securely into the backseat, returned to my project.

It wasn't that I was unwilling to kill the man - he was a vile little fellow, more than deserving of a swift bullet to the head - but I'd already made up my mind while escaping through the tunnel that I needed more from him. After all, this mission had gone to hell, and I needed to know why. Had Bishop betrayed us? Or was this whole ploy set up by Artemis, with Bishop being the one who had been framed?

The first order of business was this car. I'd always been a mechanical whiz, and it wouldn't take long to hotwire this old Peugeot 203. Bending down, I snapped off the panel beneath the steering column and got to work. This wire to that, and soon, the engine roared to life.

The safe house was on the edge of the French sector. With Krane riding jovially - or so I figured - in the back seat, I drove through the crowded city streets. I didn't have a map with me, but asking for directions with my window down was simple enough.

"Do you speak English? French?"

"Yes, only a little, sir," the man replied.

"The French sector. How do I get there?"

And so it went until I found my way back to familiar hunting grounds. I'd spent enough time in this area of Vienna during one of my previous missions that these streets were like the back of my hand. I quickly found my way to the safe house - a rather large building, no doubt owned by the Bureau - and entered quickly, locking the door behind me. Krane had begun to stir a bit, his arms fluttering occasionally as if he were in some sort of deep sleep. It had only been an hour or two since I'd made my tunnel escape, but it felt like far longer.

The safe house itself was a beautifully intricate piece of architecture. Paintings lined the walls, fabulous chairs sat around meticulously woodworked tables, and beautiful wallpaper was plastered on every wall. Even more impressive was the wardrobe, filled to the brim with weapons, guns, first aid kits, and as many tools as I would ever need.

Making short work of it, I grabbed some rope out of one of the bins and tied Krane to a chair. If he came to, I wouldn't have to worry about him. I dug through his pockets, fumbling through his personal items: a small pistol, some hastily written notes, a pencil, his ID, and even more notes. This man was an obsessive note-taker.

With a twinge of pain, I glanced down at my left arm - blood was soaking through my makeshift bandage, and I knew this took precedence. Grabbing one of the medkits stashed in the wardrobe, I sat on a couch and tended to my arm. With a wall mirror as my guide and several healthy swigs of whiskey, I felt my flesh to ensure no bullet had stuck - then cleaned, cauterized, and stitched up the wound as best I could with one hand. It was a sloppy job, but at least I wouldn't need that damn rag tied around my arm anymore.

The sky had begun to darken. I stood by the window, watching shadows cross the cobblestones. I felt cold - eerily so - and I couldn't shake the feeling that I was in trouble. I had called the number scribbled on a notepad next to the phone to get help, but there was no reply. Worst-case scenario, I'd have to kill

Krane and bail. Speaking of Krane, I heard him begin to struggle behind me.

I turned and watched as his eyes flickered open. He looked dazed for a second before fixing his piercing, calculating gaze on me, like a hawk assessing its prey. There was no doubt the man was intelligent, though I considered him insane.

"Couldn't do it, could you?"

"Do what?" I asked.

"Kill me. I'm still here, aren't I?"

"Don't get ahead of yourself. There's still time."

"Time, Max. That's a funny thing. Is there still time? Where is it, anyway?"

"The hell are you talking about?"

"Oh, you're a smart guy, Max. You know this is really about the Mirror - about what it did and what it can do again. You of all people should know…but you don't, of course, and that's the conundrum of the whole issue."

"Speaking of issues, Krane, I have a bone to pick with you." I stood up and walked over to him, grabbing him roughly by the shoulder. He let out a little involuntary squeak.

"What?"

"See - the mission backfired. It went to hell. One of my men is dead, and another is missing. Does Bishop work for you?"

"Bishop? Oh, that little twat - didn't he subcontract for the Bureau before?"

"Yes," I replied, tightening my grip on his shoulder. "And before you say anything else, don't play games. I'm not ready to kill you yet, but a weak man like you is easy enough to hurt."

"There's no reason to threaten me. I'm not trying to hide anything from you - not that I can, anyway."

"Then answer."

"Bishop - if he's working with them, I wouldn't know the heads or tails of it. Then again, maybe - oh, maybe that's what happened."

"What?"

He smiled, his mouth thinning near the edges as he eyed me. "You don't know yet, do you? Don't know how important you are in this whole charade?"

"Cut the games, Krane. I think we both know we don't have much time, so answer. Who ratted us out?"

"Why does there only have to be one?"

"The hell does that mean?"

At that moment, however, a knock came at the door. Three taps, a pause, three knocks, and a final knock two seconds later. The code. I whipped out my M1911, aiming it at Krane's face.

"Quiet," I hissed, motioning to his head. "You know I won't hesitate to shoot you if you so much as say a word."

I didn't know why, but I had an eerie feeling about this…like something was wrong. Why hadn't an agent answered the phone when I called?

An agent was supposed to be here to get us papers, passports, and a flight out. But something felt off - nobody had checked in, Bishop was missing, and potentially working for the Soviets. I waited, frozen, with bated breath.

I remembered the protocol. If nobody answered, the agent would try the same code again, then leave and alert the Bureau.

The seconds felt like hours. I slowly crouched, my eyes fixed on the door. In my peripheral vision, I saw the window behind me. It was much darker outside now, but from what I could see, the streets were empty.

Suddenly, the door exploded inward. With a sickening blast, wooden splinters cracked and flew into the room like shrapnel.

Smoke. Shouts. Russian voices. Gunfire.

CHAPTER 7
MAX CALDER

He walked along the street, hands shoved deep in his pockets, sauntering as he watched the people passing by. Against the current, as he'd always done in his life. Max Calder, however, didn't care much about the sun here in Cambridge, nor did he care about the fact that he wasn't really meant to be here. He'd forged the documents well enough, and he figured that nobody would really consider him out of place. His outfit? Acquired from the nearest clothing store to make sure he looked the part of a student. His demeanor? Well, the other students could see for themselves - he blended in perfectly. Even his voice had been altered. His usual Scottish accent transformed into a more local dialect. There was nothing that could distinguish Calder from the other students. He was a chameleon.

He'd been here for months now, studying as any good student would. According to the latest student report, he was earning fantastic grades. It was less of an indication of his intelligence and more so an indication of the lack of intelligence at the university he'd chosen.

He had originally traveled from Glasgow to Cambridge in a desperate attempt to gain some sort of knowledge he hadn't already acquired. For some damn reason, he always picked up on things quickly. If he read a book once, he didn't have to read it again - he'd memorized everything important. It wasn't that he could memorize the whole book, front to back, but rather the fact that he could memorize the important pieces - the sentences that mattered. It was the same with what he was taught.

Here lay the crux of the issue - Calder had no real interesting things left to do, except for his favorite activity: people-watching. Sure, he'd be attending a class under his forged name, but good ol' Jack Fontaine, as he'd chosen to be called on his attendance slip, wasn't much interested in the class. If anything, he was considering dropping out of the school that he'd forged documents to get into in the first place.

He paused under a tree, leaning against it and watching the students walk by, usually in pairs or groups, all talking to their friends. He was a bit of an outcast. He hadn't made any friends here, either - not that he hadn't tried. Making friends was hard when you understood so much about people even before they spoke to you. Why engage with such disinteresting figures who sauntered around, following rules only because they were told to, with no original thoughts in their heads?

He sighed deeply before he pulled a shriveled paper bag out of his pocket, from which he retrieved a sandwich. Taking a bite, he continued to stare at the passersby with indifference. That girl - yes, the one who was excitedly talking to her boyfriend. Calder could tell she was going to break up with the fellow soon. It was in her face, and her face couldn't lie, even if she wanted to. When she spoke, her smile was slightly too wide, tight at the corners, almost strained. Her eyes spoke even more than she did - they darted away ever so slightly from the young man she pretended to like, especially whenever she pretended to laugh. Her hands were a dead giveaway, too. Though the rest of her demeanor was relaxed, her fingers fiddled absentmindedly with the strap of her satchel, allowing her to pull away from someone she would have normally leaned into. Most people would have seen a happy couple excited to spend some time together on a sunny afternoon, but Calder knew better. He saw more in a situation where others saw nothing at all.

He took another bite of his sandwich, shifting his gaze away from the pair. They had given him all the information they could offer. It had always been like this, too. He'd always been able to read people and understand them at a deeper level than they had wanted.

Finishing his sandwich, he walked slowly out from under the shaded tree and along the road until he reached the riverbank. The River Cam looked beautiful, with several smaller boats and the usual punts gliding across its calm waters, and Calder watched for a while. Soon, however, his attention shifted abruptly. He'd caught the eye of two men walking toward him from a downriver direction, each at least as tall as he was. One of the men in particular fascinated Calder, prompting him to turn toward the two men slightly for a better view.

This man was heavyset, with an unmistakable air of dignity, and though he walked carefully, he held himself in the unmistakable manner that a man of military bearing would. He looked tough, although Calder wasn't sure he had seen combat in a fair while. It was clear, however, from the way that the man returned eye contact that Calder was his target.

The man and his compatriot approached, glancing up and down as if evaluating Max for several seconds before speaking.

"Jack Fontaine?"

"Yes. And who do I have the pleasure of speaking to?"

"Let me be blunt," said the man, taking a cigar from his pocket and lighting it. "I work for a certain organization that values…deductive qualities. I've had my eye on you for a while. I know your name isn't Fontaine, nor Jack, nor do you properly attend this school."

Though he did not show it, Calder had instantly tensed up, his every muscle ready to run. "How'd you figure?"

"I figure because I have powerful allies - men who find those of interest to my organization and alert me to their presence.

You, Calder, have been ticking quite a few boxes. But don't worry, I have no plans to out you to the college."

"Well then, what do you want from me?"

"I want to test how good you really are. If I'm correct in thinking you are the type of asset that would be of service to me, then you'd likely find no interest in the schoolwork here, so why attend?"

"I was curious to see what I could learn."

"Well, I'm sure that's gone well. But let's see how good you really are. Meet me at The Pickerel Inn tonight at 1900 hours. I'll be there alone - and if you're good enough, I have a job offer."

"If you think I have nothing to learn here," Calder replied, staring at the man intently, "then why would I be interested in a job that's more of the same?"

"Because it's not more of the same," the man countered. "I'll let you do your own research before then, but this is a one-time offer. If you don't show, I won't contact you again."

"My own research?"

"Sure. If you're interested, find out what you can about me - it's only fair. My name is Hugh Sinclair."

Without another word, the man turned away, followed by his companion. Calder stood there, his whole body coursing with electric excitement. This unexpected event was what piqued his interest more than anything had the entire time he'd spent at Cambridge. He felt a thrill surging through him and knew already that no matter who the man was, he'd attend the meeting. After all, this was different - this was something that existed outside of the ordinary pattern.

Still, he did his research, asking around and rummaging through the Cambridge library for any information he could find on the man. To his surprise, it was easy enough. Hugh Sinclair, as Calder quickly learned, was a man on a mission and one of the most high-profile figures in the government. As he was quickly informed by one of his professors, Sinclair was the director of Naval Intelligence - a formidable figure with knowledge and access to tremendous resources. If Sinclair himself had tracked Calder down, then Calder was truly a person of interest.

He spent the day researching as much as he could but grew impatient as time went on. Calder had never been that interested in research, though he had a knack for it. He often thought on his feet and preferred to let answers come to him as events unfolded.

As dusk settled over Cambridge like a thick woolen blanket, Calder set off to The Pickerel Inn. It didn't take long, and though he walked briskly, he was excited at the prospect of a challenge for once in his life. It had begun to rain slightly, drizzling and turning the once-bright Cambridge into a more haunted place, reminding men who walked there of the ghosts from centuries past. Calder pulled his coat over his head and quickened his pace.

He reached old Cambridge with time to spare and turned down Magdalene Street, where the old pub stood. The small windows glowed with an enticing light, and the pub buzzed with regulars coming and going. As Calder entered, he felt it was a place of definite interest.

Thick oaken beams crossed the ceiling, sagging and bent, weathered though sturdy. The pub had been standing for ages, and Calder was confident it held thousands of untold secrets. The familiar smell of smoke tickled his nose as the air thickened with the wisps curling from the ends of cigarettes, blending with the scent of liquor on breath. The men who attended this bar varied widely: river porters, students, old military men, and the occasional college professor sat at the bar and around tables, all talking loudly. Though the night had scarcely begun, the drinks had already started to flow.

Rain splattered against the windows, intensifying and nearly drowning out the noise of conversation. Calder, however, wasn't looking for any of these men. He glanced up and down the room until his eyes fell on a table in the far corner, the most secluded spot, where the man sat. There was Sinclair, relaxing and reading a newspaper as he smoked a cigar.

Calder walked up to the table, pulled back a chair, and sat down without a word, waiting for the man to speak. A few moments later, Sinclair put down his paper, eyeing Calder with something akin to shock.

"I didn't think you'd actually come."

"Why not?"

"A lot of the men I approach are afraid," he responded, shrugging. "You seemed different, but I didn't know if you were different enough."

"I was bored."

"Good - you won't be for long if you end up solving this." Sinclair pushed a paper he'd concealed in his newspaper over to Calder, tapping it with a pen.

"What's this?"

"That's for you to figure out," Sinclair replied, making a face as he took another puff of his cigar. "It's a code. You break it."

Calder glanced down at the paper before him. It looked like something he had seen earlier that day when doing his research. He had been thorough in his investigation. Sinclair was obviously involved in the tradecraft of intelligence agencies, spies, and the government, and some of this included cracking ciphers. He had seen examples as he filled in Sinclair's background, and at a quick glance, this appeared to be one he recognized as Playfair, invented for telegraphy and the first cipher to encrypt pairs of letters in cryptologic history. He had no trouble recalling this, either - it was lodged firmly in his photographic memory. It was also given away by the absence of double letters in the encrypted text. Sure enough, he solved enough of it a few minutes later. He didn't need to decipher the whole thing, as this code was relatively simple; instead, he could glean the answer from a few of the key letters within the code.

He pushed the paper back to Sinclair, tapping it. "Clever. Fontaine."

"Already?" Sinclair checked his watch and then looked back at the paper. "You've figured that out already?"

"Why? Was it supposed to be more difficult?"

"Well, for most men it is - even our most brilliant code-breakers take longer, and this is your first time seeing it... or have you seen this cipher before?"

"Maybe. But that really doesn't matter, does it?"

Sinclair raised his eyebrows, impressed. "I guess not. All that's left, then, is for me to ask - are you interested in working with me? I'm sure you've figured out by now who I work for and the organization that I run."

"Yeah. Naval Intelligence, right? What exactly would I be doing there, anyway?"

"Exactly what you've just done now, to start. You're an incredibly gifted codebreaker - I've seen few men who could rival what you've just done, Max."

"Well, I don't have anything much better to do." Calder shrugged, noting that it was the first time Sinclair had called him Max, then nodded. "I guess I'll accept your offer, then."

And so that was it. The man known as Jack Fontaine dropped out of Cambridge the very next day, citing illness in the family to his professors and the organization at large. Only men like Sinclair and his inner circle knew the real reason for Jack Fontaine's departure, which is also the reason why the records of Max Calder have since been shrouded in such mystery. Even the most powerful men cannot track Calder's past, as before this point, his life was relatively unknown, and after it, he became a ghost.

After his remarkable achievement in breaking the Playfair code, Calder was contacted by one of Sinclair's underlings the day after - a balding man, short in stature and with a rather nervous temperament.

"Max Calder?" the man asked, waiting on the steps as Calder walked out of the office. Calder had just finished resigning from

Cambridge and was feeling rather excited about the prospects his future would hold.

"Yes?"

"We're off to London."

"Where specifically?"

"You'll see. Hop in," the man replied, motioning toward a black Rolls-Royce that sat idling on the road.

The drive was brief, but Calder quickly deduced where they were headed. From his readings in the library, he'd gathered that London was the home of most Naval Intelligence operations, and he figured that was where he was being taken. This would be the first time that Max Calder ever deduced something and was wrong, but not due to any fault of his own.

As they were driven along the roads, the bald man suddenly shifted in his seat, making eye contact with Calder before speaking.

"A few details before we reach your new home. Firstly, as I'm sure you're aware, you will have zero contact with the outside world - you are operating outside of traditional govern-ment jurisdiction. Secondly, as Mr. Sinclair has requested, I am to inform you that you will not be working for Naval Intelligence."

"The hell?"

"Though he wishes it to remain relatively unknown, a few years ago, Mr. Sinclair became the director of another organiza-tion much more interested in men such as yourself and has opted to reassign you to this organization."

Calder raised his eyebrows, thinking. He assumed Sinclair wouldn't have gone to all the trouble to recruit him in the first place if he wasn't genuinely interested in his skillset. So Calder figured it was safe to assume there was no trick at play here.

"Why did he neglect to mention this to me?" he finally asked.

"Simple. You'll be working for MI6, and our organization prefers to stay under wraps. Naval Intelligence is a schmuck's dream, and we would have no issue if you told any of your

friends about it. But MI6, the Secret Intelligence Service, well...
the public isn't even aware that we exist."

"Well, lucky me then - and where exactly in London are we
headed, if not to Naval Intelligence headquarters?"

By now, the very tops of the buildings were visible over the
hills through which they drove, and London emerged from the
foggy morning. The man smiled at him, then pointed out the
window toward one of the sections of the city.

"You'll operate out of Westminster, at Broadway. At least,
that's where the initial tests will take place."

"Tests? Didn't I already ace that?"

"Oh, not all. We have much more with which to vet you and
determine your usefulness within the organization."

They had arrived at 54 Broadway, where he was ushered
from the vehicle into the MI6 headquarters. The exterior of the
building was drab, unassuming, and looked fairly ordinary
compared to what one might expect. It had a sign on the outside
that read Minimax Fire Extinguisher Company - a cover name. It
was the perfect location for a secret organization yet to be known
to exist. It was taller than the surrounding buildings, constructed
from gray and yellow stone with handcrafted, intricate designs,
and featured many windows that faced the road. Of course,
Calder knew better than to assume the building itself was ordinary. He knew a man such as Sinclair would not adopt such a
location unless it was optimal, and as he walked through the
narrow door into the office spaces where he was assigned to take
his test, he made sure to take in the entirety of the space.

The ceilings were high and lofted in many areas, with
wooden paneling surrounding several doors, while other walls
were more basic. The room he entered was one of a similar
nature, with a lower room dimly lit by the glow of artificial lighting. There stood Sinclair, leaning up against one of the many
rows of tables set in the center of the room, smoking a cigar. He
nodded in welcome and motioned for Max to sit down, pointing
toward one of the tables.

"Well," Sinclair said, nodding to Calder, "shall we begin?"

"It's another test, is it?"

Though the records of the specific results of this meeting and test have long since been scrubbed from the records, the rumors spread through the halls of MI6 like a virus. There was a gifted man who had been recruited not by one of the many recruitment officers working for the organization but by Sinclair himself. This man had been placed in a small unit within Section D of the organization and would be operating as a covert agent while simultaneously undergoing training within the organization.

It created waves within the organization, as such an occurrence was highly unusual at the time, even among the most talented individuals. For the next year or so, Calder would be mostly resigned to the code-breaking jobs he excelled at, but it was obvious to anyone who spoke to him that he had a hunger for more. His gifts were incredible - not only was he an excellent codebreaker, but his ability to psychologically profile any of those whom MI6 targeted was unmatched. Eventually, he was called to Sinclair's office for a meeting.

Calder swung the door open, taking a seat comfortably in the velvet chair in front of Sinclair's desk, instantly noticing that Sinclair appeared more stressed than Calder had ever seen him before. Sinclair was not seated. Instead, he paced behind the desk, his face visibly uncomfortable as he walked, growing more agitated until he finally spoke.

"Max, good to see you. I know you've made your way quite well in MI6 so far, and of course, mostly you've operated within Section D in accordance with the missions I've assigned. Though I realize you're likely disappointed - no need to explain why."

"Not really," Calder responded, shrugging. "It's far better than how I was spending my time before. But you're right - I'd like to do more."

"Yes, yes. You're behind a desk most of the time, but I aim to change that. You see, we've been having a few setbacks with the establishment of our Hong Kong station, as I'm sure you're acutely aware."

Calder nodded. It had been obvious to the entire organization for several weeks that struggles had begun to arise within the establishment of MI6's new anti-communist task force.

"So what is it you need from me?"

"Well, Max…I want to assign you to the field."

"Sir, I would be honored." Calder leaned forward in the chair, his face betraying his eagerness. Perhaps it was the faint glow in his icy-gray eyes or the way he shifted slightly, but Sinclair nodded and shrugged.

"Don't get your hopes up too high, Max. There are issues we've been having there, and I'm worried that even you might have difficulty, especially as you're inexperienced in the field."

"What sort of issues?"

"Hong Kong is currently becoming a key node within our network. Simply put, it's very close to two nations of significant interest within our infrastructure: China and Japan. This, of course, means Hong Kong will be an invaluable outpost for gathering intelligence - if we manage to establish it and keep it from falling to either of those nations. We need to ensure that it is secure and keep the Chinese and the Japanese from infiltrating Hong Kong, if at all possible."

"And this is where I come in?"

"Yes. I want an asset on the ground who's not only knowledgeable enough to find any double agents or weak points - as I'm confident you'll be able to - but who isn't previously known or profiled by any of the men already stationed there. A new man, if you will."

"Understood."

"But listen, Max." Sinclair clasped his hands together, staring at Calder with piercing eyes, as if trying to evaluate what the mysterious man was thinking. "This is dangerous. If there is, as I suspect, a double agent, he will try to kill you."

"I understand the risks. I accept."

"Very well…"

Max Calder set off for Hong Kong on his first field mission. But his past hadn't entirely been understood by Sinclair and those around him. While his intelligence and photographic memory were fully comprehended, Calder's ability to fight and operate in the field had been wildly underestimated.

Before even attending Cambridge, Calder often found himself in bar fights, brawls, and other skirmishes growing up in Scotland. Although the data on his childhood was limited and unclear, the most classified Bureau profiles of Calder noted his almost exceptional ability to use the environment around him to his own benefit during fights. They also highlighted quite impressively how Calder himself recalled his childhood, although in limited fashion, during one of his interviews.

If these documents are to be believed, Calder spent his earliest years in the alleys and slums of Glasgow, specifically the Gorbals area, where robbers, murderers, and thieves were prevalent. Though Calder himself seemed rather ashamed of his upbringing, he had a certain cockiness from these early experiences that stemmed from his instincts and resourcefulness. When asked years later by the Bureau during one of their routine interviews how he had managed to survive, Calder simply responded that while others had thrown themselves into the harshest environments by their own desire, he had been forced to endure out of sheer necessity.

It was this skill set, in particular, that allowed Calder to be an invaluable asset in the field, although Sinclair did not know it yet. During his travel, Calder dismissed MI6's normal route and instead traveled to Hong Kong under the guise of an academic, a method accepted by a disgruntled Sinclair. Stepping out onto the docks of Victoria Harbour, Calder was ready to begin his new life as a member of MI6 Hong Kong Station.

For the first few days, he conducted recon without even notifying the members of MI6 already established there that he had arrived, choosing to reveal himself later.

Although MI6 had no official headquarters in Hong Kong, Calder had sauntered into the French Mission Building, which was currently used as a base of operations. His rough but academic clothing and freshly shaved face almost taunted the more experienced members of MI6 already there.

The building was located directly next to Government House and was already occupied by various colonial departments, making it the perfect cover for the establishment of MI6 in Hong Kong. Calder, of course, already knew all about their cover - the third floor of the building was home to the "Office of Maritime Trade Analysis," but in reality, it was here that MI6 had set up their temporary base.

With a knock on the door, he walked in, nodding politely to the stunned secretary who watched as he entered. After a brief conversation with only a few words exchanged, the woman backed away, her face dropping in shock. She turned and pushed her way through several doors, blocking any view further into the floor.

An hour or so later, Max Calder found himself seated at a table with two of the chief officials in charge of the MI6 station in Hong Kong. Frank Lau, a half-Scotsman and half-Hong Kong native, was an elderly fellow in his mid-sixties but had the air of an experienced combat veteran and a keen, smart agent. Henry Armitage, meanwhile, was a more fascinating individual visually, with a thin face, sunken eyes, and an almost bloodshot stare that indicated he hadn't slept well in years.

"Ello, fellas," Calder said, nodding to the two men who sat across from him at a meeting table once he'd gotten initial introductions out of the way. "So, where do I begin?"

"Apologies," Frank Lau replied, being the older and more experienced of the two. "But we'd just received news of your arrival a day ago, and you're telling us you've already been here for nearly a week?"

"Yes, more or less." Calder nodded toward the other fellow, the spindly man who had introduced himself as Henry

Armitage. "I was just telling Henry, as a matter of fact, that I've already found some information of note."

"Yessa'," Henry interjected, his thin face and almost bizarrely sunken eyes revealing a strange nervousness as he spoke. "Mr. Max Calder here says he's located the names of two local smuggling rings, as well as their locations - rings with ties to the Chinese."

"If that's the case, Max," Lau said, "then we need that information. Also, however, I want you to note that I am in charge of this location, not your handlers back in London. When you're here, you do not snoop around without my permission."

Calder nodded, a slight smile on his lips. "Of course, my apologies - this is my first field mission, so I'm sorry if I overstepped my boundaries."

Lau nodded, motioning to Armitage. "Henry here will take down all the information you've found later. For now, walk with me. I have questions as to what exactly you're doing here and what task Broadway has assigned to you."

He stood, motioning for Calder to do the same, and the two men walked along the hallways of the building, with Lau occasionally pointing out points of interest for familiarity and as a way of introduction.

Eventually, as the two men passed several empty rooms, Lau spoke, his voice lower and more urgent. "I believe I already know why you are here. I sent a request to Broadway a while back... told them we needed an outside agent to evaluate our branch here. That you?"

"That's me," Calder confirmed with a nod. "I'm guessing you have suspicions of a double agent?"

It was a simple deduction. Sinclair himself wasn't on the ground, after all, and would need at least one informant whom he trusted, at least reasonably, in order to convince him that there was indeed a double agent operating in Hong Kong.

Lau nodded slowly. "Yes. And I realize you have no reason not to suspect me either, so do your job well. I will give you full clearance to the highest level to operate however you see fit. But please, tell no one else why you are here."

Calder looked carefully at the man, evaluating him. Though Lau seemed rather old to operate actively in the field, he seemed perfectly fit for a position such as the one he held, where decisions were paramount and determined the success of other men. This alone meant that Lau took pride in his work and in his longevity in the field, making him a lower priority on Calder's list.

The two men parted ways, and the next few hours were spent relaying all the information he'd found to Armitage. From that point on, Calder became an established member of the MI6 station operating in Hong Kong. Over the following weeks, he was sent on multiple key field missions, all of which were completed with a great level of success. While the MI6 station had been struggling with failed missions, Calder's recent missions were met with a strange lack of resistance. Of course, Calder himself knew what this meant all too well - whoever the double agent was, they were purposely not feeding the intel from these missions to the enemy… at least for now.

Fieldwork often included spycraft, though just as often it would devolve into irregular operations that the Hong Kong station was forced to attend to. From recruiting local informants to running safe houses, Calder took on as many tasks as he could. During this time, he found an unlikely ally in Henry Armitage, who seemed to have gotten over his initial nervousness and helped Calder assimilate greatly.

However, Calder quickly grew suspicious of the man. He seemed almost too eager to help out on any missions that didn't prove crucial, and this alone made Calder suspicious. Soon, a mission came around that seemed far too important to pass up. It was late on a Sunday night, rain dripping steadily against the small, circular glass window of the bedroom of the MI6 safe house where Calder had been holed up. He sat at a table, papers spread out in front of him. He'd opted to encrypt all his writing in ciphers, usually simple ones. Although these ciphers were easy enough to break, it would mean that anyone who glanced quickly over his shoulder couldn't discern enough relevant information for any use. Just then, a knock at the door prompted him to turn around, glancing sharply at the clock on the wall before speaking.

"Who is it?"

Armitage slipped into the room, his face more nervous than Calder had seen in a while. His hands trembled slightly as he held up a piece of paper to the light.

"Something's come in, Max. A signal from one of our informants at the docks… information about a new shipment arriving tonight - or this morning, really - that seems to be normal enough. But take a look at it and tell me what you see."

Max grabbed the paper, his eyes scanning the message. In an instant, he'd seen it - the prices listed for the shipments deviated only slightly from what was expected, a small enough amount that no casual observer would notice and could easily have come from a change in prices or a greedy dock manager. But it wasn't just a price for one or two - every piece of imported textiles was priced slightly higher, almost as if it had been practiced. A few hundred, or even more, but never more than two hundred. Sure enough, he grabbed a pencil and a piece of paper and got to work. The substitution cipher - for that was what it was - was simple enough. His mind raced as he worked, and Armitage stood behind him, looking pleased.

Only a few minutes later, a message had emerged on the piece of paper where Calder had scribbled. "PIER ELEVEN. MEET AT OH THREE HUNDRED."

He spun around in his chair, looking up at Armitage. "Where did you get this, exactly?"

"I intercepted it - brought it here, to you. Listen, Max… I know why you're here."

Calder tensed, but his countenance didn't change. "Why?"

"We all do, really," Armitage continued. "It's common

knowledge that Frank is trying to paint one of us as an under-cover agent. But I've been doing some thinking. Right now, the Chinese are ahead of us at almost every turn, like they know what we've been up to.

"Only since you've joined the task force have we seen a semblance of success. But that means the information - what's being leaked - has to come from the very top, doesn't it? That's why I poached this document out of communications... before it reached him."

"Who's 'him,' exactly?" Calder asked quietly.

"Frank Lau."

Calder sat still for a few moments, contemplating, then nodded. "If you're right, we should be able to catch them in the act down at the dock. Let's go."

The two men threw on their overcoats and rushed out the door into the rainy Sunday night. Neon signs illuminated their path as they made their way down to the docks. Calder glanced at Armitage here and again, trying to make up his mind. Within thirty minutes, the two men had neared the warehouses at the docks, their boots muddied now as they stepped through the puddles that had formed in the crevices of the road stonework. The sound of the waves was soothing and grew ever louder as they approached, almost drowning out the distant clatter of dock workers already beginning their day.

They kept to the edges of the street as they walked, moving briskly but never venturing too far into the light in case they were intercepted. Soon enough, they'd found Pier 11, a large warehouse that was particularly used for textile shipments. There were only a few lamp posts located here and there, casting a dim and flickering light on the place. The two men paused, looking around.

"Let's split up," Armitage whispered suddenly. "You take the east; I'll take the west and check out the crates."

Calder, however, held up a finger for silence, listening

intently. Armitage nodded, waiting and listening. Suddenly, Calder spoke.

"It's you, isn't it?"

"What?"

"It's you, Henry. You're the double agent."

"What? What the hell - "

"Oh, just shut up," Calder responded, watching the man for any sign of action. "It was too obvious, Armitage. You've known about my reason for being here from day one, haven't you? If you've always had this ability to intercept messages before they reached Frank, then you knew why I showed up. Nobody else knows - that was a bold-faced lie."

Armitage straightened, his eyes glinting in the light from the lampposts. "You're speaking nonsense. Walk me through this, Calder. Why not Frank?"

"Because Frank isn't the one trying to lead me into an ambush. Neither has Frank been trying to play my good side for weeks, trying to cozy up to me on missions. For me, it was between the two of you - but you've just made up my mind."

"Well, that's unfortunate, Max."

"Let me guess, Henry. If I go east, there will be at least a dozen men waiting for…"

Before Calder could finish, Armitage bared his teeth and lunged forward, a glint of steel flashing as he swung his hand. Calder dodged backward, but he wasn't fast enough. A sharp, piercing pain seared across his jaw. He felt blood spurt from his face, saw the knife glint as it rose past him, then fell again. Armitage swung once more, this time aiming directly for the center of his neck.

Any hesitation that might have crept in during his intellectual work - his code-breaking, and his jobs with MI6 and Sinclair - so far instantly vanished. Calder's mind was blank in an instant, transported back to his childhood in the Gorbals. He felt no pain, no fear, only a cold, white anger at the attempt on his life. His right arm shot upward, catching the man's arm before the knife reached his face. The two fought for control, slipping on the wet cobblestones as the waves lapped quietly against the dock. Armitage suddenly lost his footing, falling down as Calder fell on top of him, knocking the knife from his hand. The two men looked at it for a second before scrambling desperately, fighting to reach it first.

Calder struck downward, his fist connecting with Armitage's jaw, and he felt his grip loosen for a second. Armitage clawed his fingers against Calder's jaw, grabbing desperately at the raw flesh that he'd cut, making Calder grunt in pain.

But Max Calder was no mere trained soldier like Armitage was. He was a street fighter who had the experience of a man twice his age, and he brought his knee solidly down into Armitage's chest, feeling the air leave the man's lungs as he gasped desperately. That was enough. With a final lunge, Calder managed to grab the knife, his fist closing around the handle. In the next moment, Armitage was on top of him, clawing desperately as he tried to pry the knife from Calder's hands. The two men rolled, slipping and sliding down the dock as they fought, the ocean lapping below them only inches from their faces as they hung over the edge of the pier.

Calder struggled, finally gaining the upper hand with the knife still clenched in his fist. He pulled himself on top, thrusting the knife downward and into Armitage's side. The man let out a grunt, his hands trembling as they slowly went limp, and he stared at Calder.

"I thought you'd only worked at a desk. How the hell did you learn to fight?"

"Eat shit," Calder replied, standing before he kicked the man in the ribs, pushing him off the dock and into the dark water below.

Armitage fell, screaming for only a second before the waves collapsed over his head, and the dark water turned a slight shade of crimson. Calder tenderly felt his jaw, but he had only a second to inspect it.

With a resounding crack, a bullet ricocheted off a barrel that stood only feet away from Calder, causing him to duck suddenly.

Yells and shouts in Chinese erupted suddenly, and several men ran toward the docks, their faces angry. Armitage's scream had captured the attention of his allies, and the sudden footsteps meant one thing: Calder had to escape. Though his jaw was still trickling with blood, he ran, dodging past barrels and street-lamps as he ducked for cover, feeling bullets whizzing past his head. He ran up the cobbled street, the neon signs overhead illu-minating his face as he ducked into an alleyway, finally dodging past old boxes and piles of trash.

He could hear the men behind him, screaming vulgarities in their native tongue as they pursued him, but he was too fast. Though he was still new to Hong Kong, the first days he'd spent there had been crucial - he knew even these streets with a certain level of familiarity and weaved deftly from back alley to back alley, dodging finally into an open doorway of an abandoned house. His vision grew blurry, and he quickly fashioned a rough dressing out of his shirt, tearing it and using it to slow the bleeding slightly.

He leaned against the wall, eyes fluttering shut until morning arrived. When the sun first peeked over the tops of the build-ings, Max Calder stood up, wobbling as he made his way toward the MI6 safe house.

A few weeks later, Calder requested to be relocated back to Broadway for his next mission.

He sat in front of Sinclair's desk, arms crossed, listening to the man speak.

"Max, welcome back - damn, you picked up a parting gift from Hong Kong?" Sinclair tapped his own jaw, indicating that he had seen Calder's.

"Yes. I don't believe the double agent was all too pleased to be caught."

Sinclair laughed. "Well, you're clearly a valuable asset, Max.

You have my deepest thanks for your work here, but I won't ask this of you again - I'm going to assign you back to the desk for a while, then - "

"Sir," Calder interrupted, leaning forward. "If it's at all possible, I'd like to be assigned a new field mission."

At the time, Max Calder had a deep-seated hunger to do more. Although many years later he would try to escape back to a normal life, that strange glow in his icy gray eyes always led him back to the world of espionage.

As little as he liked to admit it, this one taste of action that he'd gotten on the job had kindled something more - something precisely close to an addiction.

CHAPTER 8
SELL OUTS AND SETBACKS

The blistering sun shone down on my face. I squinted, suddenly aware of my cracked lips and aching ribs. Where was I? How long had I been here? I blinked. I blinked again. I assumed I was still in Vienna.

What the hell was going on? What had happened, anyway? I rubbed my eyes, pausing only when I realized my arm was caked with blood. I smacked my lips, tasting the metallic tang in my mouth. I glanced around, becoming more aware of my surroundings. I was still too stiff to move, but more lucid at the very least. I was in some back alley - no doubt during the day, past high noon, judging by the angle of the sun - lazily sitting on a heap of potting soil which had been dumped on the ground, accompanied by loose bits of trash and other detritus.

My whole body felt sore, but I was beginning to remember.

———

They had blown the door to smithereens. I'd jumped away, rolling back from the door in an instant and firing off shots into the smoke. There had been groans, thuds as bodies hit the floor.

Bullets came whizzing back, tearing into my skin like icy-hot irons, branding me a dead man.

I'd fallen backward, then crawled my way into a room behind the one where I had harbored Krane. I grabbed a gun out of the wardrobe - a BESAL, if I remembered right - and laid into them, shooting indiscriminately. Considering I thought then that I would die, I'd gotten as many answers out of Krane as I ever would… and if he died, it would matter little.

The clip ran empty. More voices. I knew they were coming for me and crawled toward the window, my skin ripped and bloody. I bashed it with the butt of the gun, then toppled out, downward - and then, darkness.

———

I stood up gingerly from the pile of soil. Why hadn't they gone after me and finished the job? And more importantly, why the hell was I stitched up where I'd been shot? It was an expert job, evenly spaced, and something even I would have trouble matching with my current abilities. Whoever had stitched me up was clearly experienced in this field - whether the medical profession or perhaps a field of work similar to mine. I wasn't sure. What I was sure of, however, was the fact that whoever had done this had likely saved my life.

As I stood there judiciously stretching my body, I would have bet good money that whoever had done this had also spirited me off away from the safe house where I had almost met my end. But now wasn't the time to think about who had done this - I could figure that out later. Right now, I needed answers. I made my way to a pay phone a few blocks away from the alley in which I had awoken, dialing the same number that had been left on the notepad near the phone in the safe house.

The phone rang. Then there was static. Finally, there was a voice.

"Hello?"

I recognized her voice from the single word of greeting she had spoken. "Artemis."

"Calder? That you?"

"They took Krane. Withers is dead. The op's blown."

"I know. The agent who was supposed to meet you - name was Malik - is dead. Found in his bathtub with a cyanide bead lodged in his throat."

"Bishop."

"Or someone's playing him. There's more, too. We intercepted several messages from the NKVD, or whatever remains of them - they knew everything, even things Bishop couldn't know."

"Then who the hell is the mole? I have a score to settle with whoever did this."

"Not sure. Meet me at the café near Karlsplatz. Head to Kartner Strasse and find the café with the half-lit sign. I'll be there."

"How do I know I can trust you?"

She paused for a second, as if thinking. "You don't - but I don't know I can trust you, either."

"Touche."

I hung up the phone. I didn't trust Artemis - never had, if I remembered correctly. It wasn't that she was a liar; you could predict liars. It was the simple fact that even if she told the truth, it was oftentimes twisted in a way that was precisely designed to make you believe a lie anyway. And that - well, that was hard to decipher.

I cleaned myself up in a fountain along one of the city streets, then made my way to Karlsplatz. I took the train, fishing out a few of the coins I had left from my pocket. Most of my supplies remained at the safe house, and I wasn't about to head back there to retrieve them. All I had left was my Waltham pocket watch, my ring, which I always wore, my lighter, and my Colt. And, of course, an icy cold anger that had replaced my pain - the type of anger that keeps you going even when you want nothing more than to sit down with a whiskey and drink your life away. Whoever set me up - well, they were dead. I would make sure of that.

A few hours later, I was at Kartner Strasse - it was one of the busiest streets in Vienna, and for good reason. Shops and cafés lined the street, and wealthy ladies and gentlemen walked leisurely all about. It was one of the richest streets in all of Vienna, with luxury goods, tourist trinkets, and even entertainers. This was the high life of Vienna, and I had a sneaking suspicion that was why Alicia had chosen this place to meet.

She had said it, and that part was undoubtedly true - she didn't trust me. Here, I couldn't try any funny business, nor could I tip off the Russians if I were the mole. The same went for her, which guaranteed my safety. After a good ten minutes of walking, I spotted a café - its neon sign lazily blinking, only half-lit. I supposed this was the place. I entered and sat at a table. The waitresses here wore fake smiles, like borrowed jewelry, their lips thin and pursed as they nodded politely to customers. It had seen better days, I figured.

"I'll take a coffee. Black."

The waitress nodded, and she was off, returning a moment later with my cup. As I sipped it, I waited. I was certain that Alicia would show soon. Sure enough, only a few minutes later, she walked in. Her heels clicked on the floor, her body moving fluidly as if she were one with the bustling environment around her. She wore a gray scarf, a stunning red dress, and an outfit that more than fit perfectly in the high society styling of our surroundings. She took a seat next to me, gently set her hat on her lap, and glanced at me. Her gaze was piercing, her auburn hair neatly combed, and her chin slightly lifted.

"Did you sell us out?" I asked. I was in no mood to chat, as much as something about her brought out that nostalgia in me.

She didn't blink. "No, but someone did. And someone else saved your life. Kulik had a kill order on you - we know that much. I'm not sure if it was retracted or if he's still unaware of what happened."

"And Krane?"

"He's back with the Soviets. He'll be moved somewhere much safer, with much more protection. There's no point keeping any of the information from you at this point. I'll give you everything I know. Stalin himself is interested in Krane's work… and we'd best assume that he's furious Krane was nearly killed. That, and even more furious you got away. On that basis, I am guessing that Kulik isn't long for this world."

"Krane seemed to have an idea of who sold us out, but he hadn't told me before the Soviets tracked us down."

"Not surprised. He wanted to be captured. From what we can tell, he's building another prototype of the Mirror, and it's nearing completion. If he can build a stable version again…this war is as good as lost."

"The war?"

"Baruch called it a cold war…the war never really ended, anyway; it just changed clothes and blended in. It became something else."

I sat back in my chair. I knew who Baruch was. He was a financier and presidential adviser in the United States, someone I'd read about in the newspapers. If this man had called it a cold war, he was probably right.

As early as it was, I would have liked a whiskey. Maybe something stronger. I was used to betrayal - it seemed that I'd dealt with such a concept every other day - but this was different.

"Where is Krane now?"

"As far as we know? Headed to Prague. The Soviets think they're in control. But with what we know about Krane, they're not."

"Who is?"

"We're not sure. But Krane has many powerful backers, and he has his own ego to nurse."

I stared at her, and for the first time, she seemed tired.

"So, what next?" I asked.

"You go rogue. Go ghost."

"Why?"

"There are insiders… one, at least - as you found out - but maybe more, who have close connections to Krane himself. I've already cut off contact with the Bureau again. It's not safe; you can't trust anyone."

"And you?" I watched her carefully, my fingers sliding toward the trigger of my gun. I wasn't sure if I trusted her fully or not. Although I didn't want to, I planned to see this through. If she got in my way - well, I was a trained professional for a reason.

"Doesn't matter if you believe me or not. You'll need me. I can help you remember who you are."

"And who am I, exactly?"

She pulled a cigarette from her coat pocket, lighting it in front of her face. A second later, she exhaled a breath of smoke that curled upward and dissipated into the café's warm air.

"You're a ghost, Calder. Remember - you were supposed to be dead."

"A ghost?" I scoffed.

"It fits."

CHAPTER 9
CATACOMBS AND CHAOS

The journey to Prague was slow. We left as soon as she convinced me, there in the coffee shop, that there was a job to finish. We traveled together. The only stop we made in Vienna was at the safe house, where I carefully entered as she kept watch, retrieving my documents and personal supplies, which I'd stashed there and left behind in the incident.

Though I would never admit it, I enjoyed her company. Did I trust her? Not at all, but her witty remarks and knowledge of the world of espionage - a world I was so familiar with - were comforting to me. I could see why we had gotten along so well all those years ago.

We traveled by train. The railways were still operational even after the war. The train ride itself, though functional, was also an emotional passage for many travelers, connecting two cities with different political realities - Vienna, under the occupation of the Allied forces, and Prague, soon to fall under Soviet influence as the Cold War began to shape the fate of Central Europe.

We departed from Wien Westbahnhof and headed into the Austrian countryside. The train car itself was nothing to write home about. It was an old, rickety car with limited comforts - cramped seats, some of them old and patched, and the faint smell of musty upholstery mixed with the lingering scent of cigarette smoke from earlier passengers. The people on board were a mix of Austrians, Czechs, displaced persons, and soldiers, many of whom were traveling either to start a new life or to return to their homes after the war.

Outside, the lush greenery contrasted sharply with the somber interior of the train. Travelers gazed out of the windows, reflecting on the turmoil of the past, as the scenery passed by in a slow, rhythmic cadence. Along the way, passengers occasionally exchanged brief, nervous conversations - discussions about the future of Europe, the ongoing tensions between East and West, and the fear of a world still hanging in the balance.

The two of us passed our time with drinks and stories from the Bureau. I had begun to remember much more about my previous life - the part of my life that was clouded in shadows - and so we discussed whatever I could remember. The details of my work - how I'd been one of the first test subjects to "Slide," as I now comfortably referred to it, how the two of us had been on multiple missions together earlier in the war, and how I had always seemed to have a keen interest in time. It wasn't like the other passengers cared much for company; many traveled in silence, simply staring ahead or out the window, their eyes glazed over. For us, this was less personal, but for these simple country folk and ex-military, the war was fresh in their minds.

When they saw the landscape passing, the overhanging clouds, and the cold, blistering landscape, they saw the bodies of their loved ones.

"Do you remember the 1945 operation?" she asked.

"The one in France?"

"No, no - the one in New York… remember, the businessman who…"

These were the discussions that now dictated how we spent our time as the train chugged along. Every hour or so, it would be stopped and subjected to an identity check, which didn't faze us much. Artemis and I were both well-equipped with our share of fake passports, fake licenses, and information needed to cross almost any border around the globe.

Halfway through the trip, we ordered food - a basic meal that reeked of poverty. It wasn't all we could afford, but we needed to lie low and blend in with the other passengers.

As the train approached the Czech border, the atmosphere within the rickety cars subtly shifted. The border crossing between Austria and Czechoslovakia was still greatly affected by the war, and traveling across that forbidden line caused an air of discomfort from every passenger riding alongside us. As we slowed to a halt for the usual inspection, we saw them - border guards from both nations, men in uniform, accompanied by military police from the occupying forces, boarding the train for a closer inspection.

They searched items, kicking and shuffling through bags, roughly grabbing passengers who seemed a little too nervous for a more up-close and personal shakedown. For many of the passengers, this was a moment that no doubt filled them with terror. For Artemis and me, however, it felt all too normal. We were used to the conditions caused by the war. We were used to the rough travel during this time. I leaned back in my seat, lounging and continuing to make small talk with her until the guards had satisfied themselves and left.

Once across the border, the train entered the Czech countryside, where rolling hills and patchwork farmland were visible. Much of the landscape had been brutalized during the war, but occasional small villages and cattle remained, perched atop hills or grazing in valleys.

As the train passed some of the towns - many of which I recognized, like Brno and Olomouc - we glanced out the windows, pausing our conversation as we stared at the many workers who incessantly slaved away, rebuilding the country in the wake of the German occupation.

The difference between the two countries was palpable - Austria and Czechoslovakia were undoubtedly two very different sides of the same coin, a paradigm drawn as a result of the various ideologies among the men who led these countries.

Austria was still very much under the influence of the Allies, but Czechoslovakia was overshadowed by the Soviets... and by communism. I knew all too well that the underground resistance movements in Czechoslovakia were slowly being suffocated by Soviet-backed forces.

Soon enough, we were in Prague. The city had been damaged by the war, but that wasn't what made it so special - it was a land of Soviet influence, and that influence emanated from every old bone and brick I could see.

Prague was quiet as I departed from the train station, walking up the steps with Artemis trailing behind me. It wore a heavy air of deceit, ruinous tragedy, and homelessness like a fur coat - each part blanketing the city and smothering it to the ground. As we walked, however, I felt her lay her hand on my arm. It was bizarre - strange and unlike her enough that it caused me to turn to her, which was exactly what she wanted.

"Max, you're going to have to deal with Krane alone... or without me, at least."

"What do you mean?" I knew something was up - she would have never used my first name unless she wanted something and had been hiding something from me.

"I'm not staying in Prague. Near Warsaw, there have been mentions of a man there - Subject Delta."

Subject Delta - I recognized that name instantly. Locked memories suddenly came flooding back to me, my mind filling in the blanks that had been foggy before. He was the name the Bureau had covered up at all costs, so of course, naturally, we all knew it. He had been the first Slider, the first test experiment who slipped into the Mirror with disastrous results.

"Why are you going after him?"

"Because the Bureau is. And if they know where he is, it's a safe bet that the Soviets know."

"And why is he so important?"

"Things are getting weird in Warsaw. If anything, it seems as if there are some residual quantum effects from the Mirror there... but it doesn't just stop at that. Before I went off the grid, I learned from the Bureau that he's seemingly entangled with the Mirror - all instances of it."

"All instances?"

"Yes. Each time a new Mirror is built, it's like a new entanglement occurs. Subject Delta isn't just connected to the first one; he's somehow linked to every copy, like some particle caught up in a spider web. You move one thread of the spider web, and the particle moves with it - no matter the string you move."

I had caught on already. "And that means that he'll know about Krane and the Mirror."

"Not just that... he might have a clue about who the compromised agents are."

"Well, I won't keep you then. Good luck."

"You as well, Calder. Contact Cenek - he's a good man, a man I trust to keep things private that happen here."

Without another word, she turned away. With a gentle, almost pedantic wave of her hand, she bid me farewell and walked back toward the train station. I stood there for a moment, watching her, before I turned back to face the looming problem before me.

The first problem, of course, was making contact with Cenek, which I knew would be easy enough. I already knew the man. Cenek Novák was a big, bulky figure, more fat than muscle, with a pair of out-of-control eyebrows and a bushy mustache to match. The man looked like he could be jovial, though he was anything but.

He had a temper only a mother could love, if I recalled correctly from my few interactions with him.

I struck up a few conversations until I found a particularly knowledgeable local who pointed me in the right direction. According to this fellow, Cenek was holed up in a dusty shop, working as a clock repairman. I knew better, though. I knew he was a former Czech resistance fighter with a surprising number of Bureau contacts.

Though I wasn't sure if I should trust him, I really didn't have another place to turn. Artemis had told me she trusted him, and I supposed I'd rather see what information he had than go strolling around the city all night, asking for the whereabouts of a mad scientist hell-bent on bringing about the destruction of the world.

I flagged a taxi, haltingly communicating where I needed to go with a man who spoke only broken French. Soon, the cab pulled up to the curb, and I stepped out in front of the shop. The sign read "Novák's Clocks," though from the peeling paint, I could only assume I would be his first real customer since he'd set up business there. So I entered, stepping gingerly around the piles of old collectibles, furniture, and clocks scattered here and there. The door creaked shut behind me, the bell dinged, and only a few seconds passed by before he emerged.

He walked out of the door behind the counter, dusting off his face with the appearance of a man caught busy in some tedious work, all too glad to be relieved of it. When he saw me, his face dropped for a second, then a slight smile broke across his face.

"Ah, Calder. She called ahead."

By "she," I could only assume he meant Artemis. "You have information for me?"

"You need information? I am your man."

"What do you know, then? Spit it out."

He scowled, pulled out a piece of paper, crumpled it, and tossed it to me. He spat his chewing tobacco into a bin behind the counter, combed his hair with his greasy fingers, and then spoke.

"They're meeting tonight. Beneath the Astronomical Clock. In the old catacombs."

"Who's they?"

"Krane and a few of his most powerful backers. Oh, and Bishop."

My blood ran cold, and I felt an icy excitement seep through my veins. If Bishop was there, that meant at the very least that he was one of the moles. I could put him out of his misery, along with Krane, once and for all.

"Anything else I need to know?" I asked.

"Not more nor less, except the fact that there'll be multiple men there. I said backers, Calder. Don't know if you can take 'em all on yourself."

"Not your problem, Cenek. Thanks for the information."

"And one more thing - the Mirror prototype. From my sources, Stalin himself assigned his top scientists to work under Krane. If it's not finished by the time you get there, it will be soon."

"What?"

"One slider to another, thought it was important."

"Could have damn well told me that at the start."

He muttered some obscenity to himself, no doubt directed at me, but I was already striding from the shop. I had to prepare. If Krane had finalized the Mirror and taken the equipment to Prague, then all hell was about to break loose. I already had my trusty M1911, but if everything Cenek said was true, I would need more firepower.

So, my first step was to blend into the Prague underground to find the tools - the weapons - I needed. War-torn Prague was still very much recovering from the destruction caused by the battles, the bombings, and the gunfire. As such, it proved difficult at first to locate what I needed. Eventually, however, I managed to find, through back-alley talk and gossip with the homeless and distressed, the location of an underground bazaar.

This was Prague's black market. It was a notorious thing that even men from the outside had heard whispers of, and this was where I could find my equipment. Tucked away in a dark alley behind the train yards was a dilapidated street market, with vendors who only barely passed inspection or would have if the city officials cared enough to inspect. One of these men, a particularly soot-covered fellow who looked as if he'd been starving his entire life, was my target. I approached his stall, my face shaded by the hat I had carefully tucked over my eyes.

"Heard you had weapons for sale."

"You heard right."

"I need something with decent firepower - not too heavy, not too large - easy enough to keep under wraps until I need it. Not a handgun."

After a bit of haggling with the owner of the stall, I procured an M1 Garand at a reasonable price... considering the situation and difficulty it had taken to even locate a weapons dealer, of course.

Though it wasn't my first choice, I would undoubtedly be able to put this weapon to good use. I stashed it under my trench coat, making sure to keep it out of sight and against my body to a void looking suspicious. Along with some other odds, ends, and knick-knacks, I was as prepared as I would ever be.

Assuming that Krane would be heavily guarded, as the Soviets would know I was still on the loose, I needed a reliable weapon that offered more than my pistol. This wouldn't only be a mission where stealth was required, but it would be a mission that would undoubtedly end in bloodshed.

It was nearing nighttime, with the setting sun casting shimmering shadows over the brutal Prague cityscape. I finally opened up the crumpled paper Cenek had given me, spreading it out against my leg as I sat on a park bench in one of the few remaining parks this city had. It was a map - a map of the catacombs, from what I could tell. I had little idea of where the man had procured such a map, but from the small bloodstain on one corner, I assumed it had cost a life or two. I had no intention of asking, either. This was part of the job, and Cenek did his job well. If one of Krane's men went missing, their body turning up only months later, I couldn't care less.

I made my way over the brick streets until I found the entrance described in scribbled writing on the map. I swung down a ledge, planting my feet firmly on the surface of the old ground, forgotten centuries ago. It was a horribly cold, eerie, haunting place. The tunnels were narrow; lit only by the flicker of the flashlight I had bought along with my gun. It reeked of rat feces, old decaying corpses, and the stench of still water gone foul long ago.

I walked for what felt like hours, though it was likely much shorter, my feet plodding along the darkened surface. I followed the map carefully, holding it up to the beam of my flashlight every few feet to double-check that I was heading in the right direction. Eventually, however, I spotted the faintest glow ahead. Instantly pocketing my flashlight beneath my trench coat, I crept forward, my feet silent against the stones. As I turned a corner, the scene came into view, sprawling in my vision like a beautiful tragedy - a perfect one.

The catacombs opened into a wide chamber, clearly cut in a more precise way than the rock surrounding it. The chamber was dimly lit with artificial lights and had a smooth floor. From what I could tell, the very center of the room was circular, a platform raised above the rest of the more mundane surface, like a ring or arena. More than likely, it had once been an underground fighting ring converted into a laboratory at the behest of Krane himself. It had many devices there, all buzzing and alight with energy. In the very center stood what I had been praying I would not find.

There it was - alight with a beautiful, blue, iridescent light, shining out of the cracked surface like a magical mist. This newly constructed Mirror had a frame more akin to a solid oak form than the antique version I was familiar with.

Next to the Mirror stood Krane, his eyes sparkling with some kind of triumph. In his hands, he held a console, attached with wires to the frame of the Mirror itself. Beside him stood two men, wearing uniforms of importance that designated them as the superiors in the situation. These powerful men were no doubt sent by Stalin himself to ensure that the project worked as planned. Far behind him stood Bishop - his face blank, his body motionless - but his rosary in hand. Around the platform stood soldiers - five or so of them - wearing NKVD uniforms. It appeared Krane himself was, after all, in high standing with the Soviets despite the small setback I had caused in Vienna. Perhaps he was simply too important to give up.

Crouching behind one of the jagged walls that hid me from view, I silently pulled the rifle from my trench coat. I'd have to be precise - a bullet in each man who stood before me - and things would no doubt get messy. Still, it had to be done.

And, of course, there was the most important target: Krane himself. I gritted my teeth as I aimed, my rifle pointing toward Krane's balding head, his frail and twisted body radiating with that aura of devilish energy he had - a scientific excitement only a man of genius can possess.

I could tell by the air around me - thick but not yet pulsing and electric - that he hadn't begun to pulse the Mirror yet. If I put him down first, he'd never be able to start this damn device, and the other men more than likely would have no idea how to operate it.

My finger rested lightly on the trigger. I slowed my breathing, focusing. I felt the gun steady, and I saw the crosshair align directly with the center of Krane's dome.

Suddenly, I felt a hand grip my shoulder - rough, cold, and strong.

"Stay down," a low, deep voice, unmistakably that of a man, whispered in my ear. Every one of my reflexes screamed at me to fight, to spin around, grab the man who had caught me by surprise, and incapacitate him before he could alert the guards. But my mind told me two other things - first, if this man had wanted to hurt me, he could have done so by now; and second, I recognized the voice that spoke to me.

Without making a sound, I turned my head and saw the man who I thought had died, a man who had taught me everything I knew. He had been my mentor in the field, the man I had most looked up to in the Bureau. When all else went to hell, he had been the man who had pulled me aside, looked me in the eyes, and ordered me to focus on the present.

Memories came flooding back - all the memories that had remained foggy, and even the memories that I had pushed from my mind. The memories of sliding, of working carefully alongside this man in some of the most crucial missions ever. He had never cared that he was the director, the leader, or even the philosopher who had created recursion theory. He had fought alongside every one of us during the war.

There, in front of me in the darkness, I saw his familiar face. He looked older and more worn than before, his dirty clothes indicating wear and tear of ages, and his rimmed glasses scratched, but it was him - Hawthorne, the man who had directed the use of the Mirror, developed the safeguards that allowed Sliders to pass through time without harming the greater timeline, and imposed ethics on a military operation where there had been none.

CHAPTER 10
MALCOLM SHAW

awthorne was the Bureau's codename for the man none recognized but all feared - Malcolm Shaw. It was the few and far between who knew his real name, and those who discovered it oftentimes met their end in strange ways... ways that left you wondering whether they had existed at all in the first place. We're not talking death - we're talking disappearance.

Of course, many who came to know his real name speculated how Shaw had become known as Hawthorne. If those speculating had managed to glimpse within any number of highly classified Bureau files, they would discover that such code names are often deeply symbolic, just like with Raven and Artemis. Those names were often chosen by the agents themselves and submitted to the Bureau or occasionally assigned by the Bureau higher-ups when the agent refused to use the name, as was the case with Max Calder.

Regardless of how the names are assigned, the organization would take the alias as seriously as the agent themselves. The names reflected the personal journey, style, and "artistic flair" of the agent and were typically assigned based on a variety of factors such as operational security, psychological profiles, or even significant life events.

In Shaw's case, it was the symbolism that mattered. Shaw was known for the strength and resilience in all that he did, the stubborn dedication he had to the rules, and his tenacity. He was known to be adaptable but also persevered no matter the hardship, and hence was named after the Hawthorne tree, which is known for its strength, stubborn nature, and its ability to withstand even the harshest of environments. Rough terrain matters not to the tree, and Hawthorne was the same when dealing with the secretive world of the Bureau. No one remembers which higher-up first assigned him that code name, but the tongue-in-cheek nickname stuck.

Hawthorne had been in Vienna for weeks, tracking down the man who had betrayed him and the entire Bureau a few years ago. The man - Emil Krane - had purposefully pulsed the Mirror to a greater degree than he should have, killing dozens during the Rosyth Naval Dockyard incident. It wasn't an easy task - he was haunted by the memories of the past, memories that he now considered failures that should have cost him his job time and time again. Yet, he had remained, trying his best to warn his superiors of the risk posed by the Mirror.

Now, he was here - a man of action who kept his emotions locked away and unreadable, like a drawer never meant to be opened or the face of a poker hustler. And yet, here he was... was it not ironic? Here he was, tracking down the man behind the Mirror - the man who could end the world. He rubbed his face, feeling the leathery wrinkles and creases. He had grown old. All those years he'd lived. All those years ago.

———

He'd been born in the bustling streets of London in the late 1880s to an alcoholic father and a mother he never knew - as his father referred to her, a "whore of the streets." Unfortunately, this alcoholic father was also a renowned British diplomat, and so Malcolm Shaw had grown up without a single friend. Instead, he'd moved between countries, only himself and his books to keep him company.

But occasionally, when his father wasn't drinking, Malcolm had been able to understand the man behind the impenetrable curtain - and he had come to understand that his father was brilliant. There was a reason he was so diplomatically talented. A shrewd, calculating man, Arthur Shaw had instilled in his son the belief that everything could be negotiated and that every interaction was a game of balance and leverage. To survive, you needed more than just strength; you needed to understand the unspoken rules of power.

"And where will you move next, son?"

"Rook to E5."

"Why the rook?"

"Can you not guess, father? To play a game, you must play to win."

That was the day he had first beaten his father at the game of chess, yet Malcolm felt unsatisfied. He'd always felt that there was more to the world than the rigid lines of diplomacy. And so, when he first set off to university, he turned his attention to military intelligence instead. With his connections, he managed to enroll in a series of top-secret training programs as Britain and the rest of the world prepared for the looming conflict of World War I.

It was here that he met Reggie Wright - a man whose wit rivaled that of Hawthorne himself. They quickly became inseparable. As men later discovered when reading through his notes and will, Malcolm had considered Reggie his one true friend. Perhaps it was because he'd never truly had a friend before, but the friendship that he held with Reggie was unlike any other. It was more of a connection of equal minds, two men who latched onto each other's similarities and leapt for joy at any differences.

They competed, too - both were fascinated by military operations, and soon the two had become fully fledged forces in the world of espionage.

But as talented as Reggie was, Malcolm was special.

A rising star in the world of espionage, known for his sharp intellect and cold pragmatism, Malcolm didn't just use rules - he broke them. He broke each rule, manipulating it to his desires.

His ego ran rampant, his brilliant mind basking in every new problem he solved. A man of strategy, he was someone who could step up to any situation and figure out the path to success, no matter the cost.

But this worldview - this perspective - would soon come to an end.

———

Hawthorne settled back into his chair, a pipe in hand. He had much waiting to do here in Vienna, so he might as well remember… for once.

It was the winter of 1941 when Hawthorne first heard whispers of the project. They called it the Office of Temporal Anomalies and Strategic Intelligence - only later would the official name be all but forgotten by new subordinates and trainees who were recruited by the organization, and only then would it become known simply as the Bureau. For Hawthorne, however, he had known it as OTASI.

The details were sparse, as they often were in the world of espionage and government work, but the whispers were all the more intriguing. They said it was a project shrouded in secrecy, aimed at taking on the looming technological and scientific issues the world was facing as it progressed. World War II was looming, and this project was said to work in the realm of time, temporal manipulation, and the emerging science of the quantum realm.

The potential of this project, of course, was immense. An organization established for such a purpose could change the course of history, both on the battlefield and in the corridors of power. It was easy for Hawthorne to find his way into this project. His curiosity piqued, he had begun to investigate when he was contacted by the highest-ranking officials in the military - men with ranks so high that nobody knew their names.

"We know you want in, Hawthorne. We'll give you an in."

Those were the words they had said, and maybe it was because they knew the true nature of Hawthorne had begun to shift. During one of his missions, he'd seen a man die - a man he had never thought would pass. He had seen Reggie, his face drained and white, blood pouring from an open wound. He had watched his one real and true friend die...die because of a strategy that he had devised.

He'd promised Reggie it would work - the mission could never fail. And yet, it had. And it had been his fault.

This changed him. Hawthorne sat in his chair, unmoving, watching the smoke curl and dance from his pipe in front of him. Though the man would never show his emotions, his heart grew heavy as he remembered.

By 1941, when he joined the Bureau as one of its first and leading members, Hawthorne had already begun to regret his philosophy of life. As he began to delve into the technologies that the Bureau recorded and created, Hawthorne became fascinated with time itself.

This wasn't just about espionage; it was about understanding the power of the new technology before anyone else could harness it. The project, he was told, had the potential to alter the fabric of time itself.

At first, he had considered it. Could he bring his friend back? Could they clash again, mind against mind, to see who came out on top?

But he had changed too much.

So even when the science, which originally seemed impossible - unfathomable, even - became a reality, he was wary. The military had poured resources into the project, and by 1942,

Hawthorne had become one of the project's most trusted operatives, ensuring that the interests of the military were protected and that no one outside the circle of control learned of its true nature.

What he couldn't foresee, however, was the growing influence the Mirror would have on him personally. Because it was then, in the early days of 1943, that the Mirror was first created, and the consequences soon became apparent.

The more he learned of the project, the more unsettled he became by the consequences of meddling with something as dangerous as time. His role, however, continued to expand. In 1943, he was dispatched to oversee the security of the facility at Rosyth Naval Dockyard, where the device was being tested.

Though he wasn't a scientist, he quickly became involved in the operational aspects of the project. As he watched the first test results, he quickly became wary. It was then that he began to implement ethical guidelines, to the best of his ability, against the will of men like Emil Krane.

The military considered the first tests a success, but success in the military was a failure to Hawthorne. Soldiers and even volunteers were sent through the Mirror, returning with fractured memories, broken bones, and aged bodies. Some rare test subjects came back unchanged, but others came back dead and rotten. To Hawthorne's brilliant, calculating mind, which had seen firsthand the effect that death and the passage of time could have on a man, this was a mistake. The implications, of course, were terrifying - the Mirror was warping reality itself, and Hawthorne was no fool. He understood instantly that although the military would use it as such, this was not simply a military asset.

He still believed in the good the military could do, of course. To a lawful man like Hawthorne, the legal process enforced by the military was a good standard to follow. But while he believed in the good the military could do, he didn't believe they should have power such as this - power that could hold the whole world hostage and break the very rules they were supposed to protect.

He knew better than anyone, even back then, that the Mirror itself was uncontrollable. By 1944, he began warning his superiors and anyone willing to listen, egged on by a man whom he considered more brilliant than even himself. He'd discussed the project with that man, and the two had concluded on its danger. But it wasn't just his fear of the Mirror that led Hawthorne forward; it was his suspicion that the device might be, in some way, interconnected with the very fabric of reality at a level that even Krane and his colleagues didn't realize. It had him questioning the very essence of his own reality, as he would much later confess to Calder during a rare moment of openness.

And so he tried to warn them. He reached out to every official he had a connection with, imploring them to listen and heed his warnings.

The military ignored him. They viewed the Mirror as an asset, a weapon to end the war on their terms - even though they had no real understanding of what it was capable of. It was then that he began to question his allegiance to the project and the Bureau as a whole. The Mirror was too powerful for any nation to control.

———

He sighed as he smoked his pipe. It was empty now, and the last wisp of smoke floated into the air. He had been right.

In 1945, the incident occurred. The incident that caused dozens of men to die, others to go missing, and still more to be forever affected by the residual quantum entanglement the Mirror had left behind. It was this event that subsequently became known as the Rosyth Incident.

That night, he disappeared, realizing that if he stayed, the Committee of Nine would undoubtedly recognize what he had come to understand that night: he was no longer one of them -

no longer a man who would risk anything to succeed, who would sacrifice life and time itself to achieve his goals. If the Committee had discovered that, they would have disposed of him.

Using the accident as cover, Hawthorne slipped into the night like a ghost forged anew into a whisper. The war had ended, but the power of the Mirror still lingered in the dark corners of the world. Hawthorne could feel it pulling him, always connected to it in a way that only he could describe. He had become a man on the run, always a step ahead of those who sought to control him. Only one or two men knew he was still alive, but those adversaries were the most dangerous of all. They were men who would stop at nothing to keep Hawthorne from his goal: to control the Mirror's destiny and ensure it was not used.

He had always been a man of strategy, but now he was a man who had simply seen too much. Those on the Committee who wielded the most power were the men who hunted him.

He couldn't afford to stay in one place for long, and so for months he traveled across Europe, moving through the shadows, gathering pieces of the puzzle in hopes that he could finally end the Mirror and its influence once and for all.

He couldn't shake the feeling that the Mirror itself had left something behind… or let something escape from its depths that shouldn't have gotten out. Now, in 1947, Hawthorne was in Vienna.

He stood from his chair, his time spent reminiscing coming to a close. He was nearing the finish line - whatever that might be - he could feel it. The war was over, but there was a new war beginning, and if the Mirror could be used, it would decide the fate of the world.

Hawthorne checked his pocket watch. The man he needed to find was somewhere in this city, Raven.

Hawthorne had spent months tracking down Raven - the man who others knew as Max Calder. But like a raven, Calder had remained a shadowy and elusive figure, melting into the shadows of the night.

He had been all but an echo for years, a whisper on the wind that Hawthorne had only heard once or twice. But even those few scraps he could gather had been enough to reassure Hawthorne that somewhere, Calder was alive.

And now, in Vienna, Hawthorne had finally managed to find him.

That name drifted like a leaf in the wind, following the damned Mirror wherever it went. Hawthorne didn't yet know what Calder had to do with the Mirror these days, but he had known Max for years. If he knew Max, there was one thing he was sure of: Max Calder wasn't about to let the Mirror decide his fate.

CHAPTER 11
MIRROR TO MARRAKECH

t was really him. Hawthorne was beside me, somehow, down here in the catacombs beneath Prague. There was no denying it; nothing I could think of would explain away why he was here… and yet, he was.

"You died," I muttered, my voice low. It was all I could muster, seeing him here.

"No. Not quite. I was gone, very much the same as yourself."

"Why?"

"Many reasons… most of which, Raven, I cannot tell you."

"I don't use that codename anymore."

"I figured as much. But right now, there are more important things we need to rectify. For one, Krane and the Mirror."

I glanced around the corner again. The Mirror had begun to pulse more loudly, and in its shimmering light, I could see Kulik's face along with the others - the man who had been in charge of protecting Krane in Vienna. No doubt he and the rest of his men were planning something with the device. I could feel the energy begin to become more electric, more tense. We were running out of time, but I still had one more question for Hawthorne.

"Why did you leave me to die?"

"Because, Max." He shrugged, his voice still low. "You have no idea how important you really are. You needed to learn on your own."

"The hell does that mean?"

"You'll know. For now, just know I didn't intend for you to go missing… the Mirror doesn't play by any rules. But that's not important right - "

"I'm not done with my questions," I interrupted, my mind still registering fully that the man in front of me was alive. "But you're right. We need to focus. How do we stop him?"

"Like this."

Without warning, Hawthorne stood, swinging his arm up in a smooth motion. His pistol gleamed in the eerie light, and a shot rang out. Like a whip crack, it echoed across the chamber, and I saw Krane crumple to the ground, clutching his shoulder.

"Nice one," I muttered, throwing myself out from behind the wall to take aim. Hawthorne had always had his own plans - ones that he would never divulge until I found out myself.

Chaos erupted as the men tasked with protecting Krane realized what had happened. There were shouts and a whimper of pain from Krane himself. Bishop lunged toward us, a knife glinting out from beneath his coat, his rosary in hand. I saw the soldiers behind him, raising their rifles to take aim. I fired, and two of the guards fell. I heard Hawthorne beside me, panting as he dodged behind a piece of equipment that had just fallen to the floor.

But the Mirror pulsed once more - bright enough to bleach the shadows from the room and loud enough to shake the bones of the saints buried in the catacomb walls. Krane screamed, clutching his shoulder, but his hands remained on the device.

Bishop was on us now, flinging himself at Hawthorne with wild eyes. Something about his face unnerved me. It was as if he'd seen a ghost or been forced to follow the whims of these men against his will. But whatever scared him, he didn't let it show. With a hiss, he swung his knife through the air.

Hawthorne grabbed his arm, twisting it downward, and they collapsed to the floor with a thud.

"You've got to stop him!" Hawthorne yelled at me.

I ran forward, firing once more at Krane. The bullet struck Kulik this time, who stumbled backward, turning and running while clutching his abdomen. He scrambled away, tripping over rocks and loose debris as he made a break for the exit. Before I could finish him off, however, two of the guards leaped at me. I swung the butt of the M1 Garand and felt as it connected with the first one's teeth, a sickening cracking sound emanating from inside his mouth. The man fell, clutching his face.

The other soldier was on top of me and wrestled me to the ground. We struggled for a moment - neither of us gaining the upper hand - until I suddenly heard a whirring sound and the room became intensely electric. I ducked and covered my head as the soldier rolled on top of me, pulling out his pistol and aiming between my eyes.

"Die, agent," he spat, his yellowish teeth gleaming in the glowing light behind him.

"Enjoy hell," I responded, watching his face. I knew what was coming. Before he had a chance to shoot, the pulse exploded from the Mirror. It was as if a wave of electric energy, invisible yet unbelievably powerful, had suddenly struck the man on his back. His body went convex, shaking as he collapsed to the ground next to me. I pushed his body off mine and stood, glancing at him for a split second.

His face - once that of a strong, rough, young Russian man - had changed, aged rapidly, with wrinkles spreading over his every extremity, his eyes turning white as if he'd gone blind. He screamed, a blood-curdling sound - but I didn't have time to watch what would happen. I threw myself forward through the pulsing energy that emanated from the Mirror. Glancing at my hand, I saw that the soldier had managed to cut me during our fight - damn guy had skills. I looked back up, squinting my eyes as I stared at the Mirror. Krane still leaned against it, his body shaking, blood streaking the cold surface of the console.

Another wave of energy burst outward, and I dove behind a crumbling stone pillar just in time. I wasn't affected as many of these men would no doubt be...that was just part of being a slider. Still, too much time spent in the energy now pulsing from the Mirror would mess with even my head. I glanced behind me as I waited for the energy to lessen and the pulse to cease.

Hawthorne was still struggling with Bishop, but as I watched, he gained the upper hand. Roping Bishop's own rosary around his throat, Hawthorne deftly grabbed one of Bishop's knives and sliced his throat clean through. Blood spurted out from his throat, slowly rising into the air as it froze, crystalline - as if it had suddenly been released into outer space, where gravity had no effect.

The pulse had lessened, and I leaped from behind the stone pillar again, rushing toward the platform where the Mirror stood. Krane glanced up at me, his face draining as he saw me rush toward him. I'd lost my rifle in the chaos, but I pulled my pistol from beneath my coat, raising it as I ran. I was only feet from the Mirror now, only moments away from putting Krane to rest once and for all.

But I never fired.

A cold, white pain pierced my side.

I faltered, glancing down at my abdomen. A long knife protruded from my side, stuck there, lodged firmly in my body. I saw my own blood and faltered slightly, turning to see who had stabbed me. My mind was already numb, and I felt my eyes flicker slowly.

I heard Hawthorne shouting something and saw him running toward me but couldn't understand what he was saying. My ears felt like they were stuffed with cotton, and a buzzing sound rang in my head louder than the commotion around me. I stared at the man's face - the man who had stabbed me.

He grimaced at me slightly, the scar on his jaw unsettlingly familiar. I could not hear Hawthorne yelling a warning, nor Krane laughing and giggling maniacally, nor the rushing sound of the Mirror growing ever louder. Even though my ears felt as if they had suddenly turned deaf, I heard his voice ring in my head as if he were speaking inside my skull.

"Sorry, bud. Sucks I had to go and do you in, especially after I stitched you up an' all - but you can't kill Krane. Not yet."

Out of the corner of my eye, I saw Krane walking up closer behind me, still clutching his shoulder. His face looked wild, confused, and excited all at once - he glanced back and forth between the two of us, unsure who was who.

Though I realized it, I couldn't bring myself to care anymore - I was bleeding, rivulets of crimson red pouring from my wound. My vision had already begun to fade. I felt my body lose balance as I wobbled, my eyes flickering shut. I knew then that I was dying.

But right before I lost consciousness, I saw him. Running as if hell itself was on his heels, his hair disheveled and his face etched with concern. I'd never seen his face like that before, had I? It was the first time I'd ever seen even the slightest flicker of emotion on that old, weathered face of his. Hawthorne ran like the devil, dropping his gun as he charged toward us.

The other Max Calder, who had stabbed me and now stood beside me holding the knife he had pulled from my wound, moved to intercept Hawthorne, but he was too slow. With a yell, Hawthorne flung himself against the two of us, tackling us backward.

I heard Krane curse as he fell backward as well, tripping over the wires attached to the console. I felt a strange sensation…as if I was everywhere at once. It felt as if my entire body had become butter, slipping through the cracks of some bizarre cold steel. I was neither here nor there - I was everywhere, and I could see time itself unraveling in front of me.

Suddenly, I felt a mental clarity that restored me. I glanced down at my side and saw no wound. I looked around wildly, and slowly my mind realized what had happened. The four of us. When Hawthorne tackled me backward, he had caused the four of us to slide into the Mirror.

———

I glanced around. Where the hell was I?

As I registered my surroundings, I suddenly remembered exactly where I was. I knew this place. I had been here before. It was Marrakech, in December 1942 - a Bureau safe house. Dust swirled through cracked shutters, the light filtering in and illuminating the dim environment.

I heard the familiar sounds of war outside: gunshots, yelling - everything that I had come to expect from the height of the war. But why was I here? What had happened to the catacombs in Prague? From what I remembered of this mission, this was one of the first times Hawthorne had accompanied me. We'd been assigned a mission to intercept a German courier carrying blueprints for something called *Projekt Verbindung*. The device was rumored to be capable of causing slight anomalies - time freezes - that would allow the Germans to gain the upper hand in battle. Of course, it was purely a concept at this point, not yet created. That was why we had been sent here.

Marrakech was exactly as it had been described to us in the pre-mission briefings. It was a city full of contradictions that had emerged from the war but was largely still a hub of intrigue. Though the country was caught in the midst of the war, there was no doubt that the people within it were simply trying to survive. Unfortunately, survival here was difficult because it was the key location for many rival powers.

The French authorities controlled the political and military affairs in Morocco, using it as a staging point for their wartime operations. However, this was hardly the most fascinating aspect of the place.

The Allied and Axis powers had begun to focus on the region, and after Operation Torch - the Allied invasion of French North Africa - we had been assigned our mission. The brief we received from our superiors was simple - the Bureau recognized that the French Vichy government's control over Morocco was creating tension between two different factions: the Vichy regime and the men and women who sympathized with the Free French forces.

As such, it had created an undercurrent of instability and tension, running rampant through the country like a river beneath frozen ice. Marrakech had become a hub for espionage, intelligence gathering, diplomatic maneuvering... and worse. That was why our intelligence indicated the courier was here, and as such, the reason we had been dropped into this location.

I glanced around, staring at the walls of this old place - I remembered it like it had been yesterday. This - this was the safe house the Bureau had us stationed in until our mission was to execute. It was located in the old city away from the main roads and highly trafficked areas.

Tucked within a labyrinth of streets, the tall, double-story house was between a row of traditional Moroccan buildings, walls high and narrow, only accessible from winding alleyways that made it difficult for outsiders to stumble upon it.

It had been the ideal place for us to lay low. The facade was inconspicuous, unlikely to attract attention from the French authorities or the local Moroccans. Close to the market area and yet shielded from prying eyes, it offered both convenience and secrecy.

The interior, well - it wasn't much to write home about. Hawthorne and I had basic amenities, but it was designed more for secrecy than comfort. It was sparsely furnished but comfortable, with some traditional rugs, ceramic pots, and cushions. The thick stucco walls and tiled floors were inlaid with mosaic patterns of typical Moroccan design.

In front of me sat a pot of mint tea on the table - typical Moroccan hospitality. It was all just as I had remembered it.

I stared down at my cup and noticed my hands. They hadn't changed; the weathered and familiar calluses were the same, but the cut I'd gotten from the fight with the soldier was gone.

"Eyes up, Calder." I heard his voice echo beside me and raised my head to see Hawthorne standing there, sliding a pistol across the table. "We have a job to do here."

"You're here as well? Where are the others?"

"Not sure where Krane or that other bastard is."

"Who the hell was that anyway?"

"He's you," Hawthorne replied, rubbing his shoulder. "Your doppelgänger. He was... you ever heard of superposition, Calder?"

I shook my head. "Can't say I have."

"It explains everything about what's going on right now, really. Why you're no longer injured - this was the only way I could figure out to save you at that moment. We still have an unfinished job to do before this slide completes; otherwise, you'll still be a dead man."

"The hell?"

"It goes back to that superposition thing I mentioned." His eyes flickered as he scanned the dusty floor, finally settling on a rock. He picked it up and tossed it in his hand. "See this? It's just one rock. Not in quantum mechanics it isn't, Calder. When it comes to the quantum field - that's the field Krane works in, the way he created the damn Mirror in the first place - there are multiple incarnations of this rock. Multiple versions exist at the same time. These things don't stay in one spot... they can be in many spots, multiple spots at once."

"Not sure I follow."

"Quantum particles - think of this rock I'm holding - they don't just sit in a single spot. When we slid through the Mirror, we stopped being fixed in one single place. Instead, we became scattered... a near infinite number of possibilities. An infinite number of Max Calders. That's what you felt when you slid just now - every version of you, every possible version, that has ever existed across any parallel quantum field."

"So then why the hell are there two of me?"

Hawthorne looked at me, his eyes weary. "You want to know how it works? I'm not sure you really do - but the simple answer is that every time you slide... every time you've ever worked near the Mirror, there's been a possibility of echoes... copies. Think of them as doppelgängers.

"The answer is right here, in Marrakech, right now. Quantum physics...it has something called branching points. Every possible version of this rock in space and time. Every possible version has its own conclusion. Yes, I know it sounds preposterous. Our mission here, in 1942, somehow... this is where that copy of you originated from. The universe is confused, Calder. The laws are being broken, and sometimes it slips up.

"Sometimes, a version of you that shouldn't exist in this universe slips through the cracks - slides through the very fabric of reality - and ends up here. Usually, those versions never cross. They're like separate threads, separate parallel lines that run side by side but don't touch.

"And that's why the Mirror... that's why it's so dangerous. Even Krane hasn't figured it out yet. It punches a hole clean through the threads, through the parallel lines - less of a hole and more of a tiny, white ball of gravity. That gravity bends those threads - all of the parallel threads that should never touch - together. They all touch at once when you slide."

"So..." I thought for a second. "But that gravity...what exactly is the Mirror pulling toward it? Is it all the timelines, bending together?"

"Yes, Max. More or less."

"So that's how it works? It simply pulls the timelines together and chooses where to send us? So how do doppelgängers ever exist in the first place, if every slide is determined and set by whoever controls the device?"

"Well," Hawthorne said, and he sighed. "That's not all, but that's the real trouble with the Mirror. None of us are quite sure what happens at that peak moment. Quantum systems are dependent on an observing entity because that is what precipitates one reality from multiple potential virtual realities. It's all based on observation. But the Mirror is such a complex quantum system that it operates nearly by itself, even without outside prompting or instruction. It is not dependent on an outside observer and it's not like we could have built some method for observation into the system either."

"Why is that?"

"In quantum physics, any system that tries to observe itself will collapse - it self-implodes in a way of speaking. It's a fundamental contradiction of nature."

"Is that why these doppelgängers can slip through the cracks? And we really don't know how the system works at a fundamental level?"

"Precisely," Hawthorne nodded.

"So...that man, he's me. But from a different timeline?" I asked. "Think of it that way," Hawthorne responded, dropping the rock to the floor. "That man - that was you - the version of you from a mission where things went wrong. I hope we damn well never know what went wrong to make him like that...but the fact of the matter is that we're about to find out."

"What do you mean?"

"You haven't figured it out yet, Calder? We're not in our version of 1942... we're in his."

CHAPTER 12
CALDER VS CALDER

So, there we were - Hawthorne and I - the two of us stuck in 1942… until the slide completed, at least. Slides were temporary; that much I knew. I'd been on more than one, and each time the mission lasted until some qualifier was completed - usually, the Mirror was monitored, controlled, and pulsed again to move any Sliders back to the present.

But now - well, I was here, and Hawthorne sat across from me, his face shaded in thought.

"How do we get back?" I asked, gesturing around the room. "I'm guessing Krane and my doppelgänger are somewhere around here as well, so that leaves no one who knows the Mirror. Nobody to pulse it and bring us back to the catacombs."

"Well, for starters, it'll probably be a good idea to track down and kill your doppelgänger. I doubt Krane's here, so that leaves the three of us."

"Where's Krane?"

"Not sure, but the three of us are here because we have ties to the timeline. There wasn't a specific slide location set as Krane was pulsing the Mirror, which means it would simply implant each of us in the place within the timeline where we had the greatest impact…considering, of course, the fundamental intertwined nature of quantum. This nature means the three of us, at least, will likely all end up in the same spot…so here we are. But Krane - he's an outlier."

"That's good at least," I said.

Hawthorne's eyes went cold, his face darkening. "That's what I'd like to think. But who knows what kind of hell Krane can kick up wherever he's gone? We have to send your doppelgänger back to the crack in time he crawled out of before Krane manages to create some catastrophic situation for us."

"He can do that?"

"We're dealing with time. There are rules, but the rules are that whoever has the most time…the most choices within that timeframe, they will emerge as the victor. Let's go."

Hawthorne stood, making his way to the doorway. I followed, setting my empty mint tea cup down on the table. As we walked, Hawthorne glanced around, taking in his surroundings. I knew better than to disturb the man - his mind rivaled that of the greatest detective and the most cunning spy, and I could tell he was thinking. Finally, he paused, then turned down a dark and misty alleyway before turning toward me and staring intently at my face.

"I believe, Calder," he said, his face masked in shadow, "that I've deduced the split in the timeline that created your doppelgänger."

"And when is that?"

"Do you remember the courier boy? What happened?"

———

The boy stood in front of us, his face pale and terrified. He was white with fear, the blood drained from every inch of his skin. We had cornered him in an alley behind the Grand Hotel, clutching the blueprints like they might burn him.

"Give it here, boy," Hawthorne had said, extending his hand while he aimed his pistol with the other.

The trembling boy, with shaking hands, handed the blueprints to Hawthorne. With a click, Hawthorne had cocked his gun, aiming it at the boy's head.

"Wait," I'd said. "The kid probably isn't even sixteen, director. You sure you want to kill him here?"

Hawthorne had paused, his eyes masked underneath a layer of thought as usual. He'd finally nodded and walked off, striding away as I jogged to catch up. We had left the boy there, trembling and sobbing, sitting in the middle of the alley.

———

"I remember," I said, nodding. "Why?"

"This version of you, Calder, most likely found his body later that night. His body would have been in the square, shot in the head - one clean bullet to finish the job."

"...And why would that have affected him?"

"Because I shot the boy, Calder. I let you believe there could be mercy in our line of work, but I finished the job all the same."

"The hell? So you lied to me? Killed the boy in cold blood anyway?"

Hawthorne nodded, his eyes piercing through my very skull as if he could read my thoughts before I had even conceived them.

"Yes, I did. And I'm guessing - no, I'm almost certain - that this version of you found out on that night. So what will you do now that you know, Calder?"

I stood there, unmoving. I remembered that boy's face...his innocent face, his trembling hands, and the tears that had streamed down his cheeks as he sobbed for mercy. He was no soldier - merely a civilian pawn that had been used by the Germans for a greater goal they wished to achieve.

"Nothing for now," I finally said, motioning toward Hawthorne. "But hell, that didn't follow our code."

"Maybe not our code... but it followed the rules. Now come -

we have to finish what we...what I started here all those years ago."

We walked in silence. The two of us knew where we needed to go - if Hawthorne was correct that the man - the doppelgänger who was none other than another version of me - had begun his descent into madness when he'd seen the body of that innocent boy dead on the ground, then we knew where the current version of him would be.

There was no doubt that he would have anticipated this and laid some sort of trap for us when we arrived. But I was confident in Hawthorne's ability to improvise, and I was confident that a duo of Hawthorne and Raven could outsmart a lone Raven, no matter how desperate he might be.

No matter how damning or annoying I found my code name, I kept being sucked back into situations that reminded me of it.

Eventually, we drew closer to the Grand Hotel - and as such, began to move with much more caution. I blended into the shadows of the buildings that towered above, my coat drawn up to my neck. As I did, I glanced over my shoulder.

Hawthorne was gone. He had silently wandered off, and I knew that his plan had already begun. He didn't have to tell me, either; there was something I had to do, and he was confident I'd figure it out.

Though Hawthorne hadn't explained as much as I would have liked, I deduced several things from our current situation. The first was that Krane was not here - he was elsewhere, in some other timeline or alternate reality. According to my understanding of the quantum science Hawthorne had explained, there was some connectivity between the two, which would explain why my injuries disappeared. It must have meant that the quantum entanglement, which affected all of us who had come into contact with the Mirror, had healed my hand and abdominal wound - or rather, maybe those didn't exist in the first place.

It was still unclear to me how specifically the Mirror worked;

I was more interested in the science of espionage and spy work. However, this would have meant that we had more or less succeeded at our current task. The Mirror wouldn't alter the greater timeline, but the lesser timeline within our framework had already been rewritten.

That would mean, of course, that all I had to do was figure out what I had already figured out. I rubbed my forehead exasperatedly. This sliding stuff was confusing and a real pain in the arse. Why couldn't the world simply feed me the answer?

But then, suddenly, I had an idea. It wasn't about what I had to do, nor what I needed to change within this version of 1942 - it was about what I had already done, or, if Hawthorne's logic held true, what I was about to do now that mirrored what I'd done before.

The past and future, the one time and the other, were bleeding together like some great horrible tapestry. I pressed my body against the Grand Hotel's shadowy, cold stone wall and felt the pistol that Hawthorne had given me stuffed comfortably into my pocket.

I let my mind calm, closed my eyes, and focused. My mind whirred, and everything was blank - but suddenly, I saw a flicker of memories, memories I had never seen before. I saw the boy's face, heard the sobbing, and recalled the click of Hawthorne's pistol. But I saw something else as well - I saw the dead boy's body, vivid as day, lying bloody against the stonework of the square. I felt the white rage of betrayal, saw my hands as I bent down to feel his pulse, and saw his face - whiter than death. He was dead.

Then, I felt time pass, sliding past my mind, a fluid river of a thousand memories.

I saw Hawthorne walking along the street in front of me as I tailed him, a gun stuffed in my pocket. I felt the eager leap of my emotions, the excitement as I waited for the perfect moment to kill him - to get revenge on Hawthorne as I had done with the other one... the one from my timeline.

I opened my eyes - there was the answer. I moved quickly along the alley, my boots quiet on the cobblestones. The city was a quilt of darkness, shadows spilling from the buildings as the sun set in the sky. Where had Hawthorne gone?

Ah, but of course - he would have gone back to the one place I would expect him to: the safe house. If I had been my doppelgänger... Well, I was. If I hadn't been with Hawthorne when he explained it to me, I would have assumed that he was running reconnaissance, searching for me, and would later return to the safe house to report his findings and develop a plan.

That must have been exactly what Hawthorne did when he wandered off, leaving me alone here. The other Max Calder must have tailed him, waiting for the perfect moment to strike.

I ran, my feet pounding against the ground now as I glanced this way and that. Judging by Hawthorne's speed when he had walked off, they could have only gotten half a mile or so down the road, and as such, I needed to buy more time. I needed to catch up to them. I sprinted down the streets, ignoring the shocked and disgruntled looks from the citizens of this fine city or passersby, until I saw him. A few hundred feet ahead, I saw Hawthorne's signature coat and hat.

Behind him, only twenty feet away, I saw the other Calder. He was trailing behind Hawthorne, his hands stuffed in his pockets. So why hadn't he killed Hawthorne yet?

But that must have been the reason - he must have been waiting 'till they got back, back to the safe house where he'd either kill or capture Hawthorne and then use him as bait to lure me in. I closed the gap. It was almost night, the setting sun casting a golden-red shimmering glow over the rooftops as it descended for the night. Pulling the gun from my pocket, I silently advanced, becoming the hunter, closer to my doppelgänger than I had been since he'd stabbed me.

But I hesitated to raise my gun. What would happen if I killed him? My mind faltered for a second as my thoughts raced. If there were doppelgängers, other versions of me, there had to be an original. What if he, this Calder in front of me, was the original? I had assumed when Hawthorne explained the science to me that I was the Calder from the original timeline…the one who would continue to exist even if this one had been shot and killed.

So which one was I?

I saw the man in front of me quicken his pace, and a shiny object glinted from beneath his trench coat. He held a long, silvery knife and closed the gap between himself and Hawthorne with incredible speed.

I didn't have time to think - all I could do was react.

I raised my gun, taking aim.

And then, I pulled the trigger.

CHAPTER 13
SWISS SERENITY

stood there, panting, my breath raspy, and my hands on my knees. I had killed him - and yet I remained, so I must surely have been the real one. But where was I? My eyes adjusted to the dark and gloomy light, and I blinked slowly. Then, from behind me, I heard a voice.

"Steady now. Hands where I can see them, agent."

I glanced around. Hawthorne stood behind me, his arms already raised in the air and a sheepish expression on his face. Behind him stood half a dozen soldiers, armed to the teeth with guns and various weaponry. I instantly felt a bizarre jolt run through my mind, and I knew what was going on. When I had killed my doppelgänger, the timeline had glitched. Not enough to change the greater timeline, but enough to where the doppelgänger that had interacted with our timeline had caused a timeline split - a form of that quantum science I was still struggling to get the hang of.

We were back in the place, though perhaps not at the exact second, that we had left when Hawthorne had knocked us into the Mirror - beneath the surface of Prague, in the middle of the large lab at the center of the catacombs.

However, when we returned from our slide in that very

instant, Kulik's men had already rushed to Krane's defense when they heard the commotion. Except he wasn't there. After all, we had never really slid in the timeline we were now thrust back into. As Hawthorne had explained to me, instances such as this created new splits, oftentimes deviating slightly from what you might have experienced before.

Despite finally beginning to understand at least some of this whole quantum thing, that didn't change the fact that Kulik's men were here.

They had gotten the drop on us. They stood behind us, guns raised, positioned as if they were destined to be a firing squad. I slowly raised my hands into the air. I was no longer wounded, though I assumed there was some other split doppelgänger of me dying on the floor at this very instant - but that mattered little. These men most definitely had the drop on us.

The man in charge, a big, bulky fellow, stepped forward, his eyes alight with eager fire.

"Well, agents. It appears Kulik will promote me today, does it not?"

"You speak good English," I replied, nodding toward him. "Any chance you want to reconsider?"

"And why should I do that?"

"The Mirror. I don't see Krane anywhere around here, do you? But Hawthorne and I know how to use it."

The man hesitated, and I knew it was my chance. But suddenly, before I could even move, another voice broke the silence.

"Or maybe we just end it here."

Out from the darkness she appeared, her face alight with a brilliant beauty - her auburn hair shimmering in the eerie hue.

Artemis.

She emerged from the smoke, her gun raised, her trench coat trailing like a storm. Her eyes met mine, and I saw a sparkle of excitement - this was, as little as I wanted to admit it, what the two of us lived for. We relished the excitement of the chase... of the unexpected twist.

The commander hesitated, then made a motion for his gun as if to grab it, but I was too quick. I was already on top of him, tackling him to the ground. Though Hawthorne was old, I saw him dash to the side, grabbing the rifle of one of the nearest men and twisting it around.

Artemis had been the single distraction we needed - the few seconds that would allow us to gain the upper hand. As I easily dispatched the commander and some of his men, it proved to be the case.

I straightened, the blood from the final man covering my hands. I checked my pocket watch - it was splattered with blood, but it still worked. 1950 hours.

"Dirty game, is it?" I commented.

"Thanks for the kind welcome back, Calder," she replied.

"You owe it all to Hawthorne, really," I responded, nodding toward him. "I could'a cleaned this all up easier if he hadn't made a mess of it."

She laughed, nodding toward Hawthorne as he stood there, a hand on his chin. Hawthorne, however, looked grim.

"What's the matter, director?" I asked.

"I'm not sure if this is the end," he replied, his brow furrowed. "Krane's not here, is he?"

"Not that I see."

"Then he's still sliding. And if Krane is still sliding, that can only mean something ominous is still at play."

As if to confirm Hawthorne's suspicions, we heard a sound. It was a wailing sound, as if a woman in distress from some harm caused to her child, or a wild cat screaming into the night - a mountain lion or cougar of some kind. It was the kind of wail you never wanted to hear again, blood-curdling and horrifying.

It wasn't just a sound exactly, either - more like a pressure that gripped your spine, rewriting your heartbeat. Krane was nowhere to be seen, Bishop's body lay dead on the floor, and

Kulik was long gone. But the Mirror continued to wail louder, its voice screaming to be born anew.

"What the hell - " I muttered, but I never finished. Hawthorne shouted over me, his voice deep and clear even through the pressure.

"It must be Krane! He's still sliding, changing things, controlling the Mirror. We need to stop him now - destroy the Mirror at all costs!"

I grabbed the gun from Artemis's hands, firing two shots toward the Mirror. The bullets ricocheted off, leaving no damage at all. As they bounced around, however, their motions slowed as they eventually came to a stop mid-air.

Suddenly, a wave of invisible energy pulsed outward. Stones began to crack, iron corroded, and time itself seemed to switch.

"Damn it! Just run!" I yelled.

We bolted. Hawthorne and Artemis were running only steps behind me as I led the way through the catacombs, my muscle memory familiar with the path I ran, though my mind had forgotten it already. It was a special talent of mine - to stow away some map in my head and be able to follow it to pinpoint precision without ever bringing it to the forefront of my mind. The tunnels trembled, collapsing behind us as the Mirror's pulse accelerated.

We reached the surface just as the clock tower above shattered, raining centuries of masonry into the square. A piece struck Hawthorne on the shoulder, but he motioned for the three of us to keep running.

"I'm good. Just keep running, damn it!"

I glanced back at him and opened my mouth to speak. My voice never left my throat. I wanted to tell him to look out, to run, to dodge - to do something - but it all happened too quickly. I watched as a gigantic hand of the clock fell toward him like a spear.

His vision followed my gaze, drifting upward in slow motion as he registered what was above him, plummeting downward.

As his eyes met mine, he mouthed something, but I never heard it.

The hand struck the ground, and Hawthorne disappeared. In an instant, Artemis and I were thrown backward with the force of a thousand suns, hurled across the square, and solidly into a brick wall that remained standing. I felt the air leave my body as I collided with the wall, and I saw Artemis's body twist into some unnatural contortion as she hit the wall beside me.

I felt a pulse and felt myself sliding - it was one of the most powerful effects from the Mirror I'd ever felt. Then, just like that, it was all gone. There was silence around us, except for the quiet noise of falling dust.

"Hawthorne!" I yelled as I struggled to catch my breath, but there was no answer. The square around us was in utter disarray - it looked as if a bomb had exploded in the very center of the area. Bricks lay scattered all over, and a blast radius emanated from the underground - from where the Mirror had been.

I grabbed Artemis, her body limp and her eyes shut. I didn't know if she was okay… if she would even live - but we needed to escape. I doubted the men we'd dispatched were all of Kulik's men, and if they found us here, in this condition, we would be no match for them.

Prague was burning. I dodged through the rubble, which only lasted for several blocks, only to find a hectic situation beyond the area of the pulse. The rest of Prague hadn't been destroyed, but it was alight with confusion. Whole blocks were locked down, police sirens wailing. Rumors of radiation. Black cars from various government organizations were driving down the streets. Nobody yet knew what had caused the explosion, and perhaps that was for the best.

I got to the closest payphone I could find, flexing my hands as I grabbed it. I remembered the number I had used to contact Artemis from the safe house in Vienna. Though I doubted it would work, I dialed it. I knew better than to search her pockets - Alicia would never have been daft enough to keep a list of contacts on her person and no doubt had every name and number memorized.

The phone rang for what felt like an eternity as I sat there, her body still limp on my shoulder.

"'Ello?"

"This is Max Calder. Code name Raven. Who am I speaking to?"

"Oy, Calder. What do you need?"

"I need an out. At Letná Park."

"How soon?"

"Can you travel back in time?"

She laughed. "Understood. I'll be there m'self." It was a joke between us who had worked at the Bureau - or in her case, still did - as a way to verify the identity of another agent. Still, she knew what I meant - I needed her here as soon as possible.

Soon she appeared, driving an ambulance down the streets, its sirens blazing. I had no idea where Opal had managed to acquire it, but she'd clearly put some work into it. The ambulance was a relatively new Skoda panel van, white, a civilian vehicle that had been repurposed into an ambulance with a red cross painted prominently on its side. Nobody would have questioned it during the post-war chaos. It was the perfect cover, really. In such a disastrous and hectic state as Prague was in, there was no commotion over an ambulance, and people got out of the way.

"Get in. Is she hurt?"

"Not sure. I'll drive; you check her out."

"Alright," she replied, grabbing Artemis and heaving her into the back of the ambulance with the air of someone who had done it many times before. "Name's Opal."

As I stepped into the dimly lit interior, I glanced around. It was equipped with a simple stretcher for transporting patients and some small pieces of medical equipment. An oxygen tank sat in the corner, still wobbling from Opal's drive down the city streets. Mounted to the walls were a variety of bandages, first aid devices, and other cheap medical supplies. It was an actual ambulance, for sure.

Opal, as I soon discovered, was fast, angry, and didn't ask questions. But I had a lot of questions to ask, and so I began as soon as she had assured me that Artemis looked fine. From what Opal said, she just needed rest and recovery - and a healthy dose of painkillers.

"How'd Prague respond so fast to the explosion? There are lockdowns everywhere, police officers, government agents - what the hell is going on? How'd they know in advance?"

"The hell you mean, Raven?"

"Did they know we were down in the catacombs?"

"Not even the Bureau knew you were down there…until you made the stupid mistake of calling me."

"So then why is Prague on lockdown?"

"The city clock blew up hours ago. I figured you could tell me what the hell's been going on down there."

"How long ago?"

"Around 18:50. Why?"

"Nothing important."

So that explained it. Krane still had his hands on the Mirror. He must have displaced it then, not destroyed it. He must have done something while he was sliding to mess with us - bastardizing the timeline and saving the Mirror all at once. He wasn't trying to activate it; he had been trying to hide it. Not only from us, but from Kulik and the Russians. All at once, I understood - Krane didn't care about working for the Soviets…he had the Soviets working for him. He'd been playing us all.

Had this been his plan all along, or had he figured it out on the fly? I didn't care much for the answer - all I knew was that the next time I found that man, I would make sure he was dead for good.

We rode the rest of the way in silence, the back of the ambulance lit by surgical bulbs, while the front, where I drove, was illuminated by the eerie light from the streetlamps. Artemis awoke, her eyes foggy and her face weary but alive.

"Where are we headed?" she asked, her voice tired.

"The border. Switzerland," I responded. Before she had even woken up, Opal and I had decided on our course of action.

The safest strategy right now was for us to head to a safe house located on the edge of the Swiss border. Opal couldn't help us more than this, as it would likely prove to be a conflict of interest with the Bureau, especially now that we didn't know if Hawthorne was alive or not. He might have known who we could trust, but I felt like a fish out of water when dealing with the higher-ups.

Instead, we'd regroup and figure out where we could catch Krane. It would take a while to get there, driving the ambulance through the war-torn Austria and across the formidable Swiss Alps. But I had no doubt that the route was the best one, especially since we had the disguise of a medical vehicle on our side.

The plan was perfect - not a single soul suspected that a lone ambulance driving quietly along the winding roads in the middle of the night was carrying three of likely the most wanted individuals the Soviets would have paid millions to catch. The night was quiet, save for the occasional whistling of the wind through the trees and the barren landscape.

We passed only one car during our entire trip. The road was otherwise empty. Along our route, the occasional village emerged from the darkness, dimly lit by yellow-orange hues spilling from the windows of the local inns and houses.

As much as we might have desired sleep, we did not stop. I shook my head, blinking. The ambulance, complete with poor suspension not suited for these rough roads and plenty of loose equipment that bounced around, was keeping me awake. I was exhausted - but then again, I had been trained for this. A little exhaustion wouldn't stop the mission. So we drove onward, the flat plains eventually giving way to hills and the distant sound of church bells ringing out across the desolate fields.

It was still night as we drove through one small town after another. As the roads grew narrower, we began to ascend. The Alpine forests closed in on both sides, and the road went jaggedly uphill and became far more treacherous. I wasn't a man particularly intimidated by rough roads or treacherous driving conditions, but it was clear Opal's ambulance had reached its limit. It was built for city streets, and we were no longer driving in the city. The twisting mountain passes had begun.

Opal slept as we drove, but Artemis and I remained awake. I knew Opal would awaken at the drop of a button - she was a trained agent, after all - and I assumed nothing I wanted to say to Artemis would do good if it was to fall on Opal's ears as well.

We finally arrived at the Swiss border in the early hours of the morning. The road was cloaked in low clouds, the mountains rising sharply on each side, snow-capped peaks hidden in the mist.

It was a haunting, chilling sight, but it was exactly what we wanted. Here, we would be secluded.

There were still border guards, but we were well prepared. The sense of calm here was unprecedented compared to previous countries we had entered, and as such, a quick flash of our forged passports was enough for us to gain entry.

Switzerland was a land of peace amidst a war-torn Europe.

The safe house we were aiming for was carefully situated to avoid detection by any military presence in the area. While Switzerland was neutral, the precise location of the safe house was close enough to the border to merit some caution.

There were no doubt smuggling routes, military patrols, and even the potential for rogue robbers near the area. Eventually, however, we made it. The safe house itself was built far from major roads, difficult to spot unless you knew exactly where to look.

We stepped out of the ambulance, stretching our legs. I glanced at the safe house - it was old, no doubt, but still very much solid. Stone walls, steel doors, and more than likely food supplies to last for years. It was an old war bunker left off the books and looked every bit the part.

A few minutes later, we were inside. We settled in - there were indeed stashes of canned foods and other goodies - and began to eat.

Opal left us there only a minute or so later but informed me curtly that she'd have to report all the activities and information she'd gathered to the Bureau.

"I'd love nothing more than to let all this slide, Raven, but you know how the Bureau works."

"Let it slide? Cute. Tell 'em. I don't give a damn."

With that, Opal departed, leaving us alone. And so here we were, sitting on the cold stone floor with bread and canned soup, a small fire lit in the middle of the room. The only clothes she wore were her undergarments, as her clothes had been torn and bloodied. I wore all of my clothes, ignoring the discomfort. One of us undressing was enough for me.

She finally spoke, rubbing her bruised jaw as she did.

"Calder? Where's Hawthorne?"

"I'm not sure. I think he might be dead."

"Damn it. And Krane?"

"Definitely not dead."

"So what do we do? What's the next move here?"

"For now, we get some rest. We need to find wherever or whenever Krane is - and kill that man once and for all. Getting rid of the Mirror isn't enough now. We need to kill the source of the Mirror."

"I'll call my contacts when I wake up."

"Thanks, Alicia. Get some rest."

But I couldn't sleep. I lay there, staring up at the dimly lit ceiling. I had tossed my coat aside and now relaxed with only my shirt and pants left to fend off the cold. It felt good to be alive. There were no windows, and as such, the only light came from an old bulb positioned at the very center of the ceiling. We had elected to leave it on, as the light was dim enough that it only cast shadows about the place, giving it an almost haunted feeling.

I lay with my hands behind my head, a cig in my mouth, puffing occasional clouds of smoke upward. But my mind whirred. I thought of Hawthorne more often than not as my mind wandered - I wasn't sure if he was alive or not, but it seemed likely to me he had perished. From what I had seen, the hand of the clock had struck the ground where he stood. It would have struck him as well.

If Hawthorne was dead, I was out of my depth. Krane was still missing, and it was likely he was altering the timeline in a horrific manner - something I could only guess at. Would we be able to stop him? I sighed and blinked. Suddenly, a quiet voice spoke out from the darkness.

"Can't sleep either?"

I shifted, turning so I could see her silhouette backlit by the low glow of the bulb. She stood above me, clearly unable to sleep. She'd wrapped the coat I had discarded around herself, the hem brushing against her legs. Her eyes were almost entirely obscured by the darkness, but I felt a rawness in her demeanor and a softness in her voice.

She sat down beside me. I hesitated, then reached over, with my arm outward in an opening gesture. She slid closer, eventually lying down next to me, her head resting on my arm, settling into the crook of my shoulder. I felt her fingers slowly brush against my chest as she moved, slowly at first, her body relaxing as she eventually sighed.

For a long while, neither of us said anything. The place was silent, with no sound emanating from the walls or even the flickering bulb, until she finally moved.

She shifted slowly, grasping my coat and drawing it tighter around her body as she cuddled up even closer to mine. Her breath was warm against my skin. We lay there, the silence reassuring. I didn't know what I wanted to do - I knew I wanted her, but I also knew I couldn't trust anyone…not fully, at least. The Mirror had jaded me, broken me. Hell, I didn't even trust myself - the experience in Prague had proven that. My doppelgänger had proven that.

But eventually, I felt myself giving in. Her heartbeat thumped against my body, growing louder, the only noise in the room. It was rapid at first but slowed as the rhythm began to sync with my own. She traced circles against my chest, her finger as light as a feather, growing slowly more confident as it began to linger with each pass.

Her touch, as little as I wanted to admit it, eased the pain, the doubt, and the soreness I'd felt since Prague.

She slowly turned her face upward, locking her eyes with mine. I brushed a strand of hair from her face and knew I could no longer resist, even if I had wanted to. What I wanted, I didn't know. But I knew my body wouldn't allow me to take any other path.

She closed her eyes as I touched her, leaning in, her lips brushing softly against the edge of my mouth. The kiss was slow at first, but I finally allowed myself to respond. Her hand gradually moved to the back of my neck, the other pressing against my chest. The room was cold, but she was warm.

Her skin felt soft against mine as she shifted beside me, her face finally clearing from the fog and darkness I'd seen on her features when she awoke. It was the first time since I'd seen her back in Prague that she looked truly relaxed. My hands moved on their own, exploring her waist, her hip, her neck - each curve of her body, each piece of her that I saw as my coat slipped to the side.

We moved together as one, forgetting our troubles, taking comfort in our shared disaster that was our lives and the bizarre adventure that had been cast upon us. The discomfort of the hard bed and old blankets was forgotten, our exhaustion transforming into something almost electric. She gasped, and I grabbed her hair, unwilling to let go of this moment.

For a while, we were able to forget the tension of the world around us - the war-torn hellscape, Krane, Hawthorne, and everything else. There was only our touch.

Eventually, silence returned to the room, not as harsh as before. She curled against me beneath my battered coat, put to use once again. My arm rested on her shoulder, and I felt a sense of ease. I knew my body would forget it in the morning. In the morning, I'd be back to the Max Calder I knew, the one I would recognize in the mirror.

But for now, this was bliss.

An hour or so later, we fell asleep, both exhausted from the day and our night's activities.

———

I woke up and sat up, stretching and groaning. The bed here wasn't the most comfortable, especially when shared. Still, I didn't regret anything. The world outside might be burning, but for a few hours, everything would be okay.

"So," I said as she finally stirred. "We have a lot to talk about."

"Do we, Max?"

"Yes, and not about last night. We have more pressing matters - at least for now."

She shifted slightly, and I wasn't sure if it was from discontent or from a lingering question that we both avoided. Either way, I wasn't about to find out. My mind was rested and eager, ready to get started.

"Well," she eventually said. "Shall I make contact with my sources?"

"Not yet," I replied. "First, I'm curious… what were you up to while Hawthorne and I were in Prague? You only arrived near the end, and you had told me you had something to do… something with Delta."

"Oh," she said, smiling at me, her eyes flashing with excitement. "You'll be happy to hear I made tremendous progress there."

CHAPTER 14
DELTA DELUSIONS

She had taken the train, walking away from Calder, turning her back on him. She didn't want to see Calder still standing there, watching her, nor did she desire to remain any longer than she had to. She was confident that he would take care of Krane himself - if there was any agent she had complete faith in, it was Calder. There was a reason she had tracked the man down at the behest of the Bureau, traveled to Hell's Kitchen in search of him, and convinced him to reconsider his life and join the movement once more. It was simple - though there were other sliders, Max Calder was the man she felt most comfortable with and trusted the most.

So, she walked back to the ticket booth, purchased a second-class ticket, and settled down on a bench to wait for her train. It would depart in about an hour, and so she spent her time with her eyes closed for the most part. She knew Calder preferred to people-watch, but that had never been her style. She could glean all the information she needed from people while talking to them and had no use or interest in the games that Calder did.

Eventually, bored, she stared around at the train station itself. Columns were still marked with bullet notches, the glass roof still had cracks in it that were being repaired, and the station itself was far quieter than she was confident it would have been before the war. Finally, the train she had been waiting for pulled into the station, and Artemis boarded, ignoring the beggars who reached out their hands as she passed, grasping for her red scarf. She felt a tinge of sorrow for them, but sorrow wouldn't change their predicament, nor could she help - she'd killed more men than these, men whose only reason for death was that it had been ordered.

She stepped into the train, a narrow, old-looking thing that was far less accommodating than the previous train she and Calder had ridden. The narrow interior was dimly lit, and she settled herself at the very end of one of the benches, ignoring the few other passengers in the train car. She did not care for the battle-torn man who bore the unmistakable look of a soldier, nor the mother with a crying child held tightly in her arms. Artemis was focused on the journey ahead and settled in for a long trip. The train sped away from Prague, through the countryside, finally crossing the Czech border. There was a quick pause here as guards entered, demanding proof and evidence of loyalty from the individuals traveling into the country. Artemis, however, was more than prepared and rehearsed a carefully practiced story to the soldier who questioned her. She flashed her papers, and the soldier passed on. She glanced at his face as he walked past - tired, old, haggard, and worn - and she knew that he wanted to do this job no more than she had wanted to speak to him. Eventually, the train sped up once more and soon passed Katowice.

It was here that Artemis slowly perked up, watching out of the window as the Polish countryside passed. Children watched wide-eyed as the train raced by, running along the tracks with their dogs, ribcages visible in both animal and child. Finally, Warsaw appeared. She couldn't help but shudder as she saw it. The destruction of Warsaw was still fresh, and it was apparent that the city was a broken, destroyed haunt of its former quali-ties. Many buildings were still utterly destroyed, with only the foundations remaining. Artemis stared, watching as the train slowed to a halt at the very center of the city. It was there that she departed, stepping from the train into the desolate haunt that was Warsaw.

As Artemis traced her path carefully, she recalled everything from her life that had led up to this moment. Did she regret it? Yes, she did - not the espionage, not the strange pull she felt toward that man, scar and all, but she regretted ever working for the Bureau. Ever laying eyes on that damned Mirror. But she pushed the thoughts from her mind. She'd traveled all this way from Prague, leaving Max there alone, and she had a job to do.

The job, of course, was to locate Subject Delta and find out what he knew. She already had a good idea of where she could find him, of course. He'd made quite the stir here, even in the war-torn ruins of this city, and as such, she had a good general idea of his whereabouts.

His name was less than important. It may have been once, but not anymore. The Bureau called him Subject Delta. Locals whispered about him in the back alleys of Warsaw, as if his name were some kind of curse. Of course, it was - he had survived around their youth, conjuring images of a vampire or some sort of blood-sucking leech when his name was uttered.

To Artemis, he was something worse than a leech - he was a slider who'd lost his tether and yet held onto an infinite number of tethers simultaneously. This was a man more connected to the Mirror than perhaps anyone except Hawthorne or Krane himself.

She trailed her way through Warsaw, dodging past any remains of the city or humans that were still being cleaned up, watching as workers fixed and rebuilt houses, staring at anyone who dared to stare at her. They all did, of course - it was hard not to. In such a city, mourning still from the destruction, a woman who wore a red scarf and auburn hair turned heads. She did not care, however - she had no reason to blend in and instead walked quietly, thinking to herself.

She searched several buildings - old offices, hotels, and burnt-down remains of homes. Artemis had begun to doubt she would ever find the man and considered that her informants might have given her false information. Soon, however, her perseverance paid off.

She found him in an abandoned bathhouse, naked except for a shattered wristwatch duct-taped to his chest, whispering numbers into the cold air. He must have got the tape off some old ammunition boxes as that is what it was originally developed for during the war. His eyes were wide, empty, and old. His face was taut, drawn, and violent. His teeth were sharpened and yellowed from decay.

He didn't see her at first. He was nearing his end, and he would die a few days later - but Artemis didn't know that at the time. She just heard him whispering to himself, talking to the shadows and faces she couldn't see.

"Fifteen twenty-one. Loop begins again. Loop begins again. Loop begins again…"

Artemis crouched beside him, her hand on her pistol.

"Subject Delta?"

He flinched like she'd slapped him.

"Loop begins again. Loop begins again. You're too late. You're too late. You're late."

She glanced carefully at his face, wishing Calder had been there. She'd never struggled to make a decision, but now she did.

"Krane?"

He nodded quickly, a jerking motion that made some of the loose teeth in his mouth wobble. "He's going to make it sing. He's going to make it scream. Then he's going to fold. Fold. Fold. Loop begins again. Two. Maybe three. Maybe all of them. Here. Loop begins again."

"What are you trying to say?"

"Versions. Versions. Many versions. All killers. All here."

His face contorted, the skin around his eyes rippling outward as they grew white. His jaw shook as if he were having a seizure.

"Subject Delta… you need to listen to me. If you can hear me, I need to know where Krane is. What he's planning."

"He'll bring them here. Here. All of them."

"I don't know what the hell that means," Artemis spat, frustrated. "What are you trying to say?"

"No way to explain. No, won't understand. Loop begins again."

"Delta - "

Suddenly, however, the man froze. He stared at her, directly into her eyes. His gaze was piercing, and Artemis shuddered, recoiling. It was as if he stared into her soul. As if he could see every piece of her. And he broke into a wide grin.

"Oh, but you are. You're - you will understand, won't you," he said, his voice smooth for the first time. "You'll know when the time comes. Krane will go into the Mirror. You can't stop him. He'll change it all. He'll bring them here. He's brought one. He'll bring more."

"How do we stop him?"

"Calder. Calder's in trouble. He'll die if you're not there."

And with that, the man's body went limp. She tried to wake him, pushing and shaking him, but he was asleep and wouldn't awaken for another day or so. But Artemis didn't know at the time that this would be the last chance she ever had to talk to Subject Delta. What she did know, however, was that Calder's life was at risk. So, turning away and striding briskly down the street, her red scarf billowing behind her in the cold and biting wind, she made her way back to Prague as if a devil were on her heels.

———

But that was in the past. Now, here she was, falling asleep in his arms. It was a strange feeling - to finally connect with the man physically like this, intimately, after they'd shared so much throughout their past.

She snuggled closer to him, thinking of it. In the morning, she'd return to her normal self, to that reluctant separation from him, and to their normal relationship. But for now, just for tonight, she wanted to be close to him.

Though she'd never admit it, Max was her tether to reality itself. Without him, she wouldn't have known what to do when she'd first come into contact with the Mirror. She would have never understood how to tether herself to reality or how to tell the difference between her memories.

More often than not, she had memories that she wasn't sure of - memories that more than likely weren't hers. Memories of someone else.

Beautiful, terrifying memories. But the one constant throughout all of these was Calder - memories of him from when they'd met, memories she was certain in her heart weren't fake.

Even those rare, strange memories of knowing Calder before they'd met.

She shook her head, shivering. It was cold here. But he was warm. And she closed her eyes to sleep.

CHAPTER 15
CROSSING CONTINENTS

sipped scotch from a cup, feeling the warm burn travel down my throat. Artemis had just finished telling me of her experience in Warsaw and what Subject Delta had said.

"So," I said, nodding toward her as she took a sip from her own glass, "What do you think it all means?"

"I'm not sure, Max. I'd like to think that the worst is over, but I'm not sure we're out of danger yet."

"Definitely not. From what you've told me; Subject Delta was trying to warn us of some group traveling here - or some group that Krane would bring here?"

"Yes, though I'm not sure what that could mean."

"Do you think it's the Soviets?"

"It has to have some connection to the Mirror, I'd think."

"Good point," I said, sighing. "Well, in any case, our plan hasn't changed. Until we figure out what in the blazes Delta was talking about, our goal is to kill Krane, but right now we are at a dead end."

"Speaking of," she responded, a slight smile on her lips, "I should get in contact with my sources."

I watched, impressed, as she used the single phone in the safe house to dial her contacts. She had dozens - at least the ones she called now - and I knew she likely had hundreds more memorized. Every detail of her brilliant database was in her head and nowhere else. I knew she would die before she let a single secret slip from her mouth.

So on it went - she kept calling old friends and new ones, enemies, and even the occasional Bureau member who could be trusted not to tattle. I knew we had little time, but there wasn't much for me to do. I wasn't like Artemis - I preferred to work on my own and figure out the strategy on the way. But for now, I needed to locate Krane. Then, I could do this all on my own again. Eventually, Artemis struck gold. Her voice became excited, and I forced my mind to focus on her tone and what she was saying.

"Yes, and you've seen Krane there? Are you sure? He was just in Prague a few - yes, he matches the description perfectly? You sure?"

She nodded and scribbled a few things on the notepad she'd been holding the entire time. It had been hours - hours of useless calls and dead ends.

As soon as she put the phone down with a click, she turned toward me, a spark of excitement in her eyes.

"You found him?" I asked.

"I think so," she replied, "though I'm not sure how he managed to get there so fast."

"Mirror?"

"Most likely. He's in Argentina. Where the Nazis fled after the war - but you know the details."

I did. It was common knowledge for any government employee, current or former, worth at least a dash of salt. After their defeat, many of the Nazi scientists, great minds, and thinkers - who, though evil, were all too afraid of death to meet their ends honorably - had fled to Argentina. Rumor had it that many of them were alive and working there, sheltered by the leadership of Juan Perón, a fascist sympathizer.

After the war, they'd escaped through the ratlines, organized by former SS officers who hadn't been caught and the Catholic clergy. It was an underground railroad for the top dogs of the Nazi military - men who would be prosecuted if caught by the Allied powers. They fled to the foothills of Argentina via Buenos Aires - if the rumors were to be believed.

"So he's there? We haven't hit a dead end?"

"Yes, spotted by a Nazi contact…"

"You trust him?"

"More than enough. He was responsible for smuggling many refugees out of the concentration camps during the war. I helped him with a prison break while I was on a mission - infiltration."

"No wonder. You make friends wherever you go, don't you?"

"Well, that friend has information on the whereabouts of Krane… or so he claims. You know Mengele?"

"Josef Mengele? The damn Angel of Death? How the hell would Krane know him?"

"The one and only," she raised her eyebrows as she glanced at her scribbled notes again. "Apparently, my contact spotted Krane in the northern provinces, alongside Mengele. He's been tracking Mengele for months, and just yesterday, Krane appeared with him. They appeared to know each other."

"Damn."

I rubbed my face with my hands - I'd grown more weathered in the short time since being cast back into the world of espionage. I was tired. Though I could only guess, I assumed that Krane had done something with the Mirror, some sort of bastardization of the timeline that had allowed him to relocate there so swiftly. My mind raced as I tried to piece together everything Hawthorne had told me, searching for an answer to the question I now had. As if responding to my thoughts, Artemis spoke.

"I just don't know how he'd gotten there so quickly."

"I just might," I replied, growing more confident. A theory was forming in my mind. "The Mirror allows us to slide, right? Through time?"

"Yes. It's in the name."

"Cute. Well, the temporal relocation - the distortion it has on the timeline - that's a physical process, isn't it?"

"What do you mean?"

"I mean what Hawthorne had told me when I first started sliding. Time and space are intrinsically linked. You - well, think about it. Time and space are basically two sides of the same coin. You know Einstein's work?"

"Who in this business doesn't?"

I smiled slightly. Artemis was a smart one - smarter than me. "Well, space and time aren't really different. I remember Hawthorne showing me a paper by Minkowski one of the first days. We'd really just started working closely together. He called it spacetime."

"Hermann Minkowski, the mathematician?"

"Yes - you would know him, wouldn't you? Well, the way the Mirror works… if it altered time, allowing us to slide without altering space, we'd end up thousands of miles off the Earth. Hell, you might be on the damned moon."

She nodded, her eyes lighting up. "So, you're saying sliding through time necessarily means you'd be sliding through space… or distance, I guess?"

"You've got it, Alicia. Spacetime." I thought I saw a hint of a smile play on her lips as I said her name.

"So then, Krane, if he somehow managed to get hold of the Mirror's controls or influence something in time while sliding, could have used the Mirror to make his way across the globe?"

"I'd guess so."

She walked toward one of the walls, her fingers tracing the cold and dusty stones that sheltered us, her expression unreadable. Finally, she asked the question I knew she'd been wanting to ask since the beginning.

"Will you go?"

"Yes. It's what I was trained for."

She turned around and stepped closer to me, her eyes softening. I saw her face shift slightly, as if there was some foreboding notion in her head, something she held back. But if there was, she didn't share it. Instead, she said something I had known she would, but hoped she wouldn't.

"Well, let's make our way to Argentina, then."

"You as well?"

"Yes," she nodded. "I don't think you'll be able to do it alone, Max."

"I prefer alone. You know that."

"Not this time."

We packed. The next few hours were a blur. The safe house had enough resources to replenish our dwindling supplies - extra money in every currency we'd need, simple food supplies, new outfits, and even world maps. Though the old bunker hadn't been used in ages, it was still kitted to take care of any agent who needed a quick out, no matter where that out would lead.

Soon, we departed. It would be a long, arduous journey - I was aware of at least that with my knowledge of geography, and I didn't look forward to it much. Still, I thought, as we hiked toward the nearest town in the Alps, it would be worth it - to put Krane and his damned ideology down for good. He was a dangerous man, and his obsession with the Mirror would likely cast others into the shadow of it... into the realm of becoming sliders.

As Artemis and I knew all too well, this was a dangerous world filled with regret. Neither of us wanted to forget - to slide, find ourselves in places we'd never been before, with memories that were false and ideas that were incorrect. And yet we did, and we had no choice in the matter. Perhaps, if we put Krane down for good and destroyed the Mirror, we could live normal lives.

I shook my head, watching the sun set. We'd woken up late, started packing even later, and as a result, it was nearly night-time already.

Artemis ambled along next to me, occasionally glancing over her shoulder. It seemed as if she felt uncomfortable, but I wasn't sure why.

"What's wrong?" I asked.

"Nothing much… just not sure. Things are always confusing when you're a slider, you know. Is everything I remember real?"

I nodded, silent as I mused over our past few days. I wasn't sure what memory, false or real, she was referring to, but I knew she was right. When I'd first awoken to this last time, right out of Hell's Kitchen, I had forgotten nearly everything about my previous life as an agent of the Bureau. It had taken Artemis's help and guidance for me to remember everything I knew.

Even now, some of my memories were faint, some were shoddy, and others might have been fabricated - memories from another timeline that held no real purpose here. But I didn't know, and I had no real way of knowing. That was the problem.

But we'd finally reached the small town nearest to the bunker safe house, and all thoughts were driven from my mind as I focused once again on the task at hand. It was a little town, barely an adjunct to nature rather than actually part of it. The hills merged with the townscape, the houses were old and dilap-idated, and the rare car we saw seemed old and more rust than vehicle. But eventually, under the cover of night, Artemis and I managed to locate one of the nicer cars. As she kept watch, I moved my fingers deftly, working to gain entry to the vehicle, hijack it, and start the engine.

Our goal was to reach Zurich, which was far too many miles away to do without a vehicle. The car door wasn't locked, and as such, the more difficult part was hotwiring the engine itself. But I was experienced, and Artemis looked on with appreciation as I deftly fired up the car. It was a Renault 4CV, and though the quaint-looking vehicle was a newer model, I still managed to find my way through its systems with ease.

Then we were off, driving through the night. It wasn't far to Zurich - only about an hour's drive - so we arrived much earlier than we needed. In the early hours of the morning, Artemis and I found a hotel with the lights still on, and I parked the car and stepped out. The fresh air was warmer here than in the Alps, though still chilly.

I sauntered into the hotel, tapping the bell on the desk as I waited for service. I glanced around as I waited.

It was a rather shabby place, dimly lit, with red wallpaper in a jovial pattern, peeling in some places. The carpet had the look of a worn-out salesman, trodden on repeatedly for business, yet enduring all the same.

A few seconds later, a friendly-looking fellow, no older than 17, appeared behind the counter. He raised his eyebrows at me, and no wonder - I had the unmistakable appearance of a foreigner.

"Wäri Sprooch schwännsch du?"

I nodded, guessing what he'd said from the look on his face.

"French or English?"

He smiled and nodded, switching from the Swiss-German I guessed he had spoken to a French dialect. It was one of the official languages of Switzerland, thank goodness, and I had expected as much when I'd entered the hotel. I listened as he gave me the prices and room options and inquired about how long I'd be staying, then slid 20 or so francs across the counter to him.

"La chambre que ça m'achète."

His eyes widened, and a few seconds later, he nodded, directing me to one of the nicer rooms. A few minutes later, Artemis and I had unpacked and settled in. I pushed the curtain aside ever so slightly, glancing out at the dimly lit street. I would have preferred to stay on the move, but I doubted there would be any active trains so early in the morning. We'd stay here for a few hours, recalibrate our plan, and reassess any potential inconsistencies, then depart from the nearest station. So, we passed the time smoking, talking, and going over our maps and the limited information we had. Eventually, as the morning sun rose, we departed once more, leaving the building and hopping into the 4CV. It took me less time to hotwire it this time, as I'd begun to get the hang of the wiring systems, and we were off.

The next hour or so was a blur of motion. We parked at the Zurich HB train station, or central station, as I learned from a conversation with a friendly local, filtered our way through the busy lines, and soon purchased tickets to Milan, Italy. Artemis and I had decided this was the best route to find our way to Argentina, and we were soon on our way.

It was only then that I was able to relax, sitting in one of the nicer seats on the train, with Artemis next to me reading a newspaper. I stared out the window, taking in the beautiful Swiss landscape.

We passed charming rolling hills, lush forests, and grazing cattle of all sizes. The snow-capped Alps towered in the background, making it seem as if we had been cast into some fairytale wonderland. Even after the war, Switzerland remained relatively unchanged - one of the few places that could claim such a feat. Occasionally, the train would chug past a small village, dogs or children running along next to the tracks and waving at the train car. Artemis would wave back, smiling if she weren't too engrossed in her newspaper.

A while later, after I'd ordered some coffee off the trolley, we began to ascend into the Alps once more. Of course, we'd just left these mountainous, almost mystical protrusions from the otherwise tranquil landscape, but the train knew that not. The towering peaks grew closer, and the train submerged into darkness as it cut through a dark tunnel hewn from the rocky side, only to emerge a few seconds later. The views were breathtaking, with the valleys and grass sprawling below us, the train navigating a landscape that would be treacherous for any man, animal, or vehicle.

Hours had passed, but I was in no mood to sleep. The rest that Artemis and I had gotten at the bunker, as well as the time at the motel, was more than enough for my mind. I had coffee, a cigarette in my hand, and a beautiful view - what wasn't to love? The train finally crossed into Italy, and the landscape began to change… gradually, but noticeably.

We traveled through the beautiful Italian landscape, where wide plains were covered in dotted houses, quaint and peaceful. The train crossed a river, and I looked down, seeing a lone fisherman on the banks with a pole in hand. And then it was gone, replaced anew by even more fertile farmland.

This was a place that truly retained its natural beauty, even amidst the war-torn remnants that were ever-present, lingering in our path. But eventually, we arrived in Milan. Artemis stepped down from the train, walking in front of me.

"Enjoying the view, Calder?"

"I won't lie."

And so I didn't, trailing behind her at my own leisurely pace. We stopped at the clerk's desk for only a few seconds to purchase our tickets for the next leg of the trip, then wandered the city, taking in the sights. We needed to get to Argentina as soon as possible, but our train wouldn't leave for another two hours.

The city was scarred. It was vastly different from the countryside, where vast amounts of rain had regrown the foliage destroyed by the war as if it'd never been touched. Buildings were being rebuilt, with evidence of bombs everywhere and occasional blood stains. It was the capital of "fashion and design," or so I'd heard, but it looked more like a war-torn hellscape, marked by much deep-seated fear and the subdued nature of its residents. Nobody had forgotten the war.

But the hours passed like a leaf in the wind, and soon we had re-boarded the train. A nod from the conductor who stood at the entrance signaled our departure, and we were off again. This time, I slept. I slept, and as I slept, I dreamed.

———

He sat on the beach, his face masked from my view. His hands were cold, his fingers decaying, but the light from his face was nearly overpowering - a vision of radiance that shone from his eyes.

"Hello, Max."

I recognized that voice. It was younger than I'd ever heard it before, but the familiar tone and the almost warm depth were unmistakable.

"Hawthorne?"

"No… you'd think that, wouldn't you? Well, maybe I am - maybe I'm not. Sometimes it's hard to tell, with how close he is and I am."

"Where the hell are we?"

The waves washed up against the shore, against the cold stone rock he sat upon. He waved, beckoning me to come closer, but I remained motionless. Something made me fearful. I wasn't sure what - I'd never felt so uncomfortable before next to another man.

"Well, I suppose you wouldn't, would you? You've never trusted me."

"I have."

"…And you don't understand either," he continued, sighing. "There's so much in store for you, so much you don't under-stand, Max."

"Such as?"

"Such as the fact of her. She's not who you think she is, and she won't be herself much longer, either."

"Who?"

"I think you know."

He was right. The instant he had mentioned her, an image of Artemis washed into my mind as if carried by the waves on the shore.

"What do you mean?" I asked, backing up slightly. My fingers felt for my familiar gun, but it was missing. I felt my fingers touch my cold skin and realized I was wearing nothing - I was simply there. "Is she in trouble?"

"That all depends on you, Max. It's possible. She might die; she might live. The Archives hold the answers - every answer to what you're looking for."

"I'm looking for Krane."

"No, you're not," he chuckled, and the light from his face beamed even brighter. "But maybe you think you are, for now."

"Tell me what I'm damn looking for, then!"

"You're looking for the truth. I discovered the truth - he discovered the truth - Damn!" The figure grew agitated, then composed itself. "Well, in any event, one of us discovered the truth back then at Bletchley."

I knew of Bletchley. The man, Hawthorne, or whoever he was, was referring to Bletchley Park, the code-breaking facility that had closely collaborated with both the Bureau and MI6 during the war.

"What did you find out at Bletchley?"

"Another time, Max. For now, just remember to question everything. It'd do me no good to have you lose yourself yet."

I felt something beneath my toes and glanced downward. There, protruding slowly through the sand, hollow and decaying, was her face.

———

I jolted awake, still dazed from the dream. What the hell did that mean? Was it something to do with the Mirror? With Krane? Or was it simply a wild dream, driven onward by my growing concern for Artemis? But I didn't have too long to mull over the dream, as a voice spoke in my ear. It was Artemis herself, stretching and yawning next to me.

"You awake, Calder?"

"Yeah. You been awake long?"

"Just woke. We're here, I think."

Sure enough, we were. We had reached Genoa, the port from which we would leave for Argentina. It was one of the largest ports in Italy and the place where we'd depart to cross the ocean.

I stepped down from the train first this time, stretching my arms. Genoa was a beautiful port city, filled with stunning women dressed in festive and exotic outfits, crowds, and beggars. It was one of the busiest ports in the Mediterranean and was the perfect place for Artemis and me to begin our journey to Argentina. It was the "take-off" place for many ships, and so we began the initial leg of our sea journey by purchasing tickets at the shipyard. The Lloyd Italiano shipping company was my choice for travel - I'd been on their ships many times throughout my time working for the Bureau and pulling off espionage missions as if they were nothing. After a brief conversation with the agent later, we procured our tickets for the MS Vulcania. It was a large ocean liner, one of the most prominent vessels in port. As luck would have it, our journey would begin in the afternoon of the next day. All Artemis and I had to do, then, was spend our time well until then.

"Fancy a drink?" I asked her, pointing to one of the nearby bars, a sailor's place that sat near the docks with an uncomfortable number of burly men.

"If you insist," she replied, a twinkle in her eye. Neither of us wanted to spend the rest of the day holed up in some old dingy motel, and as such, we decided, with hardly a word spoken between us, that this was the far better option.

However, as we approached the bar, something happened that threw a stick in our plans. A man, tall and wearing a sailor's jacket, tweed coat, and sporting a twirled mustache, approached us, making his way in a leisurely fashion out from the shade of the bar.

"Oy, you Raven?" he asked, his voice blunt but with an unmistakably British accent.

I tensed instantly, my hand on my gun before he had even finished speaking. I didn't draw, however - that would have been foolish. Instead, I looked at the man; he was a full head taller than me, and I sized him up. I was confident I could take him, but I lived by the rule that trouble often came in pairs, at the very least.

"Who's askin'?" I replied.

"Been lookin' for 'im. Same height as you, too, I'd reckon. Same scar. Figured it must be you then, airght?"

"And what are you looking for me for?"

"I work for the Bureau. Heard from Opal there that you an' 'er were tracking down Krane and the Mirror."

"Well, we lost 'em."

"Humh." He stared me up and down, clearly trying to discern if I was lying. "And issat where you are going now, then?"

Before I could respond, Artemis spoke. "We've booked a ticket to Argentina. My mother is ill, and I want to see her before anything too grave befalls her."

He raised an eyebrow, clearly impressed by the succinctness of the answer. "Well, anyway, that's not what I'm 'ere to press you on. I need to know the whereabouts of Hawthorne."

"Hawthorne?" I asked, confused. "Didn't Opal report back what we told her? He's MIA."

"Maybe is, maybe not. Maybe you're lying."

I scoffed, stepping forward and tapping his chest. "I'm not. But if I were, the Bureau can go to hell. They're the ones who put me in this damn situation in the first place."

He stared down at my finger, his jaw clenched for a second as if he couldn't decide whether to clock me upside the head or not. Eventually, however, he loosened his muscles and relaxed, a more jovial expression on his face.

"Well, my superiors don't think Hawthorne has expired just yet. But they do think - and they think very much - that when his ugly face does turn up, he'll likely be turning up around you, Raven."

"That so?"

"That's so. Which means you'll see more of me in the days to come." He glanced over toward the ship behind us, the towering MS Vulcania, and smiled. "We'll enjoy the trip, won't we?"

I stuffed my hands in my pockets and raised my eyebrows, watching him walk away, whistling the tune to "Shenandoah" until he broke into song.

"Oh, Shenandoah, I long to see you… Away, you rolling river… Oh Shenandoah…."

I glanced at Artemis. Her face looked confused and baffled, as if she'd just seen some unsightly insect or some ghastly scene caused by an animal.

"Quite something," I said, motioning toward the receding silhouette of the man. "Isn't he? And we didn't even get his name."

"I'm not sure I want to," she replied. "But I have a feeling he's going to book himself a ticket on the Vulcania as well."

Artemis was correct. On the evening of departure, we boarded the ship and caught a glimpse of the man in line behind us. He wore the same outfit and waved once as he caught my eye. As uncomfortable as his presence made me, I was much more interested in the ship. I'd only seen the Vulcania while doing my work for the Bureau and had never had a chance to sail on such a premier vessel.

It was stunning. We were traveling first class, and our cabins were decorated elegantly with wood paneling, fine carpets, and even lavish artwork - a far cry from the subpar accommodations we had on our trip to the coast of Italy. And of course, there were the rest of the amenities - I strolled around the deck as we departed, taking it all in.

With a luxurious dining room, spaces for music and dancing, and even a promenade deck, this vessel was unlike any of the shabby ones I had been on before.

It even featured a library filled with plenty of books, a few comfortable chairs, and a more relaxed setting. I grinned to myself; glad I wasn't spending my own money on this project.

It was a glaringly hot afternoon, with the sun glinting off the waves, casting beautiful reflections across the rows of portholes as the ship slowly inched out of sight of the coast, away from Genoa's bustling port. The longest leg of the journey had finally begun, but I was busy thinking about other things. Krane could wait - after all, we had our friend from the Bureau to deal with.

I stood by the rail for a while, deep in thought. The vibration of the powerful engines could be felt best here, and something about the rhythmic and powerful nature of the ship comforted me. I stood and watched the sea spread out before me, staring into the blue Mediterranean sky.

Eventually, I heard footsteps beside me. I was known in the spy business as a "catalogue". I was the type of man to take down any information, observe everything, and remember it acutely for later use. As such, I instantly recognized her footsteps. Sure enough, only a second or so later, Artemis strolled up beside me, her face unreadable. Though I couldn't tell for sure, she seemed different. She had seemed different ever since our connection in the abandoned bunker on the Swiss border, but I wasn't sure why. Now, however, her face was even more blank than usual. But I was not a nosy man, and so I let it slide.

"We're really going, aren't we?" she asked. It was half a statement, half a question - something that held a sense of trepidation for what reason I knew not.

"We are indeed," I replied, pulling out a pair of cigarettes from my pack and offering one to her. We smoked together, watching the sun set over the deep blue waves.

"So," she said finally, blowing out a wisp of smoke. "What about the sailor agent?"

"Ah, the man from the Bureau."

"Who else?"

I shrugged. "If he plans to follow us, he's already on the ship. But so long as we're unsure of what he's here to do, it's best to keep an eye on him until we know what course of action to take."

"Observation. That is just like you, Calder."

I grinned, but it was only half-hearted. For some reason, her voice seemed distant. What could it be? My mind raced, trying to figure out the possibilities. Finally, I settled on one.

"That thing… about your mother, was that true?"

"What about her?"

"Is she sickly?"

"Yes," she said as I watched her face carefully. "But she has been for a while."

"I see." I flicked the butt of my cigarette over the railing, watching it fall into the water, lost in the waves. The ship's engine was steadier now, and the vessel was filled with activity. Dinner was approaching, and by lamplight, children darted between legs while the wealthy sat at dining tables.

But where Artemis and I stood, the ship was empty. Finally, she spoke once more, her voice more hesitant this time, as if she wasn't sure if she wanted to share her thoughts.

"I had a dream."

"Oh?"

"The night in Switzerland."

"Oh really?" I paused. "What did you dream?"

"Probably nothing important. But I don't have a good feeling about this trip, Calder. It feels like death."

I felt every one of my muscles tense, but I was careful not to show a single emotion cross my face. My mind whisked back to the dream I had had of the man who had spoken to me with Hawthorne's face. Was this related? I didn't tell her. I simply nodded, slowly.

"Well, every mission does, doesn't it? Usually, it ends in death, too, but not for us."

"I suppose so. It's late; we should get some rest."

I nodded. I had lied, bluntly. I did not fear death, nor did any mission we'd ever been on concern me in such a way. I knew it didn't usually happen for Artemis either, and as such, a spark of concern was kindled in my mind.

As we walked back to our shared cabin, I stuffed my hands in my pockets, wondering what this mission would bring. The dream flashed into my memory yet again, like an annoying gnat that wouldn't leave me be.

What had the man with Hawthorne's face meant? What was the truth I was looking for, anyway? And what had happened at Bletchley Park?

CHAPTER 16
BLETCHLEY BEGINNINGS

I n Hawthorne's early days, the Bureau would often send him to confront scientists, demanding information or assistance with the projects it sought so hard to contain. Bletchley Park, particularly, was a hotbed of scientists, codebreakers, and genius cryptographers who proved invaluable to the Bureau, MI6, and other government organizations that operated from the shadows. It quickly became the center for the greatest minds in mathematics, cryptography, and engineering, where men worked tirelessly to crack German codes and decipher military messages.

For Hawthorne, however, Bletchley Park proved to be of another use. The Bureau dealt with time anomalies and other amalgamations of tech that had previously been considered science fiction. As such, the men at Bletchley would often be called upon to discuss the likelihood of a project's success or the likelihood that the Germans had already developed such a project.

In the early days of the war, these projects were often rudimentary and unsuccessful, but nevertheless, Hawthorne still found assistance from the most genius among society here. It was on one such outing - requested by the highest authority within the Bureau - that he was put in contact with Alan Turing, one of the most brilliant minds of the century. He hadn't been sent to Bletchley Park for Turing. Originally, he'd been tasked with talking to and interviewing Alastair Denniston, the infamous man who, as one of the founding fathers of Bletchley Park, ruled it with an iron fist.

Hawthorne had arrived on the estate one cold night, the biting air seeping through the poorly sealed windows of the car he drove. His hands were gloved, his breath creating crystalline clouds of mist in the air as he exhaled. He turned the key in the ignition, and the car sputtered to a stop. He'd arrived at Bletchley Park once again. The place never ceased to amaze him.

It was a sprawling complex, with Victorian-style buildings scattered throughout, surrounded by well-maintained gardens. For those who didn't know better, the serene setting would deceive them into thinking that it was a place to relax. But Hawthorne was aware of the intense work being done inside, even at that very moment. The estate itself was a mixture of an old manor house, newly constructed warehouses, and several huts that were constructed to house new codebreaking projects.

Hawthorne ignored these buildings, walking directly toward the centermost mansion in Bletchley Park - the main building. It was a grand, old Victorian house that screamed stories of the centuries it had stood there. It was here that Hawthorne expected to find Denniston, as he so often had. But Denniston was oftentimes busy, and when Hawthorne arrived and spoke to the beautifully charming secretary at the front desk, she informed him that Denniston was busy.

"I am truly sorry, sir, but Mr. Denniston has informed me that he won't be meeting with any guests tonight."

"Did he have no contact from the Bureau? One of my men should have called ahead."

"If they did, I never received it, sir."

"Well then, who else might be here who knows the operational status of this place? I've been instructed by my superiors at the Bureau that we require a thorough outline of the individuals who operate here and their current projects, so we know what resources are available at our request."

"Certainly, sir. If you'd like to speak to one of the men most familiar with key operations here, you could try Mr. Turing from Hut 8. He tends to keep to himself, but I suspect he knows far more about the operations here than he lets on."

"Alan Turing?"

"Yes, sir. Allow me a minute, and I'll have him fetched."

That was how Hawthorne had first met Alan Turing, who led the team in Hut 8 working on breaking the German naval Enigma code. The two men shook hands, Turing nervously avoiding eye contact as they did so. At first, Turing seemed distant, only answering questions when they were required.

As their interviews stretched on, Hawthorne chose to speak to Turing even when Denniston was available, and the two men quickly began to develop a relationship fueled by their appreciation for the same sciences.

Although Hawthorne never worked directly with Turing on any of his code-breaking projects, the two men made sure to speak whenever they got the chance. When Hawthorne was assigned to some task, interview, or retrieval of information at Bletchley, he would stop by and have a conversation with Turing. Hawthorne, of course, had quickly realized how brilliant Turing was and wouldn't pass up a chance to speak to him.

He found Turing's work compelling to witness, particularly the man's brilliance when it came to the principles of computers, as well as what would later become known as Turing Machines. However, Turing would admit that Tommy Flowers was the real mastermind behind building the world's first digital computer used for code breaking at Bletchley called Colossus.

He'd spend hours engrossed in conversation with Turing , discussing animatedly not only how data could be handled and manipulated by breaking it down into pieces, but also the ethics of the whole matter. Indeed, the two men soon found themselves diving into theoretical discussions when they had reached the borders of reality itself. Although Hawthorne wasn't supposed to share the details of his work, he'd often prompt Turing with conversations about hypothetical quantum mechanics and time travel.

"You know, Malcolm, what fascinates me about quantum mechanics is how it challenges our former understanding of time and space," Turing said one day, staring at a chalkboard covered in scrawls and complex formulas. "In classical physics, time is constant...but quantum mechanics - well, time isn't so straight-forward, is it? The very fabric of reality might be in a state of flux, an infinite interaction of probabilities, if you will."

Hawthorne nodded, his arms crossed as he leaned against a desk. "Precisely. And why not, then, use quantum mechanics to emulate a sort of time travel? Rather than view time as a linear progression, we should view it as a probabilistic field - a field that can be influenced by the quantum, where the future and past aren't predetermined - hell, where they don't even exist and yet do - together in a state of superposition until we interact with them."

"Exactly."

"And how specifically would we achieve that, Alan? Humor me."

"Consider quantum superposition. Particles exist in multiple states simultaneously at any given moment. Only when we see a particle does it become a definite state."

"I'm following," Hawthorne nodded. "And for time travel?"

"For time travel," Turing continued, "we could apply this same principle. We might be able to consider multiple timelines - infinite timelines - as existing in parallel, each with different outcomes, until we collapse them into the single timeline we desire."

Hawthorne began to pace as he spoke, excitement brimming from his voice. "Parallel timelines. Multiple versions of history. But how do we interact with these timelines? How do we access them without damaging the current one?"

"Ah, but that's the crux of it, isn't it?"

"Hmm."

"But maybe," Turing said suddenly, "maybe a device capable of creating a stable quantum field…maybe that could do it. A device that allows you to interact with various timelines without causing distortion."

"Sounds advanced, doesn't it?"

"Sure, but the principle holds."

"So you're saying that if we could entangle particles across time, we could connect different points of history? Influence those points without directly interacting with them?"

Turing nodded, smiling slightly. "Precisely. A quantum link between moments in time. We could send information, perhaps even energy, back and forth. It wouldn't manipulate time, per se…but influence it."

"It sounds fragile."

Turing glanced toward Hawthorne, one eyebrow raised. "Fragile? Yes - yes, that's an understatement, I think. Time is delicate, Malcolm. Even the slightest change could leave the world collapsed to the size of an oyster."

"Well, that's a sobering thought," Hawthorne muttered. Though he had not yet told Turing, the Bureau had already begun work on the Mirror, with Hawthorne himself monitoring development progress.

"It really is."

"But you'd say it's more than theoretical, wouldn't you? It's about control, not theory. If we can measure the quantum field and adjust it - just like adjusting the dials on one of your machines - we might have the power to direct the flow of time."

"Or even send people through time. That's what you're getting at, isn't it?"

"You caught me."

"Too much power. We'd risk becoming gods of time, changing fate and destiny itself."

"But the ability to correct mistakes and preserve the stability of the world," Hawthorne said, grimacing. "It's tempting, isn't it?"

"Tempting, yes. But dangerous. Oh, so dangerous - and what of free will, if such a thing even exists? If you change probability itself, do you not remove the freedom of choice from any decision ever made that has led to that point? What happens then? Which philosophy must you adopt to use it?"

"I'm not sure. Maybe the rules of time must be followed strictly - never bent, and surely never broken."

"What rules, Malcolm?"

"Time itself is an enigma to many men. But there are rules everywhere in our universe - it's apparent, isn't it? Flowers bloom and follow the rules of their bud. Animals mate and follow the rules of their genetic code. Surely time will follow such rules, as does the rest of our universe?"

"Indeed," Turing said, smiling, though a slight sadness reached the edge of his eyes. "But remember, Malcolm. It's not just the knowledge that's important; it's the wisdom to use it correctly. Time is not ours to control, just as you would not dream of controlling the way the sun spins or the way the universe expands."

"Time is both a tool and a weapon, I suppose. But who wields it?"

"That's a different question than who should wield it. Who wields it? Any man who finds the answer first."

"I suppose you're right," Hawthorne said quietly, more to himself than to Turing. The two men sat in silence, contemplating the discussion they'd had.

The conversations he'd had with his superiors and the scientists who worked on the blueprints of the Mirror echoed fresh in Hawthorne's mind as he sat there. Was Turing right and those men wrong?

But even within the rules, there might be a way to manipulate time. To fold it, merge it, and modify it so that a greater possible outcome for all could be achieved.

And that, he thought, was his goal. To save men from themselves without ever so much as breaking a rule. To guard the rules but use them to the advantage of humanity.

Unbeknownst to Hawthorne, his most optimistic theories would be dashed against the rocks, dead and bloodied, in several months.

The initial test of the Mirror would change his very view of reality itself, haunting him until his death.

CHAPTER 17
SHIPBOARD SLIDERS

I rolled over in bed, tossing and turning. I was uncomfortable, sweaty, and I couldn't help but feel as if I'd never sleep. I wasn't sure I wanted to, either, considering how bizarre my dreams had been of late. I finally rolled myself out of the spacious double bed, making sure not to wake Artemis. We'd opted for a single couple's stateroom rather than to travel separately, as this would cull any suspicion from nosy parties - and besides, neither of us had a problem with it. I looked around the room, admiring the beautiful, plush velvet drapes framing the door, which opened to a small veranda just outside our room. It was a luxurious, almost regal place, far more impressive and sprawling than the shabby safe rooms I'd felt boarded up in for days while working for the Bureau.

To my left was a beautiful, dimly lit reading lamp sitting atop a small table, with a plush stool positioned directly in front of it. The bed, perhaps, was the nicest amenity of the room, serving as the focal point of the whole thing, with an uphol-stered headboard and cotton sheets. It didn't take away from the very attractive mirror located on the far wall, however, nor the painting of an anchor that hung to one side of it. Though the room was immaculate, I still felt trapped, as if I were sailing directly to my doom. I couldn't rest or think in such a luxurious, confined space. I wasn't used to it. I needed something else.

I needed fresh air. Though I could have easily had a smoke on the veranda, I decided instead to take a small walk to the deck, where I would have more space. I quietly dressed, put on my trench coat against the cold night air, slipped my M1911 into my pocket, and headed up toward the deck. The last time I'd been on a ship, I had done away with one of Krane's Soviet goons, and I wondered very much if this time would be the same. After all, there was an agent from the Bureau trailing us, and it was simple enough to recognize that he was a threat. I didn't need to make any advanced deductions to understand that.

I fully understood the implications of the Bureau sending this agent to track us. While they wanted Krane dead, the Bureau was also extremely interested in the latest working prototype of the Mirror. It was possible that is was way more advanced than any version they had. And if Krane currently had his hands on this, they'd likely take it by force once we'd dispatched the mad scientist himself.

As for us, I knew all too well that we had deviated from the Bureau's plans as soon as we came into contact with Hawthorne. This alone was enough to put us on a watch list from our superiors, but the addition of our fragmented nature no doubt had the Bureau's big shots on even higher alert.

I had finally reached the deck, and I leaned against the guardrail, looking out into the darkness. It was pitch black in the ocean below, and there was no way of even guessing what lurked beneath the waves. It was a chilling thought, but not as chilling as what I had concluded - the Bureau wanted to know what Artemis and I knew about the Mirror. If we gave it over to them and allowed the organization to control it once again, they would likely let us live. But if we even dared to lay a finger on it, that was what the Bureau agent was here for.

Simply put, it was clear he had been sent to kill us if we deviated from their plans.

I sighed, shaking my head slowly. It was a damned strange world I'd ended up in. The world had swallowed me now. I remembered less of my childhood than I did of the men I'd killed, the files I'd stolen, and the projects I'd seen to completion.

Suddenly, a voice spoke out of the darkness beside me.

"And so what will you do, anyway?"

I jolted, turning toward the source of the voice. I hadn't heard anyone approach, but a man stood beside me, five or so yards away. I couldn't see his face through the darkness, nor could I make out his stature, and his voice seemed masked. I couldn't identify it, but it had a familiar ring to it.

"Who the hell are you?"

"That really doesn't matter, not for now. What does matter, Raven, is that you return to your cabin."

"What? What do you mean?"

"She dies in thousands of parallels. Don't let this be one of them."

With a flick, I pulled my M1911 from beneath my trench coat and leveled it at the stranger.

"Step forward, slowly! Into the light, where I can see you."

He did not respond, but I saw what little bit of him was visible shift slightly. Then, the man began to walk forward, into the light. But as he did, when each part of the light struck him, his body seemed to crumble to dust. I couldn't see his face. As the light hit that part of him, it seemed to dissipate. Eventually, only a black, sooty trench coat was left, fluttering to the floor at my feet. As it fell, however, the man's voice echoed once more, as if he still stood there.

"Save her, Raven."

"What the hell…" I muttered, staring at the trench coat on the ground in front of me. I didn't have time to think of what had just happened. Whoever - or whatever - I had just seen, I knew too damn much about the Mirror to delude myself into thinking it was just a vision. I turned and raced down the steps below deck toward our cabin. As I neared the door, however, I heard a ruckus emanating from inside - shouts, thuds, a real commotion.

"Where the hell is 'e? You help him throw me off, did you?" a man shouted, and I recognized the voice as that of the Bureau agent.

I slammed my shoulder against the door, not even bothering to check if it was unlocked. There he was, atop Artemis, straddling her, his fist clenched as he swung downward for another blow.

I rushed forward, tackling him to the ground as he spun to face me. I struggled with him, my muscles burning as I fought to stay in control. The man was huge, as I'd noticed at the bar - a full head taller than I, with forearms the size of logs.

I elbowed his chin, knocking his head back with the force of the blow. His thick neck recoiled, but surprisingly, that seemed to have little effect on him. He grinned, swinging his head forward in retaliation. I recoiled, dodging to one side to avoid his headbutt as I grabbed onto both of his arms in an attempt to hold him down, but the man was strong.

He tore one hand free of my grasp, swinging wildly. His fist connected with my jaw, sending me stumbling backward into the wall, the impact knocking the painting of the anchor from its hooks. I blinked, seeing stars at the edges of my vision. If his fist had fully connected, I would have been out cold.

We both straightened to our feet, and I noticed out of the corner of my eye that Artemis had managed to stand as well. Her face was already bruising from the blows, her eyes livid. The man, apparently, noticed that she had stood as well because he began to slowly position himself closer to the exterior door where I stood, rather than rushing to fight either of us. I moved as well, stepping carefully to the side along the wall, in parallel with his movements, until I stood with the wall mirror behind me.

"Well, 'suppose now's as good a time as any to introduce

myself," he said, grinning. "Name's Boone. My apologies for the intrusion; thought you'd given me the slip, Raven."

"Like hell you're going to introduce yourself after that," I responded, sliding my hand into my trench coat to check that my M1911 was still there. "The hell you think you're doing?"

"No hard feelings," he responded, nodding toward Artemis. "But she's expendable; you ain't.; If I lost you, Raven, they'd 'ave my head. And don't pull out that gun, will you? Do you think I'm the only agent on the ship?"

"And who gives a hell if you are or not?" Artemis said, her voice cold. "Surely you realize we have no plan of letting you leave…alive, at least."

"Well, you'd best do it quietly," he grinned. "But look, it won't be like that - "

Before he had even finished speaking, the man flung himself at me, his clenched fist the size of a grapefruit launched toward my face like a sledgehammer.

I ducked and heard a cracking noise and the man curse. I'd been standing right in front of the mirror, which hung on the wall, and his fist had gone solidly through the glass surface and the wall behind it. He stared for a second at his fist, bleeding and cut in more places than you could count. His fingers had gone limp, more than likely from a severed tendon.

"Oh hell… You bastard!"

His eyes bloodshot, he swung with his other arm, but his fist never connected. I stood there, a smug grin on my face as I heard the sound of solid wood strike the back of his skull. With a heavy thud, the man collapsed, and I nodded to Artemis, who stood holding a broken chair leg. Her chest heaved with effort, but she looked satisfied.

"Figured I'd let you take it out on him," I said, nodding toward the man's limp body. "How'd he get the drop on you anyway?"

"Well, I was damn well sleeping, wasn't I, Calder?" she said, rubbing her sore, bruised chin.

"Still, I figured you'd put up a better fight... he didn't seem to fight as if he had Bureau training, did he?" I said as I walked up to her, laying my hand gently against her injured face.

She flinched slightly but held still as I inspected the damage. I knew my slight jest at her lack of awareness had stung more than my hand, but she knew I'd said it all in good fun. Artemis was no slouch and could have likely taken on the man herself had he not found her in deep sleep and gotten the drop on her.

Finally, she spoke. "From the looks of him, I doubt he was a sanctioned agent... most likely a contractor, like Bishop was."

I blinked slightly. For some reason, my vision began to dull, as if I were on the verge of fainting. "Think he was telling the truth about the other agents?"

"Smell his breath," she responded. "Not that you could avoid the stench, but he's been drinking. I think his truth-telling abilities were severely damaged from that."

"Well then..." I muttered, but I never finished speaking. I squinted around the room. It had suddenly become much brighter, as if the lights were glowing hotter at an unprecedented rate. It felt as if the entire room were becoming watery, rushing away into the lights as if they were black holes. I blinked again, then glanced over at Artemis.

She stared at me as if I'd gone crazy. "Max, what's wrong?"

I felt drowsy, and my head felt heavy.

I closed my eyes.

———

I sat up with a jolt, rubbing my shoulder. I felt stiff. Had I been dreaming? I rubbed my eyes, blinking as I registered the room around me. It contained a single bed, which was where I sat now. The rest of the room was covered in a fine layer of dust, and the window and door frames were chipped. The window itself was covered in rusty iron bars, remnants of a bygone age. The only other furniture in the room was a large wooden wardrobe, doors cracked open slightly. I tried to move, but the layer of dust that covered the bed upon which I sat exploded as I did, fluffing into the air as I inhaled.

"Damn," I coughed, waving at the air in front of me to try and clear it. I stood slowly, gingerly, inspecting the bedsheets. The only places where the dust had been disturbed in the entire room were the bedsheets, where it looked as though I had been asleep despite still wearing my trench coat with the M1911 in my pocket. The sun was shining through the window directly onto my face, which indicated to me it was more than likely early afternoon - probably 1300 at the latest.

I stiffened suddenly as I heard a noise from another room - another bedroom, I assumed. Fumbling in my trench coat, I pulled out my M1911 and cautiously stood up from the bed, making sure to be silent as I did so. If a single floorboard creaked, I would be discovered.

Step after step, I walked gingerly, making sure that I tested each board before placing my full weight on it. The noises from the other room continued - it sounded as if someone else was here. Suddenly, however, the noise ceased. I peeked around the corner only to find a gun leveled at my face. I sighed in relief. Artemis stood there, in front of me, her gun pointed solidly at the doorway.

"Alicia," I said, straightening up and pocketing my gun. "Where the hell are we? Do ya' know?"

"If I did, do you think I would have my gun out at any noise?"

"Figures. Do you know what the hell happened? Last I remember, we were - "

"On a ship?" she asked, completing my sentence with her own question.

"...yeah, exactly. On a ship headed for Argentina. I'm still trying to figure things out, but it seems to me like we slid."

She raised her eyebrows slightly, looking around. "I thought it might have been a dream at first, but I tried waking myself up. Didn't work."

"Well then, where are we?"

"I'm not sure, Max. It shouldn't even be possible for us to slide like this, should it?"

"You mean because the Mirror was not on the ship and had no connection to us here, right?" I paused, gathering my thoughts. "I've slid before, but only to places where I was previously - places where the Mirror was too. I had a slide the same day you first found me in Hell's Kitchen, but even then, the Mirror was there and was connected somehow. Is this even possible?"

"I'm not sure."

"Could we be dealing with some other technology? It shouldn't be possible, should it?"

She stared, confused, at the room around us. Then her expression slowly cleared. It was as if suddenly, she'd realized something. I waited patiently - I could tell her mind was whirring, and I didn't want to interrupt.

"I think I know where we are," she said, finally, walking toward the window. "I think I know why, too."

"Well?"

She stared down at the street below the house for a while before responding. "We're in Montevideo, Max."

"Montevideo... in Uruguay? What the hell? I remember this place from the beginning of the war. The British navy beat a German pocket battleship called the Graf Spee. Captain scuttled it rather than get captured. I think it is still in the river somewhere. Weren't you born here?"

"Not just born here. I recognize this place, too...this old Bureau safe house, I mean."

"Do you think that's why we slid here?"

"I think so. Do you remember what we were talking about at the safe house in Switzerland?"

I smirked. "We did more than talking there; you'll have to be more specific."

She scoffed and rolled her eyes, walking away. "About space-time and temporal relocation, Calder...more generally, about what the Mirror is capable of."

"Yes, I guess I remember. But what does this have to do with the slide?"

"For some reason, whenever the hell one of us sliders end up, well, sliding, it typically has to do with our past or future. It's not just relocating us to times or places at random. There's an algorithm to it."

"I guess that makes sense," I nodded. "When Hawthorne and I were talking, while we were sliding in Prague, he alluded to the fact that entanglement is a core, fundamental piece of how the Mirror works. If this is the case, wouldn't it be possible that the Mirror can create this quantum 'spooky action at a distance,' as Einstein called it, like we're experiencing now? That it might not even need us to be next to it, so long as the connection has already been established?"

"That makes sense from what I know about quantum science," she responded.

"Damn. Then, do you think that Krane might be responsible for this?"

"I don't think so. This place is connected to me, not to you or Krane. And I've been seeing this place, too."

"What?"

"Do you remember those dreams I mentioned, Max? This damn city has been popping up in my dreams. I'm just not sure if it's a dream of the past or something that has yet to happen."

"So then you think the Mirror pulled you here because of your dreams? Or maybe your dreams are because it was going to pull us here."

"Who knows," she said, shrugging. "In our world, it seems that time is less of a constant and more of a suggestion."

I sighed, rubbing my face with the palm of my hand, feeling

my weathered, tired skin. "I can't wait to blow that Mirror back to hell. This quantum stuff is confusing."

She laughed, nodding in agreement. "We should do that, then!"

We made our way down to the ground floor of the safe house. Artemis described it as we walked, and I stared around in awe, taking in the place. Apparently, she'd been assigned here during one of her first missions, and from the looks of it, the place hadn't been used since.

The ground floor itself looked more dilapidated than the first, with dust covering every surface. There was a dining room where a small table sat in the corner, surrounded by scattered empty chairs, and old pots and pans still hanging from their hooks. The living room had a large velvet curtain hanging across the window, and the old armchairs were stained and bleached. On one wall was a fireplace, appearing to have been built by hand with various stones from the surrounding region. Next to the fireplace leaned a fire poker, and on the mantle, there were a variety of sticks and other items.

Eventually, we came to a stop in the middle of the living room, where Artemis bent down to toss aside a large throw rug that lay in the center. I watched, impressed, as the rug went flying and a cloud of dust was flung into the air, revealing what looked like a trapdoor. I raised my eyebrows.

"What's this?"

"Well, this confirms it," she said, pointing. "The Montevideo safe house I stayed in had a hidden bunker beneath it. And here it is. Give me a hand, will you?"

I nodded and bent down, tugging at the rusty rung in the center of the trapdoor. It groaned and protested, but eventually budged, giving way as I heaved it upward. We both stared down at the flight of concrete stairs descending into the darkness.

"I don't suppose you have a light, do you?" I asked, nodding in her direction. She shook her head, so I shuffled through my pocket, pulling out a Zippo lighter I'd procured several days before we'd departed on the MS Vulcania to more reliably light my cigarettes. Artemis watched as I bent down, tearing off a piece of the rug. I walked over to the fireplace, grabbed one of the longest and straightest sticks I could find, and fastened the cloth onto it before lighting it on fire. A cloud of smoke billowed from it, replaced in a few seconds by a reasonably bright flame.

"Not bad," she shrugged. "Shall we?"

"Ladies first," I said, but led the way into the basement regardless, holding the torch out in front of me to see if I could spot anything useful. We descended the steps, taking an unusually long while to reach the bottom. Eventually, however, the ground leveled out in front of us, and I spotted an array of old crates, boxes, and equipment. Though many of these items were now decrepit and useless, the basement itself still proved useful. Along one wall, there was an assortment of shelves, each containing unique items that only Bureau agents could have placed there. From old passports to stacks of ARS bills, the keys to our upcoming journey in search of Krane.

I grabbed some of the cash and pushed it into an old suitcase made of fading leather but still usable. Artemis looked around the room, squinting in the dim light.

"I spent weeks here, you know."

"Did you?" I called over my shoulder. "What assignment?"

"Back in 43," she responded. "The Bureau had reliable information that there were certain Reich officials already planning something on this continent, and Montevideo was a source of much interest. They had several devices here too - nothing remotely as impressive as the Mirror, but minor temporal manipulators that could temporarily slow time within a small range. You've heard of the LTDDs, right?"

"Yes," I responded. She was referring to the early German technology that had threatened the Allied forces to such a degree that the government had assigned millions of dollars to be spent to create devices of our own. Though rare, these Localized Temporal Dilation Devices, or LTDDs, had been used to turn the tide of battles depending on the usage. They could apply a force field of electromagnetic energy at such a specific pulse that the actual time fabric was warped around the source of the device, making things within the area occur slower than outside. The devices were huge, hulking things that looked almost like cannons, but facing entirely upright and mounted on the chassis of tanks. Only ten or so had ever been recorded, but the Allied powers viewed the very existence of these temporal manipulators as a huge threat.

I finished packing the suitcase and stood, nodding to her. She followed me back out of the basement, and we shut the trap door behind us, making sure to cover it again with the carpet. Though it seemed unlikely, any hooligans who stumbled upon this safe house would do no good if they managed to find the tremendous amount of supplies that lay in the basement.

"So," she said, looking at me as we stood there. "What should our next step be?"

"Our next step, I think, would be to figure out exactly where Krane is located. You got any sources for that?"

"I had sources, but they're dead now. The only person I know here in Montevideo is my mother. And while I'd love to see her, I doubt she'd have any information about the ratlines."

"You think?"

She smirked. "That being said, there's an office up on the first floor. I'd be willing to bet we could find some information stored there, if there were agents assigned here after I left."

I nodded. "Assuming, of course, we decipher any codes."

"Assuming they haven't changed since last I was here," she replied. The Bureau was infamous for storing all of their information in ciphers and codes that were given to only the specific agents assigned to the cases. They were memorized and then destroyed, ensuring only they could access the contact information within that locality.

And just our luck - the information was still there. The office had locked file cabinets for added security, but I was able to force my way into the locks, gaining access easily. Bureau agents were so confident in their encoded ciphers, of course, that they rarely paid too much attention to the quality of locks protecting any information. A few minutes later, I had a plethora of papers spread out on the floor before me, scattered here and there so we could see them all at once.

Artemis stared down at the papers, her face wrinkled as she focused. Her auburn hair dropped down past her eyes, and she pushed it out of her face and behind her ears, a look of annoyance flashing in her eyes.

I laughed quietly to myself. She was the type of woman who'd wish that her hair were shorter - not for the style, of course, but for the convenience. But she'd never cut it, as our jobs required us to blend in, and her style was well-suited for that. Nobody would suspect such a charming, delicate figure to be one of the most dangerous spies and government agents of the Allied powers.

It wasn't long before Artemis spotted something. She bent down, grabbed one of the papers, and held it up, inspecting the words closely. The paper was covered in mostly gibberish from what I could see, but I knew that only someone assigned to this specific safe house could discern the method behind the madness. Sure enough, only a few minutes later, she'd broken into a wide smile.

"There's a man here who can help us…or at least, there was - I don't know if he's still here."

"What's his name? We'll soon find out."

CHAPTER 18
MILONGA TO MENDOZA

amiro Sosa, as we soon found out, was still very active in the community, but not in the ways we expected. When I first mentioned his name to a local, they went white as if they'd seen a ghost and scampered away, hiding inside their home. Artemis tried next, and as a native of the place who spoke the local languages and had a local accent, she had much more success. As she conversed, however, I saw her raise her eyebrows slightly, then finally turn and face me as the local moved cautiously away.

"Well, Sosa is still here… but I'm not entirely sure meeting him will go our way."

"Why? Is he still on the Bureau payroll?"

"Anything but, actually. Sosa runs Montevideo and the local gangs. He's notorious on the streets as part of the port mafioso."

I sighed. It would be just our luck. However, we had no choice. We were out of our depth here and had little time to plan ahead due to the bizarre slide we'd experienced aboard the ship. We located Sosa's hideout and took a taxi to the other side of town to make his acquaintance. His hideout was a nightclub called El Pony Pisador, and as we approached, it became clear that he was the main attraction. It was an unsightly, more intimate club built for sailors, smuggling crews, and any other societal rejects who had no other place to turn.

Located near the docks, El Pony Pisador was a well-known "milonga," as Artemis informed me on our taxi ride. Milongas, as I soon found out, could be for the rich, the poor, the good, or the corrupt. This one, however, was for the scum of the earth.

A shabby neon sign was hung lopsidedly above the smoky entrance, but that was hardly what drew my attention. Two tough-looking goons stood outside the doors, their faces rough and weathered. I strolled up, Artemis lagging behind me. One of the men, a particularly buff-looking fellow who had his hair shaved in a pattern and tattoos covering his face, stepped forward, blocking my path. He squinted at me, wrinkled his nose in disgust, and then spoke.

"A foreigner. British?"

"Correct enough," I replied, taking the cigarette from my hand and putting it out against my jacket. "I'm here to speak to Sosa."

He laughed, throwing his head back as his fellow guard joined in. Finally, the big man straightened up again, grinning at me. Several of his teeth were replaced with gold fillings. "No."

"And what do you mean, no?"

"He's busy with his women."

"His women? Don't tell me your mother works here?"

I heard Artemis chuckle behind me, but the guard looked far from amused. He cursed, pulling a knife from his belt and swinging it at me. I ducked beneath him, landing my elbow solidly on his solar plexus. I heard the wind fly out of his body, and he stumbled backward, crashing to the ground as the other guard lunged for me. Quickly, I dashed to the side, grabbing the back of his head as he overextended and using his acceleration to smash him headfirst into the orange bricks of the street. He didn't move, and a second later, I straightened back up, pulling another cigarette from my pocket as I did so. I pulled my lighter from my pocket, puffed once, and motioned to Artemis to follow me into the club.

The smoke inside was thicker than that of my cigarette, the clouds forming a wall that filtered the flashing lights as we entered. The aroma of tobacco, alcohol, and sweat was repugnant, and I wrinkled my nose in disgust. Yellow, flickering light bulbs hung from the ceiling, their incandescent light almost invisible through the cover of smoke that hung in the air like a blanket. There were neon signs hung here and there, dancing women, and more goons. They, however, had little idea of what we'd done to Sosa's compatriots who guarded the club, and as such, left us alone. The floor was wooden, though it had the look of a rotten corpse that had been trampled on one too many times. Boards were mismatched, replaced when they finally could stand the pressure of booted feet no longer. Men sat in circles around the crowded mismatched wooden tables. I glanced around, my eyes settling upon the bar. I hadn't had a drink in ages, but this hardly looked like the place.

I wasn't stuck up, but a place like this felt too dangerous even for me to get drunk in. One wrong move, and even a trained agent could find themselves attending their own funeral, likely resulting in a watery grave and a meeting with Davy Jones. The liquor bottles lining the wall behind the counter were half-empty, some even partially broken or cracked. As we walked, music purred from a rusty old jukebox that sat along one edge of the wall, resolutely playing Benny Goodman in a bid for attention amid the sea of rowdy, drunken voices.

Finally, at the very center of the room, I spotted a man who could only be Sosa.

He was a large, bulky fellow with a convex stomach and chubby cheeks, his long black hair tied behind his head in a man bun. He smoked a cigar, his bejeweled hands tightly clutching a glass of whiskey as several women fawned over him. I walked forward, pulled out a chair, and motioned for Artemis to sit before I grabbed another chair and did the same. Sosa turned his attention from one of the women, finally looking at me with something that almost resembled respect.

"Who are you?"

"Calder. Max Calder. I'm a Bureau Agent."

He sneered, motioning to the women to disperse. "I helped during the war," he said finally, taking another puff of his cigar, "but no more. There are new organizations at play here that will have my head if I help your little organization."

"You don't really have a choice, Sosa," I responded, motioning to the building around him. "You think we didn't come prepared?"

He glanced around, almost uncertain, before focusing. "What do you mean?"

"The Bureau has captured an LTDD...I'm sure you know what that is, don't you?"

"They were destroyed in the war."

"Most were, yes. There was one remaining, which is why my compatriot and I are here. The Bureau now has control over this artifact, but we're not finished."

"And if I don't help?"

"You know what it can do, don't you? You and yours won't have a chance."

"What do you want?"

"I want information," I said, gesturing around. "We already know about the ratlines, the Reich officers...you name it, we know it. That's not what we're interested in. We want a specific man, and word on the street is you might be able to tell us where he is."

Sosa sat back in his seat, his eyes angry, but his posture relaxed. "Who?"

"A man named Emil Krane. He's one of ours. Give us information about him, and the Bureau will be out of your hair again."

"I've heard of him. I don't know much, but he's been making waves around here."

"How?"

"Things have been changing. Some of the men here - they didn't escape the Allied forces...or they weren't supposed to. But they showed up here all the same."

"What do you mean?"

"Rumor has it," Sosa said, leaning in and lowering his voice, "that this Emil Krane fellow helped them escape. Hell knows how, but he did."

"And where are they now?"

"Somewhere in the foothills of the Andes, past Mendoza. You'd want to go there first."

I nodded and stood up. "Well, that's what we came here for. Now we can leave."

Sosa watched me, a glint in his eye. As I turned around, however, he finally spoke.

"I have not heard of any Bureau presence here, you know."

"And what of it? You know how we operate."

"I do not want to believe you are lying to me, Mr. Calder. But if I find out you are - " he motioned grandly at the nightclub surrounding him, " - we will find you. Track you down. Kill you. I do not take threats lightly, especially if I ever find out those making them cannot back up the threat."

"Glad I can, then," I responded without so much as a backward glance. As Artemis and I walked out of the club, she shot me a look.

"We need to get the hell out of Montevideo," she muttered.

"I agree. The faster, the better - if Sosa finds out we're not even Bureau agents anymore...officially, at least...he'll give us hell."

We walked briskly down the street, the eyes of the men staring out of the dusty club windows following us. There was no doubt in my mind - Sosa was a dangerous man, and I believed he would keep his word. The question, then, was not whether or not he would find out, but how soon it would be. I motioned a cab down as soon as I saw one, and Artemis and I stepped into the rusty old vehicle that looked as if it had seen better days. She breathed a deep sigh of relief, but I held up a finger before she could say anything.

"You speak English?" I asked the cab driver, a weathered old man who looked as if he'd lived in Montevideo his whole life. He shook his head silently, then pointed to the roughly written sign attached to the back of one of his seats, which informed us of prices, common locations, and how we could communicate with him. Artemis nodded and directed the man to drive toward the train station.

"Can't be too sure of who will report to him or not," I said, and I knew she understood. Sosa was on both of our minds, and it was for the best that he had zero inkling of what we were discussing.

"Agreed. Now, what should our path be? The Andes foothills?"

"Yes, but I figure we'll have to get to Mendoza first, don't you? And perhaps contact your original informant from there?"

"More than likely that's where he'll be anyway," she responded. "And if not, I should be able to find one of his friends there."

"Good to know. Now, I suppose we get the hell out of this town before he realizes I fed him a cock and bull story."

She nodded, and we settled back in the taxi, watching the town pass. Montevideo was clearly still underdeveloped, and the effects of the war had exacerbated this. Everywhere Artemis and I went, we saw those effects - even places that hadn't been at the core of the conflict. We passed streetcars, automobiles, and many horse-drawn carts and buggies. It wasn't at all what I was used to as we arrived at Plaza Independencia and left our taxi. We were aiming to board a train. We made our way through the crowded and bustling streets to Estación Central. It was only a few minutes' walk, and we quickly arrived at the ticket booth. Since I wasn't well-versed in the local dialects, I allowed Artemis to do most of the talking while I took a more observant approach. I people-watched, my favorite pastime, and a good way of keeping an eye out for any potential danger Sosa might pose.

If he had yet gleaned that we did not actually have the backing we had alluded to, not a single event or action made indicated otherwise. The square, though bustling and crowded, was filled mainly with normal pedestrians, beggars, and locals. It seemed a peaceful place, and so I watched carefully until Artemis turned from the counter, two tickets in hand.

"I've got us tickets to Fray Bentos," she said, waving the tickets in my face. "But that's as far as this rail line will go… at least, for us. We don't have the right papers to cross the Argentinian border, so we'll have to sneak around."

"Fray Bentos?" I asked, grinning incredulously. "You're going to make me hungry."

"Hungry?"

"I grew up eating canned steak and kidney pies - that's the brand name back home. It must be produced there."

"Well, then, maybe we'll have to stop for a bite to eat when we get there."

"Fair enough," I said. "When do we leave?"

"The next train leaves tonight at 1800 hours."

"Well, we've got a little time to spare until then," I said, glancing around. "Figure we ought to lay low so Sosa and his gang don't find out what we're up to?"

"You read my mind."

We silently slipped into one of the alleyways, retreating into the darkness of the tall buildings where we would be less likely to be seen. The noise from the crowded square faded away, and we were soon in the back alleys of Montevideo. While Sosa's unseemly crew was more likely to be found here, there were far fewer people overall, and we were far less likely to attract attention. I finally spotted a small shop with a weathered sign that I motioned toward, and Artemis and I entered. Though it looked as if it had not seen a new customer since the war, with dusty floors, crowded counters, and cracked windows, it had exactly what we wanted.

Artemis and I were here to shop, and this small clothing store would provide exactly what we needed to blend in with the locals. We browsed for a few minutes, expertly selecting new outfit that would allow us to fade into obscurity. I chose a pinstripe suit and leather shoes - and although the items were less casual than I would have preferred, their weathered and worn appearance gave off an air of poverty that I appreciated.

Artemis, of course, opted for a simple, clean dress with padded shoulders, completing her look with a pair of leather gloves. Although the rest of our outfits were new, I kept the gloves I always wore. I was loath to part with them, even in a situation such as this.

Eventually, we left, paying the old woman at the counter, who grinned at us toothlessly, and made our way down the street once more. As we walked, Artemis quickly fixed her hair, expertly imitating the hairstyle of several women who passed us by. She was, after all, an expert in disguise, and although neither of us had access to our preferred methods and technology, which for Artemis included hair dyes, she was nearly unrecognizable. For the next few hours, Artemis and I enjoyed the sights of the city, discussing our plans to deal with Krane and the other high-ranking Nazi officials who had fled with him.

If Sosa told the truth, we were likely to run into an issue. After all, if Krane had assisted several Nazis with their escape - and from my deductions, if he had used the Mirror to do so - it would not only mean the Mirror was operational but also that Krane had powerful allies in Argentina. However, that was not my only concern. The more I thought about the slide we'd experienced, the less it made sense.

Eventually, I landed on an idea - it seemed outlandish to me, but I couldn't see another option.

"Do you think he suspects we're here yet, though?" I asked suddenly as we walked.

"What do you mean?"

"Think about it - you said it yourself, Krane likely had nothing to do with this slide. Do you even believe he suspects it to be possible?"

"Surely he knows of the capabilities; he built the Mirror himself."

"But what if he doesn't?" I held up a finger as I thought, cocking my head slightly. "I can't say I know much about how the Mirror itself is designed to operate... Hawthorne would have known, but he's likely dead now. But get this, Alicia - we know from our experience with slides so far that men such as Krane are able to control when they happen and how."

"I'm following."

"Right. If that's the case, then how in the world could the Mirror have caused the slide that we experienced? Even, say, if the Mirror is connected to us through a sort of quantum entanglement, how would that action ever take place without an actor to first set it off?"

She stopped in her tracks for a second, and I could see her expression shift slightly as she thought. "So, what would that mean? There would have to be an actor behind it?"

"Precisely what I'm thinking," I grinned. "Do you think it's possible someone wants us here? Someone who has access to the Mirror and somehow knows how to use it?"

"That seems to be the only explanation," she responded, nodding. "We were so busy and shocked by the fact that a slide was even possible without us being next to the Mirror that we didn't pause to ask what had even initiated it in the first place."

"Precisely, and it must have been someone who knew us... or you, at the very least."

"And why would that be?"

"That's the question, isn't it? But I can't see how it would be possible otherwise. Think about it, Alicia - look around you. Not only did we slide to the city of your birth, but we slid to the specific safe house where you were once holed up."

"So, it must be someone who knew about my involvement here?"

"That's what I'm thinking. And Krane doesn't, which only confirms what we've already deduced... he had nothing to do with this."

We walked in silence for a few more seconds, contemplating the idea. I was slightly disturbed by the notion of a mysterious benefactor, especially one who knew such intimate details about Artemis and even potentially me. I couldn't help but shake the weird feeling that it might have been connected to my dream on the train or my vision on the ship, but I felt a strange urge to keep those experiences to myself and said nothing.

Instead, I glanced down at my pocket watch, raising my eyebrows in shock as I read the time.

"Would you look at that - it's about time we headed back and boarded the train."

CHAPTER 19
RAILWAYS AND REVENGE

watched her stare out the window, her face a picture of melancholy. Though I wasn't sure, I guessed the reason had to do with her mother. If her mother were ailing, surely Artemis would have considered visiting her. Bureau agents were largely cut off from their families, and the only information Artemis must have gathered about her mother's condition likely came after she left the ranks, opting to become a free agent rather than a Bureau employee. It would have happened sometime after the dockyard incident.

It would follow, then, that Artemis would be loath to leave her hometown without visiting her mother, or at the very least checking in on her from afar. But we had more pressing matters, such as Sosa and his crew. As the train rolled out of the station, I leaned back on the bench, smoking a cigarette as I watched the crowd. I saw nothing out of the ordinary, but I doubted I would even if there were some forces already at work. We were in Sosa's territory, and we had to be cautious - at least until we crossed the border into Argentina, where I was sure rival gangs would prevent Sosa from making any bold moves, aside from a covert operation of some sort. A stark contrast to the rail networks in Europe, this train was a frail, uninteresting thing that chugged along slowly, as if it were already aging and ready for retirement.

Wooden bench seats lined both sides of the train car, their once-rough look worn to a polish from hundreds - perhaps thousands - of uses. The hanging bulbs above us flickered softly, their orange light glowing steadily in the dusk, which slowly crept over the Uruguayan landscape.

Several other passengers sat around us, mostly in modest business attire, which comforted me. Artemis and I blended in, our attire similar down to the most minute detail. The flow of conversation was sparse, and when it erupted, it was low and monotone, almost urgent. The people here were cautious, even scared, though I couldn't discern why. The sound of the tracks, the clinking rhythm of the wheels, and the monotone voices were enough to make any man tired, and so I fell asleep.

I woke in the middle of the night and quietly glanced over at Artemis. She was still asleep, no doubt tired from the trip and activities we had engaged in over the past few days. It was almost a relief to have to take a train to the border because trains meant relative safety from any gang affiliates who might be searching for us. Sosa himself would never catch up, and so the most we'd have to deal with were goons stationed along the railway at one of the towns, if that. It was very possible; I thought it was quite possible that Sosa would never find out we had no real Bureau backing until after we'd left the country and crossed the border into Argentina. Still, it was possible he discovered it sooner, and we had to be careful.

So I leaned back against the bench and closed my eyes. There was still ample time left in the trip. We were estimated to arrive in Fray Bentos at just past 0400 hours, and the clock had just struck midnight when I had awoken. But I could not sleep and instead spent my time theorizing about the Mirror and how it could have been used to pull us here.

We knew that we had been heading to Argentina to kill Krane, but who else did? I knew the answer to that question, but it was none too satisfying to consider. The only people who would have known were Krane, the Bureau, Bureau agents assigned to our case, and, of course, Artemis and me. But if those were truly the only people who were aware of our current task, then who could have prompted the machine to instigate the remote slide that we experienced?

The landscape rolled by as I thought. I watched the Uruguayan countryside, illuminated by the light of a full moon, coast past. It was a beautiful place with rolling hills, grazing cattle, and small villages that dotted the countryside here and there. Every tiny piece of this place seemed to be alive, glowing with a sort of unique warmth that I couldn't quite put a finger on. But these puzzle pieces simply couldn't help. No matter how I turned it over in my head, trying to piece together the answer, it eluded me.

Was there even an answer? How could Artemis and I have suddenly arrived here if not a single person who knew about our quest could have instigated our slide? I shook my head, muttering a string of curse words as I grew increasingly frustrated. Perhaps the slide had been instigated to a location at random, chosen simply from the consciousness of Artemis and me, and it had landed upon Montevideo by chance? But how could that have even been the case?

Though I did not know the specifics of how to prompt the Mirror or instruct it when beginning a slide, I figured it would be nearly impossible to achieve. I shuddered suddenly, feeling a chill run over my body. Though I wasn't quite sure, I kept seeing that dream - the vision I had of a young Hawthorne sitting on the beach. The dream in which I saw her face beneath the sand.

I rested my face in my hands, thinking as hard as I could. It was connected - I knew it. The answer to how we'd arrived here was somewhere in that dream, and yet the dream itself seemed to have nothing to do with it. Was it Hawthorne? But no, there would be no way he could be with Krane, and definitely no way for him to instruct the Mirror.

Suddenly, however, I felt her light fingers on my shoulder and glanced over. Artemis was awake, looking at me with concern.

"What's wrong, Max?"

"Nothing. Just thinking, and I can't figure out what I need to figure out."

"What about?"

"How did we arrive here? Who could have brought us here? Who instigated the slide?"

"I'm not sure," she said, yawning. "But at the very least, it seems they're on our side."

"I'm not so sure," I muttered, but our conversation ended there. The train was pulling into the final stop along our route - the place where we had to figure out our own path forward - Fray Bentos.

There stood the city, intimidating in stark contrast against the night sky, just beginning to color itself with the morning light. It was a beautiful town, set against the Rio Uruguay riverbank, overshadowed by the brick towers of the two main manufacturing companies that exported from the city. Both were meatpacking plants, titans of the Fray Bentos workforce and the primary landmarks of the town.

As Artemis and I departed the train, she inhaled, wrinkling her nose as the scent of processed meat hit her nostrils. I, however, had a different reaction - this was a smell I was familiar with, the smell of food I had grown up eating. I grinned at her, motioning for her to follow me through the early morning fog along the streets of the town. It was clear that the town, though still active in the early mornings with freight barges loading and unloading their goods on the riverbank, had seen the effects of war.

Most prominently, I noticed that the area had begun to bear the signs of German presence. Though it was scarce, I saw hints as we made our way through the streets. Names written in scrawling words on several shipping crates were not in any language commonly spoken in England or Uruguay, and several of the men who gathered around pubs appeared to be of foreign descent.

For any untrained eye, these unique aspects might go unnoticed, but to Artemis and me, it was all too clear that we were beginning to see the effects of the ratlines. The war, of course, was over, but here, the remnants of the men who had lost were still standing strong. Of course, I had no interest in dealing with them and so continued to blend in, walking along the dimly lit streets.

The light was still faint, and the glimmer of the morning sun had only managed to break through the thick clouds and fog that covered the riverbanks in small rays. From Fray Bentos, we would make our final travel plans to reach Mendoza, though I knew our trip was far from over. Despite our comfortable train ride through Uruguay, over a thousand kilometers still lay ahead before we reached the final leg of our trip. Right now, however, we had more pressing matters on our hands than the remaining train ride. First, as Artemis and I had decided at the very beginning, we'd have to find our way through the border crossing into Argentina and make our way to the town of Gualeguaychú, from where we'd be able to hitch a train ride the remainder of the distance. We continued through the town, walking briskly and ensuring we were not followed. Eventually, as we neared the edge of the river that bordered Argentina closest to Gualeguaychú, where we'd need to cross, Artemis and I came to a halt.

"Remember how I said we wouldn't be able to cross without the proper papers?"

"I do. And I also suppose you have a plan?"

"Well, you could say that," she responded, nodding toward the riverbank. "Money talks, and we have a lot of it."

"And what do we do with it?" I asked, though I already knew her answer.

"Well, Max, I suppose we'll need a boat."

We walked down to the riverbank, the thick fog parting before us like a curtain as the river finally came into view. It was picturesque but clearly influenced by the local industries that I knew all too well. Above the river, confidently protruding from the landscape, stood the meatpacking plant of the Anglo-Uruguayan Meatpacking Company, locally known as Frigorifico Anglo. The Rio Uruguay itself was a majestic river stretching across the horizon and a major trade route for both Uruguay and Argentina. Fishing was common, with wooden huts, small rickety jetties, and ancient-looking dinghies used by the locals. Steamers and cargo vessels docked along the riverbank nearest to the city, with cranes loading and unloading goods, many of which were meat products. Along the roads nearest to the bank were horse-drawn carts and the occasional old truck, transporting their cargo to and from the ships. Though it was tempting, we weren't aiming to use any of these boats or any of the ferries to get across the river. It was far too dangerous, as Artemis and I didn't have the papers or forgeries we would have needed to make our passage convincing on the off chance that an official decided to check.

Hence we continued along the bank, past the bustling port and toward a less populated area. Further along the river, there were dense patches of trees and lush green shrubs - much better for us to conceal ourselves. This part of the river felt far more peaceful. We saw more small docks and boathouses that looked like they belonged to local families and fishermen. Artemis and I ignored the larger commercial vessels and sought out something much less conspicuous that we could use to get across the river into Argentina unseen. Eventually, we found a small rowboat that sat anchored near the river's edge with a local fisherman sitting on the stern.

Artemis called over to him, and when she'd convinced him to give us a minute or so of his time, she offered a proposal. I could tell, too, from the look on his face that he'd already accepted, and though he haggled for a minute or so, we were soon allowed on his rig.

As I stepped onto the small boat, it wobbled, splashing water on my ankles. I grimaced, wondering how I'd fallen so far as to find myself in such a situation. It wouldn't have happened had I still been in good standing with the Bureau, but then again, I was not going to hesitate to do what had to be done. Disguised by the morning mist, we pushed off from the bank, following the nervous fisherman's instructions. The man, though he glanced around cautiously, guided the boat with expert precision. We crossed the river, and he paddled the boat still further, diverting us into a smaller tributary that ran deep into the Argentine landscape, giving us extra cover.

In many ways, the Argentine riverbank was a mirror of the Uruguayan side, but with its own unique character, distinct in several ways. We were surrounded by farmland - corn, wheat, and soybeans. Argentina was, after all, an agricultural powerhouse. There were patches of dense forest separating the farmlands, and willow trees lining parts of the river's shoreline, their long drooping branches gently swaying in the morning breeze. It was very much a contrast to the heavily industrial nature of Fray Bentos and a perfect environment to hide our arrival from prying eyes.

We landed in Argentina in less than thirty minutes, and Artemis turned to me after a final word with the boatman.

"He says we're about four kilometers upstream from Gualeguaychú," she said, pulling the promised cash from her pockets and handing it to the man. "He brought us as close as he could without raising any suspicion. It'll be twenty minutes or so, and we can reach the town before the first train departs."

"Well, that was simple enough," I said, nodding to the man as a way of thanks before stepping gingerly off his craft to avoid capsizing it. "I guess we should make a move."

Artemis and I trekked through the trees, still covered in morning dew, until we came into sight of the town. There it was, emerging from the foliage in front of us, with two cathedral towers rising above the picturesque town. It was a beautiful sight in the morning - a tranquil and peaceful town that seemed almost perfect. Though the streets were busy as we approached, the town itself was quiet, as if the residents had managed to escape the terrors of the war that almost every other town, city, or country we'd set foot in so far had.

"This place is beautiful," Artemis murmured, and I couldn't help but agree. The avenue on which we now walked was wide, lined with vividly green trees and picturesque buildings on either side. Most buildings were only one story high, allowing the rays of the morning sun to shine brightly over the top of the city and cast a beautiful orange glimmer on the streets.

We walked past the heart of Gualeguaychú, staring up at the impressive towers that rose jaggedly from the ground.

"That's an impressive building," I said.

"It's been here for a long while - Cathedral San José," Artemis spoke, her voice low in reverence.

"So where now?"

"Now, I suppose," she said, "we get on another train."

We passed the cathedral quickly, carefully finding our way with the help of a few friendly locals to the train station. It was a busy location, even this early in the morning, and had undoubtedly been upgraded recently. Argentina had seen a burst of productivity in the past decade or so, and this was a testament to that fact. I allowed Artemis to do the talking as usual - her native tongue was recognized here, but mine would likely be scoffed at. In only a few minutes, she'd procured us tickets for a ride to Mendoza. We sat on a bench as we waited for our train to arrive. I watched people as they passed, making bets with myself and occasionally sharing snide comments with Artemis about those who intrigued me. She, meanwhile, sat quietly, engrossed in a newspaper she'd picked up for 0.10 pesos.

A few hours later, the train rolled into the station, wheels clacking loudly against the rusty rails, likely caused by the constant moisture in the air. Artemis shook her head slowly as she stood, likely attempting to clear the fog in her mind. I stretched. It had been a boring wait, but there wasn't much else to do here. The city, though beautiful and picturesque, was too quiet for my liking. I was used to dark alleyways, slums, and drug dealers, not this sort of environment. We boarded the train, and I noted how primitive the seating seemed compared to some of the previous parts of the trip we'd been on. Certainly, there was no first class here that would suit a businessman from Scotland - luckily, however, I felt comfortable in this environment.

I sat back, relaxed in one of the seats, and flashed my ticket at a guard as he walked past. Artemis did the same, and soon the train began to roll out of the station, slowly at first, then picking up speed as it left a plume of smoke drifting alongside our windows. The car we had picked was busy, unfortunately - a couple, their parents, and at least seven children had chosen this specific train car as their resting place, and so Artemis and I kept quiet as the hectic environment only worsened as the trip progressed.

It would be a long trip, likely ten to twelve hours at least, and I expected that we'd find little rest on this leg of the journey with such a crowded environment. I said nothing, however, as I was preoccupied with the beautiful landscape that swept past. And beautiful it was - the train steadily chugged past the lush area near Gualeguaychú toward the plains of central Argentina, the scenery changing swiftly as we traveled. There were green fields, rolling hills, and beautiful tropical trees, with occasional breaks where houses with red roofs stood, and even the sight of a clock tower or windmill in the larger towns.

Three hours had now passed, and the landscape grew drier. The carriage remained as noisy as it had been since the beginning, but I had grown accustomed to it. Every time we passed a town whose name I could not discern, I nudged Artemis, and she whispered the name to me. Up ahead was another town. I glanced over at her and saw her already looking at me, a slight smirk on her face.

"Villa María," she said quietly.

"Am I that predictable?"

"You never stop trying to remember things."

"Our memories are jaded enough as it is from the Mirror. Let's not forget anything else."

We sat quietly for a while longer, watching the train draw ever closer to Villa María. It was a deceptively long distance away, but we were nearing it. In about twenty minutes, we'd arrived in the center of the town. The train came to a halt, slowly at first, its brakes screeching as we stopped. I glanced over at the family who sat in the car next to us - they were preoccupied, playing and screaming. Unfortunately, it did not appear that we'd reached their stop yet. I glanced out the window, watching the town carefully. The station itself was a large structure, built of bricks and stucco, standing proudly as a centerpiece of the town. Here in Argentina, it was clear that the new rail lines were of utmost importance to any city or town through which they passed.

Families rushed around, boarding and exiting the train as it finally came to a stop, the small streets crowded and full. As I watched, my attention was quickly drawn to a strange individual who stood about fifty feet from the train car. What caught my eye wasn't particularly his outfit - though he wore odd, dark clothing. Nor was it his face - a bald, gleaming head, covered in foreign tattoos a thick nose, and a thicker scar running from his cheek to his temple. It was the way he looked at the train as if he were searching for someone. He stood there, arms crossed, scanning the train cars carefully with a piercing gaze. As I watched, we made eye contact through the window, and the man shifted ever so slightly, then turned and meandered away. In an instant, I grabbed Artemis's arm, and she turned toward me.

"We need to get off this damn train. Now."

"Max - why?"

"Follow me."

I stood, threading my way carefully down the car toward the caboose of the train rather than the front, where most individuals were exiting and entering. Artemis followed quickly behind me like a shadow, muted and silent. She was an excellent agent, and in the few seconds we'd spoken, she had understood exactly what I was afraid of - she'd heard the urgency in my voice and quickly realized that we were in danger.

She didn't know what I suspected, though, as I walked briskly down the center of the train car, shoving past several men who stood talking in the middle of the aisle. The man who had been watching the train had been looking for me specifically; I was confident of that much. His face had shifted slightly when he saw me, only the slightest amount, but I had deduced instantly that finding me had been his goal.

There were two possibilities if this were the case: one, that he was an agent of the Bureau; and two, that he worked with Sosa. He couldn't work with Krane - the man wasn't even aware we were there. So we were left with two options, neither of which was ideal, especially considering what Alicia and I had done to the last Bureau contractor who had located us.

But I didn't have time to think because suddenly, gunshots erupted. The car we had just left was riddled with bullet holes - I saw the children, mother, and father who had sat there fall to the floor, crimson blood dripping from their bodies. Their eyes were blank, their bodies limp. They'd been killed in an instant.

"Run!" I shouted, and Artemis and I sprinted through the train cars, shoving bystanders out of the way as we dodged through each car. I heard foreign voices behind us, yelling, followed by more gunshots.

I pulled out my M1911 as we ran and saw Artemis do the same with her Beretta. We'd reached the final train car, and we slammed the door behind us, latching it shut and bolting it. I breathed heavily, the scent of coal and smoke mixing with the metallic scent of blood. Artemis glanced at me, her face stern but calm. I nodded, motioning to her.

There was one small, narrow window on this car, set firmly into the door we'd just latched shut. Several smaller windows lined each side of the car, but they were set high in the air, slightly above our heads and barred. I moved silently, peering through the window from one of the sides, making sure I stood with my side toward the outer wall, my body as flat as possible. Outside, it grew eerily quiet. The screams from the train and the pavilion outside had ceased, replaced by a cold calm. Through the foggy window, I couldn't see a single sign of life - dead bodies slumped against the seats, heads drooping, but the perpetrators were nowhere to be seen.

Suddenly, yelling erupted from directly outside the caboose, and the car was riddled with holes. The bullets pierced the thick wood, splintering it and leaving holes inches from Artemis's head.

She recoiled silently, dodging lower to the ground as a rain of more bullets followed.

"This won't hold long," she said tensely. "We need out of this damn train."

I nodded, glancing around. The caboose was cramped, small, and felt like a prison on wheels rather than one made of iron bars. It was full of furniture. I'd had my fill of that in Vienna, and it hadn't ended well. I carefully held up my pistol, aimed it through one of the holes, and fired several shots. If they knew we were armed, it was likely they wouldn't approach the car directly. Instead, they'd wait us out or fill the car with bullets until they were certain neither of us could have survived.

None of the options were tenable, but I had bought us a few precious extra seconds as the men outside decided what to do.

"We need to get out," I said, nodding toward the vaulted ceiling of the train car. "If this is anything like the models in England, there'll be an escape hatch up there. Guessing they know that as well, though."

"It's likely."

I cursed quietly, then shook my head. A few seconds later, I ducked as a fresh hail of bullets erupted through one of the barred windows, shattering the glass. As soon as the fire ceased, I leaped up, glancing through the glass. I saw a man reloading his gun, took careful aim, and fired. I saw him drop to the ground, his body collapsing as I ducked back down into the car. I'd hit him dead between the eyes, but the return fire only seconds later indicated many more men surrounded the caboose.

It was the first time in my life that I'd felt trapped. Though I'd kept my eye out for Sosa and his men, the Bureau, and any other number of nameless entities that had likely been hunting us, I'd let my guard down once we were well past the border of Argentina. I hadn't expected those hunting us to follow us this far…a mistake that might cost both my life and Artemis's. I glanced over at her.

Her auburn hair was disheveled, her face sweaty, and her beautiful eyes squinted in the dim light.

Not her. I didn't want to lose her - not after all we'd been through together, the countless missions we'd run, and everything else. I glanced around - I had to think of some way out of this. The ceiling trapdoor wouldn't do; they'd suspect that. The doors on either end of the caboose were also tricky. The windows were too small, and even if we managed to squeeze through, the men surrounding the caboose would see us long before we could slip away. I thought back to our time at the Swiss border, our trip from Prague, the safe house in Montevideo…and suddenly I froze.

As more bullets struck the side of the car, closer to where we crouched this time, I remained perfectly still, my mind whirring. Would it work? Could it work? I didn't see a reason why it wouldn't - after all, it had happened once. But how would it even happen? How could we trigger it?

"I think there's a way we can get out of this. I just don't know how to…"

"What is it?" she asked tensely.

"The Mirror. We need to trigger a slide."

"How?"

"I was thinking about this on our train ride through Uruguay - I think the only solution is that something about us triggered the slide."

"Which means?"

"If we know what triggered it, we could trigger it again."

We sat up against the wall, trapped between a line of fire, a gang, and the almost impossible method of escape that I'd proposed. I could hear her breathing - quick, rapid, but steady. Finally, she glanced at me, her eyes searching my face.

"And I'm guessing you have a theory as to what it was?"

Although the spray of bullets had ceased for nearly a minute now, I knew the men were still outside. I took off my jacket and held it up to the window for a second, recoiling as only a fraction of a moment later it was scattered full of bullet holes. The men were playing it cautiously, which meant that there was someone giving them orders. These men were no amateurs. I shook my head, thinking. This was the only option.

"The first time - from the ship to Montevideo - the Mirror initiated that slide because we were traveling towards it and because you'd been thinking of the place, and it pulled us away after our fight with Boone."

"Maybe it was the danger? Or just the right circumstances."

"Could be. But I think it's more than that. I think whatever instigated that slide... it knew us. And I think... it might have been the Mirror itself."

Artemis smirked slightly. "Are you saying it's haunted?"

"No. No. Programmed, connected, tuned, maybe even part of us – thinking of entanglement but I'm not sure. Hawthorne would have known... and I damn well wish I were wrong, because he's likely dead."

"You still haven't told me your idea, Calder. How do we get it to instigate a slide?"

"We have to recreate the circumstances. Retrace our steps. What exactly were we thinking about before the slide? What happened then - "

Gunfire erupted from outside, interrupting my train of thought. A bullet pierced the wood directly above my head, shattering it and chipping the wall behind me. We would have to move quickly if we wanted to find a way out of this damn hellscape.

"What were you thinking of when the slide happened?" I asked, glancing at her.

She stood there, poised, her back pressed against the caboose, her auburn hair dangling in her face, and opened her mouth to respond.

But at that moment, the world went to hell. It felt as if the world had frozen. I watched, in slow motion, as the wood behind her shoulder blew to smithereens, heard several loud gunshots ring out, and watched her stagger. Crimson blood seeped onto her shirt just beneath her collarbone, and she dropped her gun as she stumbled forward. The gun clattered to the floor, and she closed her mouth, her eyes registering a strange emotion - shock, maybe, though for the first time in my life, I couldn't tell.

I caught her as she fell, my hands desperately pulling at her shirt, trying to pull it away so I could see where she had been shot. I felt the blood beneath my fingers - warm and seeping - and I felt her skin as I tore off her shirt. She gasped, her breath ragged as she stared at me for a second.

"Max..." Her voice trailed off as she coughed. I pressed my hand desperately against her wound, trying to keep the blood from gushing out. My mind was blank - I couldn't see or hear the gunshots or yells getting closer - I just saw her.

Another round of bullets brutally decimated the walls, sending splinters flying into the air, but I couldn't bring myself to move. As I sat there, resting on my knees with her in my arms, I felt the world spinning. My vision went dull, and I blinked my eyes. I didn't see her face anymore. I didn't even see her. Where was Artemis?

I blinked again, trying to focus my vision. Had I been shot as well? The light within my vision grew brighter, making it hard to focus. I heard voices outside. But the voices weren't yelling or screaming, and there was no gunfire - only the sound of birds and carts on a cobbled street.

CHAPTER 20
CONFUSION AND CONNECTIONS

I sat there, my mind blank. Where was I? The lights in my eyes were still bright, and I could barely see the blurry shapes around me. What had happened? The last thing I remembered was seeing the town, Artemis telling me its name had been Villa María. She had told me before I'd even asked her - but what had happened? Suddenly, my memories came rushing back, and I shuddered. I remembered the gunfire, the blood, the caboose - everything that had happened at the Villa María train station and the ambush we had narrowly escaped. I felt as if I was missing something, some key piece of information that I'd forgotten, but I didn't know what. Where was Artemis?

The slide had worked, I supposed. My vision began to clear, and I glanced around. Sunlight streamed through wooden planks nailed over windows and holes in walls. It looked like an old, abandoned warehouse. No more gunshots, no yells in a foreign language, no men hired by Sosa to kill us. Dust floated through the rays of light that pierced into the building, and I could smell the metallic scent of blood.

I glanced down and, with a sinking, piercing feeling in my heart, remembered the one thing that I had forgotten - Artemis was beside me, her body limp against the floor, her eyes lifeless, unmoving. The floor beneath her was stained with fresh blood, and her clothes were dyed a crimson so deep it outshone her auburn hair.

Later, I would learn that we had slid to Mendoza. I would learn that we'd arrived at the very city we'd risked everything to reach.

But in that moment, as I saw her lifeless face, I couldn't think of anything other than her. I crawled to her side, a pain piercing my own side as I did, grasping at her face with my hands. I shook her slightly, desperately, hoping she would move.

"Alicia..."

My voice was hoarse, but I called her name again. The bullets that had pierced her even as we slid had been too much - too fatal - for her to survive. There was nothing I could do - nothing my years of training or my time in Scottish bars could do now. She was dead. I sat there, numb, and felt my hands fall limply by my side as the harsh reality set in. I couldn't feel my own face, couldn't force myself to breathe, couldn't even remember how to move my body. I had never expected this.

Though we'd made a living tempting danger, I had never anticipated her death. I stared at her face - her beautiful lips, perfect auburn hair fallen haphazardly against the old, dusty floorboards, her eyes glassy yet still as hauntingly perfect as the day I first saw her.

The numbness remained. I don't know how long. I don't know how long I sat there, kneeling on the floor of the warehouse, but at one point I found myself holding her in my arms again without knowing how. Maybe it was minutes, maybe it was hours - but I stayed there, unwilling to leave. My side was throbbing now, sticky with what I realized was my own blood, but I didn't care. I couldn't abandon her - not here. I couldn't even close my eyes; I forced them open to look at her face a little while longer.

Eventually, however, I moved. It was well into the night, and the coldness in my own body forced me to act. I became acutely aware of a buzzing in my own head that I had felt many times before from lack of blood. I let her fall to the floor once more, gently covering her with my coat as best I could. I had no other resources, no way of giving her a proper rest, but I vowed to return. Finally, driven only by my body's overwhelming desire to survive, though my mind had long since given up its love of life, I left the warehouse, stumbling away from it, my mind blurry and my feet moving on their own.

I walked slowly, my mind jumbled and confused, as if I were living in some sort of sick fever dream that I was only now waking from. I stumbled over sharp rocks, falling several times, forcing myself to my feet only to continue on. The searing pain in my abdomen was almost unbearable, and I realized fully I'd been nicked by a bullet that had grazed my side.

Out of the only instinct I had left - the instinct of survival that had driven me out of the streets of Scotland all those years ago - I found a nearby home, communicating in broken Spanish and gestures that I needed help from the woman who'd met me at the door. She nodded quietly, ushering me kindly inside and bandaging my wound with some white linen cloth from a basket of clothes she had standing in the kitchen.

The second she finished, I stood, thanked her, fished some coins from my pocket, and tried to pay her, but she refused, her wrinkled face kind as she nodded, attempting to indicate I should stay to recover. But I couldn't - I left, thanking her once again and stumbling through the bright streets.

I passed vineyards, carts chock-full of bottles of wine, and beautiful, tree-lined avenues. But I didn't really see any of it. I spotted a hotel and walked up to the counter, weak but careful to keep my wound out of sight. Slamming some money down on the counter, I motioned to the man who stood there for a room, and only ten minutes later, I lay down on the bed.

There, I remained, staring up at the ceiling of the stucco-covered room. The heat was unbearable, the noise from the streets outside deafening, but I didn't move. Though I couldn't be sure how long I had stayed there, I could feel my body growing weaker, my mouth becoming parched, and my mind fogging to the point I could barely think. Eventually, I pulled myself to a sitting position and then stood, swaying slightly. I made my way to the sink, turned the faucet handle, and drank. The water was cool.

Now, six days after I'd arrived in Mendoza, I set out on the streets, wearing a fresh pair of clothes I'd paid a delivery boy to bring me. My money was running low - it would likely only last a day or so more at this hotel, and therefore, my outfit bordered on poverty. The shirt was plain - a white cotton piece that was slightly too large for me and had several patches, likely a second-hand garment. The pants I wore now were made of a sort of wool, unwashed, brownish in color, and stained. But they were clothes that did not have blood on them, and that helped me to focus.

I walked through the streets briskly, heading for the one place I knew here - Mendoza was not home to any official Bureau presence, but in almost every city such as this, after the war ended, there would be a single agent - Bureau or otherwise - assigned to such a place. But Artemis had given me a key detail: she had an informant here. This, of course, made my entire plan much easier. If Artemis knew someone, I needed to think like she would have done to find them. Luckily, I knew Artemis - had known her, anyway. And so I walked through the streets, carefully treading my way to one of the local hotels frequented by the rich and affluent.

An informant of Artemis wouldn't have been a random pickpocket, a homeless man, or any other inconsequential individual. Her contacts were carefully selected - individuals who could keep an eye on everything that happened within their region and were more than capable of hearing even the most well-kept secrets within the city. I deduced that her contact would be someone with a hand in the very core affairs of the city itself - a hotel clerk, a priest, a chief of police, or even a government official. My plan was simple - cause a commotion at a very central point within Mendoza and have myself arrested. The worst-case scenario would itself be beneficial. I was confident that, given enough time, I could break out of any jail cell they threw me in, but positioning myself in such a place would also put the city on high alert. Any individual here who was keeping watch for the unusual would be alerted to my presence.

I arrived at the hotel, across from which was a noisy bar where businessmen, vineyard owners, politicians, and tacticians took their meals. It was there, I wagered, that a commotion would spread quickly throughout the city. Any event out of the ordinary here, of course, would be the talk of the town the next day.

I walked through the doors, pushing my way roughly past several of the men exiting as I entered. They turned, and one muttered something about foreigners, but I ignored them. If I were here, I might as well have a drink first.

I sat on one of the stools and rolled my shoulders. "What's the best wine here, anyway?" I asked loudly.

The bartender, a short man with an impressive mustache, raised his eyebrow slightly. "If you're a tourist, why not some Vino Leon? We make it here."

"Well, your finest, then."

He nodded, disappearing through a set of doors for only a second before emerging with a glass of wine. I sipped it - the mouthfeel was smooth, and the taste exotic.

I took a deep breath, then downed the rest of my wine. I didn't have the time to enjoy my drink much more than I already had, and it didn't give me much enjoyment anyway. I glanced around the room, looking for a man who would make it believ-able. Scattered about were several elderly gentlemen, calm enough, and unlikely to allow me to escalate any commotion. A woman and her husband sat at one table, disinterestedly discussing matters of love.

But there, in the corner, I finally spotted a man who I

deduced would serve my purpose perfectly. A young, handsome-looking fellow in a suit sat at a table surrounded by other men his age, all in their late twenties or early thirties, talking loudly to each other. Every time the waitress - a beautiful woman with black hair and dimples - walked past their table, the man in the suit would reach beneath her skirt quickly, laughing as she flushed and walked away, nose held high, ignoring him.

He was important - that much was clear; otherwise, his behavior wouldn't have been so readily tolerated. He was also buzzed, alcohol clouding his judgment. Those two elements were all I was looking for, and so I stood, adjusting my shirt before walking up to his table and putting a hand on his shoulder.

"Hello, friend," I said, looking down at him.

"Tha hell you want? Get lost, drunkard." He turned around, anger clouding his flushed face. His voice was thick with an accent, though it seemed misplaced - a mixture of Argentine heritage and some other accent I couldn't quite place.

"The hell I want?" I said, slurring my voice as if I were drunk, speaking loudly enough that the room went quiet. "The hell I want? I 'eard you took a pass at my wife!"

He opened his mouth to speak, but I didn't wait - I swung, my fist connecting with the man's jaw and sending him toppling from his chair. The room erupted into chaos. The men who had been sitting next to him scrambled out of their seats, lunging at me and cursing in Spanish.

I dodged backward, swinging back as my fist met another man's jaw. The next few seconds felt like ages as I swung at any of the men who charged me, kneeing one in his stomach and slamming my fist into another's ribcage. I was tackled from behind and pulled to the ground. I saw the original man whom I'd struck scrambling to his feet, bleeding from his lip where I'd hit him. He glared at me, then pulled a knife from his coat, eyes wild with drunken rage. I grinned at him before kicking forward into his chest as he lunged, sending him flying backward yet again. I twisted, fighting the man who held my arms when I heard shouts.

"Policia! Policia!"

The men backed away from me, with the suited man turning with fury toward the two mustached police officers who had entered the room. He yelled something at the officers, blood dripping from his mouth, and one of the officers walked briskly toward me.

"¿Hablas español?" barked one of the officers, but I shook my head.

"Keep your damn mouth shut," I spat back, slurring my voice for continued effect. "He was after my wife...the Bureau will hear of this!"

The officer grabbed me roughly, pulling me to my feet. "You will come with us."

As he dragged me roughly from the bar, I glanced around the room. The entire room was quiet, staring at the commotion I had caused. It was the perfect scene for what I desired. The whole town would know of my presence by morning, and those who had power and influence would find out who I was. A foreigner who assaulted a rich man at one of the city's finest bars was sure to attract attention, and if my mention of the Bureau traveled to the correct ears, they would understand exactly who I was.

Though I also risked Krane learning of my presence, I highly doubted any of his Nazi goons would recognize the colloquial name of our organization unless they were the highest-ranking officials in the military.

The doors swung shut behind us, and we walked out through the street, the air thick with moisture. The drizzle had become a steady rain, and puddles lined the cracks of the streets, small rivers flowing near the gutters. The officer dragged me roughly along, my wrists twisted behind me, but I let him. I was in trouble, and I knew where I'd likely end up as they pulled me toward a police car waiting on the corner. The two men shoved me roughly into the back of the car, water dripping from my clothes onto the old, faded seat, and we were off. They drove silently through the dark streets of the town, their faces stoic, only illuminated by the occasional glimmer of streetlamps.

Eventually, we reached what I could only assume was the jail. A taller brick building stood out like a sore thumb from the other, more traditional buildings surrounding it. I was roughly offloaded and, only a few moments later, found myself released into a holding cell where other rough-looking men sat - many sleeping, others passed out from what I could only assume was alcohol. None spoke a word as I was thrown into the cell, and I shuffled to the back before sitting down against the wall. Now, I had to wait.

Hours passed, but I didn't sleep. If help were to arrive, it would likely do so before a day had passed, and I didn't feel like resting. Whenever I closed my eyes, I saw her face, and I remembered how she'd died.

So I sat there, my head bent, my eyes only half-open, waiting. The darkness outside the one barred window in the room began to grow lighter, and I heard the rain slowly cease. Eventually, I heard footsteps approaching the cell, and I raised my head. A suited man walked toward the cell, accompanied by two guards. As he approached, he motioned for the men to disperse, and they did.

I glanced up at him. He wore a loose-fitting white suit, a thinly striped shirt beneath it, and a pair of glasses that gave him a scholarly appearance. He was relatively short, and his short, dark hair curled slightly. He was clean-shaven, but I could see the faint remnants of stubble that indicated a fresh shave was almost due again. Though I couldn't be sure, his face seemed young, and I guessed he was in his mid-twenties.

He stood there in front of the holding cell for a minute, watching me, then finally spoke.

"Who are you?"

"What do you mean?" I asked.

"Come, let's cut to the chase," he motioned toward me as he spoke. "You caused that commotion on purpose, didn't you? The Bureau."

"Eh, maybe. What's it to you?"

He sighed and stuffed his hands in his pockets. "Well, we'll discuss your reason later. For now, I need to get you out of this cell."

"Why the rush?"

"You found one of the worst guys to pick a fight with. One of Don Furlotti's sons."

"Who? In case you couldn't tell, I'm a foreigner here."

"The Furlotti family is one of the most well-known here. Almost every damn vineyard you've seen belongs to them."

One of the guards reappeared, and the man with glasses spoke to him quickly in Spanish, motioning toward me. A moment later, he pulled a few bills from his pocket. The guard shrugged, pulled a key from his pocket, unlocked the cell, and roughly pulled me out while speaking.

"What's he saying?" I asked.

"Nothing that matters to you," the man replied. "He's more than happy to help after that amount of money. Come."

We walked through the station, and I rolled my shoulders, stretching. Though I wasn't sure who this man was yet, he had seemingly gathered enough information about me to help, and for now, that was enough.

"What's your name?" he asked as we walked.

"Max Calder," I replied. "And you?"

"Antonio di Benedetto," he said, turning to me with an intrigued expression. "Calder? Rings a bell. Do you know Alicia Rayes?"

CHAPTER 21
APPARITION TO ANDES

We sat at a table in a small, back-alley café less than thirty minutes later. Benedetto watched my face intently as he held a steaming cup of coffee in his hands. When he'd asked me about Alicia as we walked from the holding cell, I had brusquely said, "Later," and inquired if there was somewhere private we could go to talk. Though he'd opened his mouth, likely to protest, he must have caught sight of the pain that flashed in my eyes and decided better of it.

Now, however, as we sat at the table, he finally asked again. "You know Alicia?"

"Knew. She's dead."

The man's face fell, his eyes widening in surprise. "Dead? The hell? How?"

"We got cornered. A local gang."

"Ahh," he said, running his fingers through his hair. He looked distressed, as if he was unsure of what to say. "I - I'm not sure what to say. She was one of the best damn agents - hell, she fed me more than enough stories to write... I - I'm a journalist, see."

"She trusted you, then."

"I suppose so."

"Then I need your help," I said. "We were tracking a man. Heard from a reliable source he was here, near this area." I didn't want to speak of her - not when I spent every sleeping moment of the last few days dreaming of her, and every waking moment hoping to hear her voice.

Benedetto sighed deeply, composing himself. "Yeah - suppose I can help. She spoke highly of you, ya' know? Alright then, who are you tracking?"

"A man named Emil Krane."

"Emil Krane… doesn't ring a bell, I have to say."

"He's been spotted somewhere in the foothills of the Andes - past Mendoza. Possibly with German defectors, Nazi sympathizers, and the like. The Angel of Death was one of them."

Benedetto's face flashed with anger for a second. "Josef Mengele? Now that man, I know."

"What of him?"

"I wrote a piece on him a while back. Vile, disgusting bastard he is. He's near here, alright. I don't know the specifics, but I may be able to help you pinpoint him."

"You have local sources of information?"

"It's the job of any good journalist."

"Alright, then," I nodded. "Only issue is that my stunt probably put me in bad favor with the community here."

Benedetto laughed loudly. "Yeah. So you'll want to lay low, likely."

"Possibly, but I'm going to need even more information. I need to make a call to someone with insider information - someone who's probably tracking Krane as well."

Benedetto sighed and then stood. "Come. You can stay at my place for the time being."

I nodded in thanks and stood, following him. He tossed a few coins on the table, waved a friendly goodbye to the waitress, who blushed, then walked briskly through the door.

"Let's avoid the main roads, if we can?" I asked.

"Of course," he replied, changing course.

I followed him as he sidestepped a cart that rolled clacking through the streets, stepping behind a large pile of barrels and into a narrow side street. The man walked deftly, dodging through the town as if he knew it like the back of his hand, which I suspected he did. I trusted him - I could tell from the instant I met him that he was precisely the kind of man that Alicia would have recruited.

But there I was again, thinking of her. I could barely focus on where we walked, couldn't even remember the streets we'd turned down or the distance we traveled. It would have been a disaster, normally, if I had failed to catalog each step I took in a new town or city, and yet here I was.

I shook my head. I would have time to mourn when this was over - when Krane was dead, and I had dashed the Mirror against the damn rocks until it never worked again.

Benedetto finally slowed down, turning quickly onto a busier street when no one seemed to be watching, before sliding through a narrow doorway into a small house. It was low to the ground, with only two rooms, and seemed a testament to the work he did. A good journalist, I had long since learned, never grew rich from their work.

The walls were white, streaked with stains from rain and moisture, and the ceiling seemed to sag slightly. The air was thick with the scent of coffee, ink, and paper. The room we had entered was fairly empty, with only a small wooden table and chairs, a rug, a radio, and stacks upon stacks of newspapers. Along one wall was a bookshelf filled with books of all shapes and sizes. I recognized books in English, some in French, and several others in Spanish and even German. I couldn't help but be impressed by Benedetto's collection, and even more impressed by how he'd fit it all into such a modest room. As if in answer to my unspoken question, Benedetto himself walked toward the other side of the room, which had a small cast-iron stove, chipped pots, and cabinets.

"It's not much," he said. "The other room is my bedroom, but

I'll make up something for you in the living room… or kitchen, or office - it's multi-faceted."

"Your book collection - it's impressive," I said. "I read some of these at Cambridge."

"You went to Cambridge?"

"Unofficially," I said. "You got a phone?"

"Ah, right - yes, I do. It's in the bedroom. I keep it hidden away - just in case the home is ever raided, you know. I do make some enemies in my line of work."

"I'm not surprised," I said. "I'll keep my voice down."

Benedetto led me into his bedroom - a small, haphazard room that was little more than a segmented piece of the larger room we had just been in, divided only by a half-wall and a curtain. Here, I saw a small, battered cot, a wooden nightstand, and a large wardrobe where his clothes hung loosely. He smiled, then bent below his cot, digging and rummaging through his trunk.

"I don't keep it hooked up while I'm out," he said, pulling an old rotary phone from the bottom of what looked like a pile of knick-knacks and plugging it into a small port in the wall. "Only when I work."

"Thank you again."

"Don't mention it. I'll leave you to it - want some coffee or a cig?"

"I'll take some coffee, thanks."

"I run on it," he laughed, though his voice was strained. "I'll put on a kettle."

He stepped back into the other room, and I could hear him rummaging through his kitchen supplies.

I sat on the edge of the cot, holding the phone. I knew the number to call, but I wasn't sure it would go over well. After all, my last interaction with her had resulted in a slightly disastrous situation. I suspected she would have had it rough from the Bureau, especially after Alicia and I had caused so much trouble. Nevertheless, with a deep breath, I dialed the number. The phone rang, and I waited.

Nearly twenty seconds passed, and I felt myself losing hope, but suddenly the ringing ceased, replaced by a faint static, and I heard her voice.

"Ello?"

"Hello, Opal." I had remembered the number I'd used to contact her, and before her, Artemis. I had gambled, hoping it would work, and it had. There was a pause for a long while, but she finally responded.

"Calder?"

"I need your help."

"The hell?" She sounded infuriated. "Do you realize exactly how much hot water you got me in with the Bureau? You and Artemis - the damn both of you. If I so much as hear a single tick of information about your whereabouts, so help me - "

"Artemis is dead."

"Dead?" she asked, quieter. "How?"

"Shot. We were cornered. Listen, now's not the time - I realize this goes against all Bureau training, but I need help, and I have no one to ask but you."

"...what do you need help with?"

"You know Krane's alive, I'm sure. The Bureau is tracking him, aren't they? What's the latest information you have on his whereabouts?"

"We don't know much. It's difficult to track him in a country where we have so few contacts. Artemis was the main agent the Bureau had for any jobs in South America... but..."

Her words stung. I knew she didn't mean any harm, but whenever she mentioned Alicia, I felt a cold, burning pit in my stomach. "Well, any details that can help?"

"Only one - a name. We think he's taken up refuge in a temple somewhere... got the information from a Nazi defector we tortured before he died: El Templo Silente."

"Any clue as to where?"

"Beats me. That's where the Bureau is hung up at the moment - there are no locals who are willing to speak of it...

even if it's clear they know. Hell, even interrogation techniques don't seem to work."

"You're damn sure? Nothing else you have?"

"Sorry, Max..." Her voice trailed off for a second, as if she had to collect her thoughts. "Listen, I wish I could help more. And hey - I won't tell the Bureau about any of this. But that's all I have."

"It's enough. Thank you."

"O'course. Sorry about Artem - "

I set the phone down, and with a click, the call was over. I didn't want to hear it. It wasn't Opal's fault, I knew, but my mind was still fresh with the pain. Instead, I stood and walked into the main room, where Benedetto stood awkwardly at the stove, holding a cup of freshly brewed coffee.

"Just finished up making it," he said, motioning toward the table where we sat. "Any luck on your end?"

"A little. Have you ever heard of El Templo Silente?"

"Hmm. It rings a bell - though I'm not entirely sure where I've heard it before."

"Do you think any of your local informants would know?"

"Absolutely. Tell you what - I'm not even thirsty. I'll go have a run at it right now and come back as soon as I find out anything. You just stay put. There's food over by the stove as well."

I nodded. "I'll wait here, then."

Without another word, Benedetto stood, pushing his chair back loudly and ducking through the low doorway as he left. I sipped on the coffee he'd made - it was black, with a strong, brutal flavor, and it woke me up. Bored, I grabbed a random book from the shelf and flipped through the pages before putting it back only a few minutes later. There was nothing here, and without anything to entertain my mind, I found myself thinking of her.

I could still feel her skin against mine, see her hair, her beautiful, haunting hazel-green eyes. It felt as if she was still here with me, though I knew I'd never see her again. I cursed, slamming my fist against the table hard enough that it felt as if I'd broken something. Why did she have to die?

Maybe - but no, it would never work. I stood suddenly, pacing back and forth, kicking up dust as I did. Could the Mirror fix everything? What if I used it to save her? Of course, I knew it was a dangerous idea - I had no clue how to use the Mirror in the first place, and from what Hawthorne had described to me, the Mirror itself never really fixed a timeline… it just created a new one, or moved you there, or shifted that timeline here. Although it was tempting, I didn't want a doppelgänger - I wanted the real Artemis back, alive.

I sat again, leaning my chair up against the frame of the doorway and resting my eyes. I was tired. After this damn thing was over - after I'd dashed the last pieces of the Mirror against rock and ground Krane to dust - then I would rest. Maybe I'd get a job as a journalist somewhere, or maybe just hide away as a hermit with a typewriter. Maybe I would spend my hours watching people and drinking away my thoughts when I was alone. It sounded nice.

At that moment, I heard a faint whisper from the other room that caused me to sit bolt upright. The air felt almost electric, and the hairs on my arms stood on end. I heard it, faintly, but it sounded as if she were just around the corner. And there it was again, louder this time.

"Max," she whispered.

I froze. The empty coffee cup slipped from my hands, clattering to the ground. I hadn't even realized I was still holding it. For what felt like an hour, I didn't dare to breathe. I must have been imagining it.

"Max."

I stood, arms shaking slightly, and walked as if in a trance to the bedroom of Benedetto's home. There, on the small bed cot, the faint air draft wafted strands of her hair as if caressing her head. Not a wound on her body, Artemis sat with legs drawn up beneath her, her eyes soft as she glanced over at me. She looked at me - she didn't look like a ghost, a specter, or even a memory - she was vivid, full, and alive. She smiled slightly, and I felt a jolt of pain course through my body as if I'd been stung. She wasn't alive... was she?

"Alicia... I - "

"What's the matter, Max? I just woke up. You look as if you've seen a ghost."

"What - but you..."

"Oh, come on," she said, standing. "We'd best be leaving, if we're to catch Krane, that is."

I didn't know what to do. She looked perfect - perfectly alive, as if she'd just awoken and sat up in the very bed she had just stood from. She smiled, a look of questioning on her face, a warmth passing over her countenance.

"What's wrong?"

"You - you're dead."

She looked shocked. "What do you mean I'm dead? I'm right here, Max."

"No, no - " I blinked, then stared back at the spot where she had just been.

Artemis had vanished. The room was empty, the bed uncreased, the air stale again, and the electricity and current I had felt were gone. I heard noises outside again and realized I must have been standing there for an hour at least. The shadows had darkened instantly.

But she was gone. I yelled in frustration, kicking the leg of the cot on which she'd sat. What the hell had happened? Why was my mind playing tricks on me? Was it my mind - or was it the Mirror?

"Damn it!" I shouted, pacing back and forth. "What the hell do you want from me? Who's doing this?"

But there was no answer. The wind whispered silently by the small house, and people and carts in the street still passed by, making faint noise. I leaned down, hands shaking, and slowly lowered myself to the floor, back pressed against the wall. I felt drained - the memory, apparition, or whatever the hell I had seen - she had felt so real. Alicia had been there, in that very room, but now the house had fallen silent. Even the wind seemed to wait, with bated breath, to see what would happen next. I stared at the walls, my eyes unseeing, waiting as the seconds inched by. I wanted to get up, run through the small home, shouting her name, but I knew it wouldn't matter.

She was gone.

Eventually, from somewhere far above the city, I heard the solemn toll of a church bell, as if heralding the return of night. I must have been waiting here for hours, but I couldn't be sure. I didn't even bother to check my pocket watch to see what time it was. Still, Benedetto did not return. How much longer would I have to wait before he found his way home, if only to relieve me of the thoughts that threatened to burst from my mind?

I reached out slowly, picking up one of the newspapers atop a stack that leaned precariously near me. Alicia had always enjoyed reading the strip cartoons, so I thumbed through the paper till I landed on the page. I read the comics but couldn't bring myself to laugh. I flipped to another page, reading an article on a new vineyard that was being built, but my mind failed to register what I had read.

At last, however, I heard footsteps outside - purposeful, heavy boots that heralded the return of Benedetto and hopefully some good news. The man slipped inside, his hair awry and sweat covering his brow as if he'd been running. He glanced over at me on the floor, raised an eyebrow, and strode over to the table before pulling out a chair, turning it round, and sitting down to face me. He glanced at me, at the coffee cup lying haphazardly, and the newspaper that sat next to me.

"Anything wrong?" he asked.

"I'm good. What did you find out?"

"I found it," he whispered, lowering his voice. "El Templo Silente. It's rumored to be haunted - cursed, what have you. I had a tough time getting the locals to talk. Even my informants were hesitant, but I finally got it. It's deep in the Andes...there before the Incas. It's hidden past the foothills, in the very peaks of the Andes themselves. From what my informant said, it lies in a valley hidden from anyone but the most intrepid adventurers."

"Great," I said. "So it'll be hard to find?"

"Well," he said, tapping his breast pocket. "Sort of - but also, not really. It's about halfway between here and Uspallata on the road over the Andes to Santiago in Chile. You follow the Rio Mendoza. No one goes there now. A lot of locals here used to stop by on the trek between cities...but anyone who goes there now vanishes. At least, that's the way it's been for months now."

"Do you know how to find it?"

He nodded and handed me a slip of paper that he pulled from his pocket. "If you're going after Krane, then this is where you'll probably find him. But damn, Calder - you could walk away, you know? I don't think anyone would blame you at this point. Not even her."

"I have to go. I can't live a normal life - not until I finish this." Of course, I wasn't sure I had any plans to live a normal life. The more I thought of it, the more I convinced myself that maybe it would be good for my life to end here - after I'd destroyed the Mirror for good. There would be no way for anyone to pull me back in. "I wish I could pay you for all this."

"Any friend of Artemis is a friend of mine," he said, smiling slightly.

"I appreciate it and all your help," I said. "But once I leave, stay out of all this - there are dangerous people who will kill to get to me."

He reached out, clasping my arm with a tight grip. "You're a good man," he said. "I can see why Artemis spoke so highly of you."

———

Scarcely thirty minutes later, I was off. I made my way down to the bustling market, strolling around and looking for supplies. It was nearly dusk now, and there were few merchants still around, but it was still relatively busy as Mendoza was a bustling city even at nighttime. Bumping roughly into a rich-looking fellow, I apologized profusely in English.

"Oh, oh, I am so sorry!"

"¡Mira por dónde vas, turista!" he grunted angrily before walking off.

I waited until he turned the corner, then opened my hand to examine the results of my stunt. I held his purse - a beautiful velvet piece he'd carried stupidly in one of his coat pockets. Carefully, I opened and rummaged through the contents. There were photos, a notepad, and enough money to buy what I needed and then some.

Though it was only a ten-hour walk, as Benedetto had informed me, the journey would be into the mountains, and I needed to be prepared for rough terrain. Approaching one of the vendors, I quickly bargained my way into renting a mule and some supplies for my trip. With that, I was ready to set off, walking away from the town and passing the weary travelers who were heading into Mendoza for the night. The road was winding, and by the time I'd reached the start of the foothills, the moon was high in the sky. The sun was nowhere to be seen now, and I could only make out the distant, snow-covered peaks of the Andes ahead of my path.

I trudged along, leading my mule. It followed silently, grunting now and again as it walked alongside me. Each kilometer I walked seemed to haunt me even more, and I felt memories of Alicia pressing heavily against me as if attempting to suffocate me. I glanced over my shoulder and saw the distant silhouette of Mendoza, almost out of sight now, only visible due to the faint yellow glow from streetlamps. Above me, the stars shone bright, unending, formidable, and cold.

I shut my eyes for a moment, feeling the wind hit my face as I stood there. I heard a distant noise - some animal I couldn't place - and almost felt at peace. I knew what I had to do now. With Alicia dead, I had nothing more to lose. I opened my eyes once more and began to walk, trudging forward through the night and into the foothills of the Andes. All that remained for me was El Templo Silente. That, and Krane.

Then, I could rest.

CHAPTER 22
QUANTUM QUANDARY

had walked through the night, squinting as the first glimmering rays of the sun peeked over the mountain peaks. I was tired, but I trudged onward. If I had followed the rudimentary map that Benedetto had given me correctly, I was now far off the beaten track and should have almost made it to the location of the temple. About thirty minutes later, my suspicions were all but confirmed. I heard voices - so faint that I almost ignored them as phantoms inside my own mind, but unmistakably human. I paused, pressing myself against the rock face next to a small, old, barely visible trail. The mountains here were jagged and sharp, and the wind blistered against my face as I stood.

The only path to the temple was, according to my map, through a narrow mountain pass. It was a winding route, past glacial streams and high-altitude forests. The cold, biting air felt thinner. Until now, the only sounds on my journey had been the wind and the distant calls of condors which soared above my head, but now… those voices signaled that I was almost there.

After another ten minutes, as the path descended, I parted ways with the mule. I figured it would find its way home - or at the very least, find a pasture to graze in until some wandering shepherd found it and added it to their menagerie. I had no need for resources any longer, no need for food or even water - the only items I took were the items I needed - my keepsakes, such as my pocket watch, my gloves, a small flashlight, and my gun. I'd kept my gloves, though I hadn't worn them in Mendoza because they seemed too foreign. Now, however, I had no reason to avoid wearing them and pulled them onto my heavily weathered hands before continuing. I couldn't help but feel as if I was deteriorating as I did so - my hands were beaten, weathered, rough, and old. But it mattered little. Whatever happened here would put an end to it all.

I finally began my descent through areas where the path nearly ceased to exist. It was slow and treacherous, as the rocks, cliffs, and ravines posed an ever-present threat. Nevertheless, I continued, descending lower and lower into the valley while keeping a lookout for any guards. I could see the temple now, though it was still distant. The valley around it was covered with green grasses, quinoa, and corn, all of which ran rampant. It was clear that one day, far in the past, this temple had held signs of life - but it was overgrown now. It was here that I first ran into trouble. As I finally reached the valley floor, moving slowly behind rocks and making sure each step was taken quietly, I saw them - a pair of tall, rough men wearing what looked like faded uniforms. Though their clothes were far too faded and weather-worn to tell, I was sure of it. These men were likely Germans, sent to guard Krane and whatever devilry he was up to inside the temple.

I slowly and stealthily inched around the rock formation I was hiding behind. The two men were looking generally in my direction, but the tall and overgrown grass and corn blocked their view of me almost entirely. I crouched, moving silently through the tangled undergrowth and vines, my eyes focused on the two soldiers. There were large, jagged boulders here, and I used them to my advantage. I would have preferred, of course, to remain silent until I reached Krane and the Mirror itself, ensuring he couldn't find a way to escape me this time, but maybe I did not have a choice.

I steadied my breathing, noticing for the first time that it had become almost raspy. The height was triggering altitude sickness, and the air was thin enough that it felt as if I was breathing through a narrow tube, or trying to take a breath with a cigarette still in my mouth. Fortunately, the two guards didn't notice me - they stood at ease, talking in a low, foreign language. It was German. I recognized the shape of their weapons now as well - old Mauser rifles, probably looted as they had fled Germany after the war. Though I was unclear of their rank, I wagered it couldn't have been too low - they were likely personal guards of Josef Mengele if the story was right, men he had recruited when the fall of the Reich had already begun. And, like rats fleeing from a sinking ship, they had followed Mengele and the other prominent Nazi figures who had managed to escape prosecution. I shivered - there was a chill in the air - and I pressed my gloved hand to my forehead in an attempt to focus. It wasn't fear that gripped me now. I had no reason to be afraid. Even death was something I had come to terms with. Instead, I felt a weird, guttural fear, recognizing in the air that menacing electricity, that buzz that I only felt when it was being pulsed. It was very clear that the Mirror was here, and it was active.

Something shimmered suddenly to my side, flickering and glowing in a pulsating, nauseating way. I jumped but kept low, watching it move. It looked like some ethereal cloud at first, flickering here and there, like a group of fireflies, but my eyes were unable to really make it out. As I watched, it slowly materialized - broad-shouldered and limping slightly. Though this figure was more battle-torn and more bloodied, I recognized him at once. It was me. It was another Calder, limping along, crouched, hiding in the overgrowth as I did. But the next second, I blinked, and he was gone. He'd disappeared into thin air as if he never existed. But I saw in the soft ground a set of boot prints that matched mine.

I shuddered. The border between timelines was thin here, like a razor-sharp edge of paper only split by a few hairs.

I crouched lower now, almost crawling, as I pressed forward. The two men had turned their backs to me now, glancing up and down the valley as if they were waiting for some sort of signal. As I pressed forward, I heard strange noises - voices and other footsteps aside from my own - but each time I glanced around, I saw nothing. I realized it must have been an echo. Was the Mirror causing this?

I focused, ignoring what I was hearing, and crept up slowly behind the first guard. The harsh wind howling overhead made it so the man had no idea I was there. The overgrown grass grew shorter here, and the rocks became scarce, so I moved quickly. I swept up behind him in one motion, cleanly hitting his temple with the butt of my gun. He fell, his body collapsing almost instantly - he'd lost consciousness the very second the gun hit him. The other man, startled, whirled around, but it was too late. I grabbed him, my hand over his mouth, and pulled a knife from his belt, repeatedly thrusting it into his side.

Blood gushed from his body, splattering silently onto the grass. He collapsed soon afterward, struggling, but I knelt and held my hand clamped firmly over his mouth until he stopped moving.

I stood, walking briskly now - I hadn't seen more guards, and it seemed likely the next men would be positioned inside the temple itself, if at all. I would kill them one at a time until I found Krane. And then I would kill him.

I moved like a shadow, darting forward toward the temple. A stone path had become clear now. On each side were erected large stone pillars, too weathered to make out the hieroglyphs and carvings engraved on their sides. The temple itself was almost formidable. It was built from large, evenly cut stones, each looking to weigh at least a ton, though they fit together seamlessly. I could scarcely see the cracks between them, which seemed strange to me. Though the temple itself seemed aged and weathered, the architecture seemed almost otherworldly.

I glanced up at it in awe as I walked. The temple was built into the face of one of the mountain cliff sides, the entrance framed entirely by large, monolithic stones hewn with delicate carvings, of what I couldn't tell.

Above the pitch-black entrance was a stone archway, intimidating and covered in the same carvings as the stones from which the temple was built. I slowed my pace, walking closer to the pillars, making sure that I kept an eye on the darkness in front of me. Finally, I reached the gateway - at least, that was what it felt like. I could feel the electricity buzzing inside, the air thinning even more than it was already outside. I stepped into the temple. Though the temple was quiet, it wasn't empty - the echoes that bounced from each step I took resounded along the walls, but other sounds returned. Shadows glimmered against the walls as I retrieved the flashlight I'd packed and flicked it on.

The passageway inside was shockingly narrow, a far cry from the expansive exterior. I slid silently along the walls, careful not to make a noise. Though I was unsure of where the guards were, I thought I would be careful in case a trap awaited me. As I turned a narrow corner, I saw a sickening sight. There, lying on the floor, were several aged bodies, the very portrait of decay.

They lay there, crumpled to the floor, their wretched faces almost unrecognizable as human, yet their clothes were clean and free of dust. I bent down to inspect one of the outfits. Sure enough, the markings were unmistakable - these were the clothes of a German guard. I stood once more, flicking my flashlight off as I heard a commotion further down the corridor. I flattened myself against the wall, holding my breath and remaining perfectly still.

"Zurückmelden! Damn bastards. When I find you - "

A man strode furiously into sight, holding a flashlight. His eyes glowed with a fiery intensity, and his face was filled with anger and impatience. As he caught sight of the bodies on the floor, however, flicking his flashlight over the corpses, his face paled slightly. He sprang backward, hands shaking as he stared at their faces with a horrified look.

"Was zum Teufel...?" he muttered, glancing around. He flicked the flashlight around the room, but before it reached me, I was on top of him. I'd sprung from the wall where I was hiding, grabbing his gun hand and flinging it aside, sending his flashlight clattering downward onto the musty, damp stone floor. He tried to shout, but I drove a knee into his stomach, knocking the air out of his lungs before he could even finish. He crumpled, gasping for breath as his eyes bulged, but I didn't give him the time to recover. I grabbed his head, smashing it against the wall. Twice. Three times. His body went limp, but I smashed his head against the cold stones once more just to verify his death. I knew better than to play games of survival when the Mirror was already affecting the men here, already changing them… aging them. I glanced at my own hands - for whatever reason, the Mirror had never had such an apparent effect on me.

Though Alicia had noted my aged look when she'd seen me all those months ago in Hell's Kitchen, I hadn't aged nearly as rapidly as the men who lay decaying in a pile behind me. I worked swiftly, stripping the gun and knife from the dead man's belt. The flashlight, still rolling on the ground from the swift action, cast eerie shadows on the walls, as if begging for something to happen.

"Müller? Alles gut?"

I froze, listening. This second voice was sharper, more defined, and slightly deeper than the first. I could tell, instantly, that this was the voice of a man used to his orders being followed. Footsteps echoed through the halls, and I heard whatever the man had called out begin to move closer. I pressed the dead man against the wall, making sure he was hidden behind an old, weary pillar that jutted out from the wall, supporting the heavy weight of the mountain above it.

The bootsteps drew closer, and a tall figure came into view - a man wearing a uniform better kept than the others, his brass shining in the light of the flashlight which lay on the floor. He was a high-ranking official. I could discern that much from his badges. The ones on his collar looked like SS. I pressed myself tight behind a pillar, watching as he walked. He walked slowly and cautiously, his pistol already drawn as he glanced around, finally stooping down slowly to inspect the flashlight. I heard him curse in a low, guttural voice before he straightened again. As he did, he glanced around, walking closer and closer to the pillar I stood behind. Though I knew he was unaware of my presence, I felt every muscle tense, every inch of my body ready for action.

When he was a yard or so away from the pillar, I moved - silently and without hesitation - raising his comrade's pistol up ever so slightly and cocking it. Though I had previously thought it likely that Krane had many more guards, the two dead bodies rotting and decaying in the corridor told me otherwise. There would have likely been frequent guard changes had there been more men positioned here, and the high-ranking men who had come to check on these two guards indicated they were all but out of foot soldiers to do their dirty work.

So, as he neared, I stepped from the shadows, gun raised and fired a single shot. The man barely had time to register my shadow before he was dead, a bullet hole between his eyes. The shot echoed throughout the corridors, and I saw a figure move in the distance. I leveled my gun at the moving shadow, only to drop it again as I saw another version of myself - younger this time - walking along, seemingly oblivious to my existence. This version of me was indistinguishable from reality; he'd clearly been here longer than the previous specter I'd seen... a doppel-gänger almost tethered perfectly to our timeline. I watched as he walked slowly along the corridor, his gun raised. He was careful, more cautious than I, and I could tell that he'd been in the field for less time. But I ignored him - whether he was real to others or only to my eyes, I didn't know.

Instead, I pressed on, even deeper into the temple. If Krane had heard the gunshot, he would likely know that an intruder had arrived. However, since I'd fired with the guard's own pistol, any trained ear who was potentially guarding the most interior chambers would assume that it was a shot fired by one of their own men. At least, that was my hope.

I didn't have time to think - didn't have time to notice the strange, almost mirage-like qualities the walls of the temple had taken on as I walked - no, nearly ran - through the corridors, the stones echoing beneath my boots.

The Mirror was close and so was Krane. I recognized the static in the air. It felt the same as it had felt every time, right before a controlled slide operated by the Bureau. Its presence was intimidating, but I pressed onward, shining my flashlight ahead of me as far as I could see. The light glimmered and flickered, and suddenly, with a slight spark, my flashlight went out. I was left in almost pitch darkness, and yet there, in front of me, was a distant light. It glowed an eerie blue, a color that shimmered and shifted, casting faint shadows on the wall. I ran fully now, holding my gun tightly as I did. If Krane was fully pulsing the Mirror, there was no telling what could happen. If I didn't get there in time, all hell would break loose if it hadn't already.

I ignored the flickering of the shadows, which grew brighter, ignored the strange, moving figures in my peripheral vision, and ignored the dead, old bodies of Nazi guards that lay strewn throughout the corridor. Finally, I reached it, sprinting around one final bend and coming into full view of the amphitheater of the temple. In the center stood a sort of jagged stone altar, raised above the floor, surrounded by stone carvings and old, brittle bones from what must have been ancient offerings.

But that wasn't what captured my attention. Instead, I saw it - at least, what could have only been it. It stood there, towering and elegant, almost ceremonial in nature. The frame was brass but had been carefully etched with symbols and various scribbles that I didn't recognize. The surface was different, too, shimmering as if it were made of a liquid metal, and yet never breaking tension. In front of the Mirror stood Krane himself - thinner than when I'd last seen him, but unmistakably the man I was searching for. Beside him stood a tall, hardened-looking man wearing the most ceremonial outfit I'd seen yet.

At the sound of my boots, the two men turned, staring in shock at my face.

"Calder..." muttered Krane, his face a mix of confusion, fright, and excitement. The man beside him reached for a pistol strapped to his belt, but he was too slow. I steadied my pistol toward his face and pulled the trigger. He crumpled to the floor, crimson blood pooling around his body as I strode forward.

"You - you damn bastard, do you know how much you cost me?" I asked.

"Ah - ah, Calder. I didn't realize you'd be here. At least, not this you. We can all see it now, you know." His voice trembled, but not from fear. It sounded instead dangerously close to excitement. He backed away from me, quivering as I continued walking forward, his nervous eyes darting toward the mirror. The eerie light flickered on his face, illuminating his hollow cheekbones and his wild eyes. His hair - what was left of it - was tousled and messy, as if he hadn't touched it in weeks.

I stepped past the dead body, my boots splashing faintly in the crimson puddle as I walked. I stopped directly in front of the Mirror, directly in front of the altar. My arm steady, I leveled my gun at Krane's heart. He flinched but remained standing there, facing me.

"You should have known I'd kill you here," I said, my voice cold in a way that I almost didn't recognize. "You. You're the reason I've had to deal with all this hell."

"Me?" Krane laughed, his voice high-pitched, his eyes bulging. "Me? The Bureau. The Bureau is blinded by its own rules. They are the ones who caused all this."

"How? You - you're the one who blew up the damn experiment in the first place. You broke everything to steal this damn piece of junk."

"No, no," Krane spat, pulling himself upright as he stared at me. "You're right! It wasn't the Bureau. It was the damn Architect. He's the reason all of this happened. But you - you're oblivious to all of this, aren't you? Ever wonder why the Mirror keeps you so well-groomed? Why do you walk free through the echoes while others don't?"

I felt a white-hot rage fill my body. Did he know of Alicia's death? Was he taunting me? I stepped closer, pressing my gun to the very center of his forehead, the cold steel against his skin. "Enough. I don't give a damn about your philosophy," I said. "Any last words?"

Krane grinned, his teeth flashing in the light. "You just don't get it, do you? You don't understand, truly, what the Mirror is. I will be it. It will be me. Just wait - a little while longer."

"Too late - " I began, but a sudden voice behind me interrupted.

"Too late? Damn, Max. Don't you wonder why you haven't shot yet?"

I spun around, and from the shadows emerged a man. He stood there, a slight grin on his face, his icy gray eyes glowing faintly. His hair was almost all gray, but the deep scar along his jaw was unmistakable.

"Another damn one of you?" I asked.

"Oh, just hear me out. Why haven't you shot that pathetic man yet, anyway?" He motioned to Krane, who had turned his attention from us back to the Mirror, his hands tracing along its brass frame, whispering words to it.

"I… you - you have always been alive, haven't you? You - you don't deserve to live. I'll replace you. I'll replace it…" Krane muttered, his eyes darting over the complex surface.

"I wanted to know - know if he felt any damn sorrow for what he did," I said.

"No, you didn't," the other Calder responded, walking

slowly closer. "You wanted to know, somewhere deep inside, if the Mirror could save her."

"I..." I couldn't finish speaking. I knew he was right - he was a version of me, after all.

"Look, it's happening now. See? The Mirror. Watch. It's showing us something."

I glanced around and watched the surface of the mirror flicker, glow, and crack - and then it blinked. I could feel myself watching, as if from above, through some sort of conscious door, the scene that unfolded inside. It wasn't like staring at a painting or even a movie - watching the world unfold through the cracks in the Mirror's surface felt as if I was there - as if I could instantly see every edge of the world surrounding me. It was almost like an astral projection. It felt as though my consciousness had left my physical body.

There sat another version of me, reclining in his armchair, a desk and typewriter in front of him. In one corner of the desk sat a glass of whiskey, and he smoked a cigar as he read the papers laid out in front of him. Though he had the same scar, and I could see the tiredness in his eyes, I also saw something else - peace. And though he wasn't me, I could feel his mind as if I were connected to it somehow, experiencing his satisfaction as he read through the papers. Was this quantum entanglement?

"After MI6, you went dark. Left the life of espionage," Krane suddenly said, his eyes fixated on my face. He watched me carefully. "No Bureau. No war. No Artemis. Just a quiet life in Lisbon with a typewriter and enough whiskey to forget the rest."

I could feel the older Calder standing beside me now, but I didn't care. The Mirror - it was all I could watch. It flicked again, blinking slowly, and the scene changed. There sat another Max, leaning up against a balcony under neon lights, smoke curling from his lips. Rain fell gently down, hot and misty, into the busy city below. I didn't recognize the place, but I knew it instantly as if I'd been there before, and unfamiliar memories flooded my mind. It was Tokyo. This Max was calm but haunted.

He'd become a detective, never worked with MI6 - didn't even have his scar. He worked cheap cases, frequented night-clubs, and spoke far too often when he drank. There was no gun in his hand, but he'd been in more bar brawls than you could count.

The Mirror flickered again, and there was another Max - this one was a war criminal, hunted and running desperately from the men he'd once worked for. And another - a priest, trans-formed from a life of pain to one of healing. A hero. A drunk in a Paris gutter.

All versions of me. All possibilities.

"It's not just showing you the options," Krane said, stepping beside the glowing machine. "It's inviting you. Take the life you want. Any life. Be the man you never let yourself be."

I stood there, unmoving. I could feel the Calder behind me inching slowly closer, and I could see Krane watching me intently. But was it true? Was Krane telling the truth? Could I simply take on a life as one of these doppelgängers, replace them in their own timeline, and fade away from this one? I stared, unsure.

And then, I heard a voice. It didn't seem to come from anywhere at all, but it erupted from everywhere at once. Inside my head, outside of it, and inside the head of every version of Max I could still feel the memories of.

"They are lying," the voice said, and I recognized it instantly. The cadence was unmistakable, the voice unique in a manner I knew couldn't be replicated. "Don't choose."

It was the same voice, the same figure I had heard during my dream all that time ago on the train from Zurich to Milan, though he no longer sounded as much like Hawthorne as he once had.

I glanced around, but didn't see anyone. "Who - who are you?"

Krane scoffed, a slight smile flickering on his face. "You hear it too, don't you? But it doesn't matter. It'll be dead soon."

"What is it?"

"It has many names. El Cuadro is one. The Mirror is another."

I stood there, unsure. For the first time in my life, I didn't know what to do. Could I find a life where I was happy and where Alicia was there with me? In my trance, I barely even heard the other Calder as he spoke, his voice filled with impatience.

"You're taking too long, Max. Time's up."

But the next second, a voice shattered me from my daze, ringing across the amphitheater. Her voice was unmistakable - hoarse but loud and clear.

"Max! Look out!"

I spun around, the feeling of uncertainty dissipating as if I had been doused with ice-cold water. There she was, standing at the far side of the chamber, clutching her side, blood seeping between her fingers. Artemis. Her hair was matted, her body covered in scratches, but even though she seemed almost ethereal, I could see her - and she seemed real. Her mouth formed words, and I heard them without even registering. "He's behind you! He's - "

I spun around as the older Calder, his face filled with fiery rage, lunged at me. I barely avoided his wild, downward swing - a glinting, thin, and curved blade in his hand. His face was filled with loathing, his anger seeping through every feature. He fought like I did, but more brutally - more unrestrained, as if he had nothing to hold him back. I staggered, my boots skidding on the stone covered in slick blood, tripping over the body of the Nazi general I'd killed.

The other Calder lunged at me, his face twisted into a snarl. "You! You could have just disappeared, and then Krane would have given me what I wanted. You think only you deserve this?" He drove the knife toward my chest, and I tried to swerve out of the way, feeling it slice through my shirt as I grabbed his wrist and twisted. The knife clattered to the ground behind us. He cursed, slamming into me and kneeing my gut. I gasped, desperately yanking his leg to pull him off me as I tried to regain my breath. He scrambled to his feet, dashing backward to grab the knife while I regained my footing.

"Why help Krane?" I asked as I stood, backing away and glancing around. I could see Krane to my side, stooping over the console that controlled the Mirror, his fingers flying over the keys. I knew that whatever he was doing was bad. He'd said he wanted to replace "it," whatever that was. On my other side, I could see Artemis, still clutching her abdomen but circling behind the older Calder.

"Why help Krane?" the older Calder spat as he responded mockingly, venom in his voice. "You don't get it, do you, Max? He promised me everything - everything I've ever wanted. MY Alicia is dead. Yours? She'll be dead after this, but Krane…if he gets what he wants, he can save mine."

He rushed at me again, knife raised. I ducked, dodging his swing and grappling with him. I knew that I wouldn't be able to avoid his blade much longer, not with his skills. My only hope was to turn our fight into a brawl and keep him moving so he didn't have time to think ahead. I shoved into him, my fist connecting with his jaw as he swung again, the knife scraping against my side and drawing blood.

A gunshot echoed through the chamber.

For a second, I didn't know who fired, but I saw the older Calder standing there, crimson blood seeping into his flannel shirt. He stared at me, then glanced at Artemis.

"Y-You…" he stuttered, sinking to his knees.

As he fell, I saw Artemis stumble, her hand pressed tightly against her side, the smoking pistol falling from her fingers. Our eyes met, and I saw her stumble toward me once more before steadying herself. I rushed to her, grabbing her in my arms to prevent her from falling.

"Alicia…you were dead. What? How are you here?"

"Max - " She coughed, trying to pull herself from my arms. "Don't let him - look, Krane..."

I whirled around. I'd forgotten about Krane. I had not been watching him amidst the chaos. He stood there now, his face glowing in an unholy blue light. He was pressed against the Mirror, his face aglow, his body feverish and slick with sweat. He had discarded the controls now, tossing them to the floor in a jumble of wires, his hands resting on the brass frame of the Mirror. The cracked surface of the Mirror seemed to expand, splintering as we watched. Krane screamed - from pain or triumph, I couldn't tell - the sound echoed throughout the chamber, haunting and ethereal.

Reality split.

Everything in the chamber bent backward, merging and separating at once, as a wave of energy pulsed from the very core of the Mirror. The wave burst outward, electric, leveling the chamber as it flashed through the air. I ducked, shielding Artemis in my arms, protecting her as best I could.

Figures erupted from the shadows. Some versions of me, some Nazi soldiers, and even the figures of dead Bureau agents. Some screamed in agony, bending over themselves, while others yelled in rage and lunged toward us.

Krane's silhouette was barely visible in front of the Mirror.

"He's trying - trying to use it - force it to bend to his will," I said, covering my face with my hand as I spoke with difficulty, trying to shield myself from the energy.

"The timelines..." she said, her voice softer now, staring almost blankly at me. "The timelines switched when I almost died. I don't know where I've been, Max."

"It's okay. You're here now."

"Stop him. I'll be here when you're done. If he gets full control of it, he won't just rewrite this, Max. He rewrites everything."

Her fingers slid gently over my cheek as she felt my face. I held her for a second longer, then gently let her go and turned to the Mirror. I staggered forward, my knees buckling under the weight of the pulse. The air crackled, rich with electricity, but I kept walking. I felt my skin burning now, aging, and looked down at my hands to see the wrinkles begin to deepen.

I looked up and realized I was hunched now, being dragged backward and downward in time. The Mirror - whatever it was - no longer controlled itself. Krane was in charge. But I fought - fought with every fiber of my being, shoving past the energy and breaking free. I inched forward again and again until I reached him. With one final burst of energy, I lunged toward Krane, grabbing onto his shoulder and pulling him backward with me.

"No! No! You don't understand what you're doing, you - " Krane screamed as we fell backward, and I wrenched him away from the Mirror.

A pulse blasted out - blistering white, searing my eyes, blinding me. A tremendous sound, like a dam breaking, emanated from the Mirror. It was as if a thousand lifetimes, a thousand realities, were there at once. I saw more than I could remember, each flashing before my eyes, shifting, and volatile. Krane collapsed to the floor next to me, writhing and screaming, covering his eyes. And then, the world collapsed. It was as if darkness suddenly crept in from the edges of our vision, surging in to swallow the entire world. All the doppelgängers and copies - versions of me, Nazi soldiers, beggars, Bureau agents - disappeared in an instant.

And then, in the darkness, I heard his voice right before I lost consciousness. I didn't hear the Mirror mimicking him, nor did I hear a younger version of him. I heard the man I had known, the man I had thought was dead.

"Well done, Max," Hawthorne said.

CHAPTER 23
ARCHITECT AND ARCHIVES

My eyes snapped open, and I felt my consciousness returning. I glanced around - it was dark, much darker than the blinding light I'd seen only moments ago. It was a reddish-black sort of dark, only broken by the flickering of a yellowish, glaring electric light overhead. I felt cold - a chill that pierced my bones, different from the mountain air I had felt and unlike the chill you feel after being shot and losing blood. I felt the sort of cold that made me think of an earthly burial ground, a subterranean consciousness waiting to strike.

For a brief moment, I debated whether I was dead. But then I remembered that the blinding light had struck my eyes just before I heard his voice. I sat upright, head spinning, coughing as dust floated around my peripheral vision. Some particles lodged in my throat, and I bent over, coughing more.

But I was not alone - I knew he was here somewhere. I wasn't sure how, but I could feel it. I stood, glancing around. A corridor melted into a darkened expanse in front of me, narrow and made of reddish brick, with condensation dripping from the ceiling. I walked slowly, feeling the ache in my side where I'd been cut by my doppelgänger. The walls, the faint ticking of the clocks, the constant drip of water from the ceiling - I knew where I was.

Though I'd never been this deep in the building before, something about the air of it was unmistakable: 27 Beaufort Court in London. The headquarters of OTASI. The place from which all Bureau agents had operated. But this part was deeper - a legend among agents, a name only whispered behind closed doors.

I was in the Archives.

I'd dared to ask Hawthorne about the place once, and he'd told me, though his eyes had grown cold as he spoke - a sign I interpreted as a mixture of lies and truth. The Archives were located two levels underground, past a steel-locked door, down a narrow stairwell where the air was thick and pipes hummed at irregular frequencies.

Nobody in the agency knew what was stored down here. Somewhere above my head, I could hear noise - as if I wasn't alone here, whatever time or parallel reality I'd been cast into. I staggered along the corridor until I came to a door. It was that door - the steel locked one Hawthorne had told me about, though it was unlocked and slightly ajar. The label on it read "AUTHORIZED ACCESS ONLY - D. ROWAN CLEARANCE REQUIRED."

I pushed it open and stepped into an open chamber beyond. The bulbs above my head flickered, pulsating in rhythm with the clocks, dimly threatening to extinguish.

The room I had just entered was a circular place, lined with twelve clocks. This antechamber was dark, but in the dim light, I could see that the hands of each clock pointed to a separate time, and from the almost constant ticking, I guessed that none were synced. In the very center sat one more clock - its hands frozen at 03:17:48. I shuddered.

Though I was no coward, this place filled me with an uncanny, almost bizarre desire to run. Suddenly, I heard footsteps. I tensed, glancing around, watching the darkness beyond the clocks.

Then a figure stepped forward into the light, his hair a classic gray color, his face exactly as I'd remembered it that day in Prague. There stood Hawthorne, his trench coat hanging as well-fitted as it had ever been, his face gruff but no older than it had been months ago. He smiled at me, his eyes wrinkling at the corners slightly, but the light behind his eyes was empty.

"As I was saying... well done, Max."

"Is this real?" I gestured around the room. "I feel alive... but you died. I saw you die."

"Death is a difficult thing to come by for a man such as myself," he said, almost sadly. "I don't know if it would have let me die, even if I'd wanted it."

"Are we alive, then?"

"As much as anything here would count as alive. This is the core. The Archives, as I'm sure you've already guessed."

"I have."

"And she should be arriving soon."

There, through the door, her eyes bedazzled and confused, walked Artemis. She was wrapped in her bloodied coat, but she didn't hold her side, and her face bore no marks of pain or a tortured countenance.

I rushed to her, grabbing her in my arms. "Alicia. Are you okay?"

"I think so. Where...when are we?" she asked, her voice quiet.

"I've brought you both here for a reason," Hawthorne said behind us. "You both need the truth if you want to survive."

"The truth?" I turned toward him again, still holding Artemis. I didn't want to let her go again.

"Follow me."

Hawthorne turned and led us out of the room, past the clocks, into a much larger chamber, where a tilted sign labeled "Room 9" hung over the doorway. As we entered, I heard Artemis gasp. The room resembled a gigantic warehouse, filled with thousands of gray boxes, shelves, and drawers. Each drawer was padlocked, and Hawthorne continued to walk, pausing for only a second to speak to us.

"I tried to keep the Bureau honest, Max. I tried, really. But eventually, you learn only too harshly that it's impossible to do."

He turned once more, his coat trailing behind him, his silhouette blending into the shadows of the room. We passed row after row of the archives. Artemis was next to me, and though she walked confidently, I was scared that at any second she would collapse. I wanted to ask what had happened to her wounds, but I didn't - whatever had cured her, I didn't want to undo it.

The dust was even thicker here, a heavy layer on shelves, the ground, and particles floating around the light bulbs like moths to a flame.

"Where are you taking us?" I asked.

"You want the truth, don't you?" Hawthorne asked. "I'll give you the truth. This is where it all began. This is where you'll learn the truth about your past."

"My past?"

"When the Bureau was founded, I was recruited on a simple premise. I joined, believing at that time that safety lay in knowing everything - recording everything, filing everything. And in the end, it served a purpose, didn't it? You're part of something bigger than you think, Max."

I glanced at Artemis, her eyes intently focused on Hawthorne. I could tell she didn't trust him, and that at this very instant, she was tense, ready for action if the need arose.

"What happened, Hawthorne? After the clock fell, that is - Prague. Where did you go?"

He remained silent, and we pressed forward through the narrow, dusty aisles. I didn't speak again. I waited until he was ready. I didn't know what the truth was or what had happened in Prague, but I knew he would eventually tell me. Though Alicia didn't, I trusted Hawthorne enough for that. He had always been a man of his word, valuing the rules above all else. He finally came to a stop, a buffet of dust echoing from beneath his boots. He didn't turn, but stared at a particularly dusty set of shelves, speaking more to the wall than to us.

"Prague. Yes, Prague. That feels as if it happened a thousand years ago." His voice was heavy, darker than I'd ever heard it.

"After the clock fell, you disappeared. We thought you died."

He glanced at me finally, his face stretched and tense. "You saw me die, yes. At least one sort of me. This version of me - " he said, holding out his hands, looking toward the ceiling. "This version of me never vanished. It's difficult to describe what really happened, but I was captured into the electronics within the Mirror itself. Not the whole Mirror - more like a piece of it, trapped within an archaic part of the system no longer used. I'm still not entirely sure, but it wasn't just a slide. It was full exposure, a raw, unfiltered connection to the Mirror.

"My mind split into a million pieces, each one splitting into a million more, each piece spreading throughout reality itself. Have you ever heard of panpsychism, Max?"

"No, I haven't," I replied, but from the way I felt Alicia tense up next to me, I knew she had. "What is it?"

He smiled sadly. "The Mirror - it has some sort of consciousness. It's what Krane was mumbling about before I brought you two here. See, the process of the universe is built upon the quantum fields. The Mirror, when it creates infinite parallels in a pulse - or rather, gives access to those parallels - doesn't only use the rules, system, or console controlled by Krane. It links to the two of you, interconnected, hearing your inner voices, but making its own conscious decision over what happens.

"And somehow, I - my mind was tangled into this. I don't know how long it took. Time doesn't really matter here - minutes, centuries, the scale of the death of the universe, and beyond. Take your pick. Either way, it allowed me to die but survive, to remain a part of it, all in the same breath."

I felt a chill run over my body, and I heard Artemis's breathing quicken slightly beside me.

"You merged with it," she said slowly. "That's why you're here now."

He nodded slowly, then spoke. "Prague was the second lesson. The first was the Rosyth Naval Dockyard. That was the true test. That night, when Krane accessed the Mirror, when he pulsed it even though no experiment was supposed to take place, killing a dozen of ours… I let it happen."

"The hell?" I stuttered, my mind numb.

"I could have stopped it. I knew Krane was unraveling, even then. But it was no good. I'd tried to warn them… warn my superiors. But they wouldn't listen. And so I let the rules of nature take their course, and on the same night, I disappeared. I became a ghost."

"So you let him." I couldn't believe what he was saying.

"I let him," Hawthorne nodded, his voice tinged with sadness, "Because the Mirror could have caused hell and destruction if that version had survived. It didn't destroy the Mirror, really, when Krane broke it. Every Mirror ever created is a quantum entanglement of the others. But it delayed the use."

"Didn't you damn well think of what it would do to us, Hawthorne? That damn incident," I said, and I felt anger surge through my veins, "it caused ALL of this."

He shrugged. "The Mirror needed rules. Still does. But I can offer it that. Back at the Bureau, in the early days, I was called the Architect. And now, in this bizarre twist of fate, I have become it."

My mind flashed back to Krane's words. He had said the Architect had ruined it all. Was it Hawthorne?

"What did you want? Why do all this?" Artemis asked, confusion etched on her features.

Hawthorne nodded. "I don't want power. I don't want Krane's ambition, nor the Bureau's schemes. Time needs to stay a constant."

"But what schemes?" I asked, my voice bitter. "What did you try to stop?"

Hawthorne looked at me, his eyes tired. For a long moment, he didn't speak. I heard the clocks ticking - faintly but constantly - and it felt as if an hour had passed. Different ticks, out of step, without rhythm.

"You want the file. I thought as much, and that's why I brought you both here. You'll go back soon, you know - back to the instant I pulled you from. But here." He bent down, pulled a key from his pocket, and slipped it into one of the locks, opened the cabinet drawer, and pulled a small, thin file from the depths. He held it out to me, his face blank. "You always wanted to see the final twist, Calder. But that's the trick - everything has been the twist."

I stepped closer, grabbing the file and holding it up. It was dusty, as if it hadn't seen the light in years. I flipped through the pages of the file. There were rows of photographs - agents, locations, and logs. On one page, my own photograph was prominently displayed. On the next - my heart dropped. There was Artemis, her head turned slightly away from the camera, a smile on her lips.

"Read it," Hawthorne said.

Artemis stood beside me, leaning closer so she could read as well. Her fingers lightly traced the words on the page:

PROJECT CALIBER - PROGRAM DOCUMENTATION
SUBJECT: RAYES, A.
SLIDER STABILIZATION - CONTROL KEY/NEXUS

My heart dropped as I read it. The words echoed in my mind, and I could feel Artemis's breathing quicken as she read the same words I did. The whole file felt as if it would break at a page's turn, and yet we turned the page in unison, both reaching for the yellowed paper and flipping it. There was another page on Artemis - another page with her photo, and scrawling handwriting covering the page:

Program Phases:
•Locate subject, convince subject to join necessary programs
•Embed subject among field agents, acting as a common

Bureau spy

*•Suppress memories of initial project, employ mind erasure to
phase out any remnants*

•Anchor subject's consciousness to Mirror circuit via the key

*If the Mirror is to destabilize, the Caliber Protocol will be triggered
- subject can be used as a system override.*

Next to her name was another photograph, this one of a younger Alicia. She wore a uniform, smiling, though her eyes appeared haunted. And though the name beneath it was hers, it had been scratched out, replaced with the text in bold, block letters "PROJECT CALIBER."

Artemis took a step back, steadying herself against the shelves. She glanced at me, then glanced away, her eyes darting around, her breathing panicked. "What the hell - God - what did they do to me? That's why my memories…that's why I can't remember - those gaps. They did this to me?"

Hawthorne nodded. "They believed it was necessary. The Mirror was breaking, slowly. Any agents who were used in the initial tests, any agents recruited to be sliders… we picked you, Alicia, and groomed you into an agent capable of not only resisting the Mirror but shutting it off entirely if needed. What you remember of your life - your mother, your father…that is true. But at some point along the way, your memories are false. Not untrue - at least, not all of them. But there are gaps… engineered to prevent you from escaping. You're the fail-safe."

I felt her grip my arm, her fingers squeezing as tightly as they could. I could feel, without even glancing at her, the panic that had set in. I glanced at Hawthorne - he stood there, unmoving, his eyes almost unfeeling. Anger coursed through my veins.

"So, what was she, exactly? A circuit breaker?"

"The Mirror is dangerous. Even the Committee of Nine - my superiors - knew that. You, Alicia - to put it simply, the Mirror employs a system of entanglement, a system of superposition, to expand all parallel timelines into possibility. But when this happens, things… destabilize. Your consciousness - your mind -

has been intricately connected to the Mirror, entangled with it to ensure that reality itself syncs with you as the singular branch. If the Mirror were to ever destabilize - ever collapse - we could use your linked consciousness to reset reality to a semi-coherent state. You are the key."

"And how the hell do you activate the key?"

"Her death is the trigger to the key."

I stared at him in disbelief. "So her death is the only way to stabilize the Mirror?"

"It should have been. But not quite."

"The hell do you mean?"

"I mean exactly that," Hawthorne said, crossing his arms and staring at the flickering lightbulb above our heads. "We don't have much more time, so I'll be quick. You, Calder, are the exception."

"What?"

"That's the incredible thing, Max. You're the bug in our plans, the piece of the puzzle that never fits. As such, I believe you're the only one who could stop this... because you were never meant to be part of the plans in the first place."

I could feel Artemis tense again, and from the corner of my eye, I saw her glance at me as if seeing me in a new light.

"What the hell are you saying?" I asked, my voice quiet.

"Our project. The Bureau's plans for the Mirror. Krane's plans. None of these accounted for your bizarre addition to the timeline. Keep in mind that, other than Alicia here, all other sliders risked consequences when they slid beyond simple memory lapses or paranoia. That was until you came along."

"You mean... you never expected me to succeed? My first slide..."

"Precisely, Max. You were expected to fail. And yet, somehow, you were the perfect candidate - the only one who could withstand the psychological strain of reshaping history. And that's the most interesting part, Max."

"What do you mean?"

"You were supposed to fail," Hawthorne continued. "We were commanded to use you as yet another test subject, maybe for one or two slides, until you collapsed like the others. But somewhere, somehow, it never happened."

"So - every mission, every choice I made - it was all designed to fail?"

"Exactly," Hawthorne said, and I sensed a tinge of pride in his voice. "But failure is a beautiful thing, Max. You see, failure teaches us what we're truly capable of. And you... you've always surprised me. You were an exception we never expected. And that - that is why I believe you can end it."

"Krane... is that why Krane seemed so interested in me back in Vienna?"

"Yes. Though he suspected that the Bureau had designed another key through training and brainwashing, as we did with Alicia. He never once thought that you had simply inserted yourself into the timeline... somehow, successfully. He suspected you were the key - the master plan within the plan. But you're not. You are the error. The bug in the system."

"So then... I can stop it?"

"Yes. You can stop it - destroy the Mirror once and for all. It's why you survived. Though even I am not sure how."

The Archives had fallen silent now. The faint dripping of water was the only sound. The clocks themselves had all stopped, and the bulbs flickered slightly, as if waiting for something to change. Finally, Artemis broke the silence.

"If Max destroys it... what happens to us?"

Hawthorne sighed. He looked tired, worn, and his eyes glimmered with an unfamiliar emotion. "You can choose to run. You can choose to fight. Or you can choose to destroy it once and for all. But I'm not sure what any of those choices will lead to."

"How do I destroy it?"

"A good friend of mine, Alan Turing, once warned me about the consciousness of the Mirror. Though I'm unsure how, this consciousness has become interconnected with the two of you in ways I never thought possible. And that is the key to destroying the Mirror. If you destroy the consciousness within it, the Mirror itself will cease to function."

"What does that mean?" I asked, although I already suspected.

"You're the second key, Max," Hawthorne said, then glanced upward. The bulb had begun to sway back and forth, and the ticks of the clocks resumed. But this time, the ticks were in sync. "Prepare yourselves. The slide is ending now. It's up to you."

Something deep beneath the brick floor rumbled, like a seismic being awakening from its slumber. I noticed a glow at the edges of our vision.

The clocks began to chime all at once. The bells rang and rang and rang.

CHAPTER 24
COSMIC CONSCIOUSNESS

Hawthorne shuffled the papers on his desk uncomfortably. He was unsure. Though he had always been a man of action, betraying a man he respected tremendously - a man who had long been considered his friend - as still a horrible concept to come to terms with.

But he couldn't be sentimental - not now. He suspected that, in some way, the Mirror itself might have begun to develop a primitive consciousness.

In many ways, Hawthorne's fears were stoked, fueled by earlier projects he had worked on and philosophies he'd studied. His fears had been stoked by the very man he now sought out - no matter the cost - Alan Turing.

So now, with his work on the Mirror becoming ever more perilous and his suspicions growing, Hawthorne made a decision.

It had taken several weeks of careful preparation. Although Turing was a friend, Hawthorne knew the man would never accept an invitation. Turing, while always engaging faithfully in discussions, was never a fan of the philosophy of the Mirror.

Once he had found an angle to persuade him, Hawthorne struck carefully and precisely, as he had been trained to do. He was cautious, as he thought it would be against his target's better judgment to give him any help or assistance, but he knew he had no other choice. He cornered Turing at Bletchley Park one cold winter evening. Hawthorne was bundled up in his overcoat and scarf, waiting on a park bench until the man headed home for the night.

"Alan."

Turing turned, his face red from the biting wind, his cheeks flushed. "Yes? Good heavens. It's you, Malcolm."

"Yes - and I need your help. Your understanding of math and code could be a great asset to me and my colleagues. Likewise, your understanding of the quantum world... surely, you've gathered from the hints I've given you during our conversations what I speak of."

"Yes, I know your idea for a device. But you know I detest it."

"I need your help anyway."

"Why should I do that?"

"As I am about to tell you, you don't really have a choice... but then again, I believe the topic may be intriguing to you as well."

"No choice?"

Hawthorne hadn't mentioned at that time that only he was the man who wanted this assistance - that none of his colleagues even knew he had contacted Turing. But Turing did agree to help. Indeed, Turing didn't have a choice.

Hawthorne had been very careful in his research, formulating a plan in order to strong-arm Turing to assist him before he ever sought him out on that cold winter night. It had worked, too - Turing was afraid of the consequences that Hawthorne outlined for him in their conversation, as his sexuality and private life were at the time still hidden aspects of his persona. But Hawthorne had discovered this and used it unscrupulously to his advantage.

Turing was simply too valuable an asset and opportunity to

pass up. He was a pioneer in cryptography and the theories of computation, and he was the very man who Hawthorne believed could assist him.

It was a theory Hawthorne had developed during his time working on the Mirror… a theory that left him unsure of how to proceed in his relations with the government. So late one night when he was sure the lab was empty, Hawthorne had snuck Turing into the lab to have a look at the device in person.

Turing had walked up and down, looking at it for a long while. Eventually, however, he set his fingers - long and thin, as if they were the legs of a spider - upon the electronic instruments used to control the device.

"And you believe this Mirror might have its own will? Its own consciousness? You think it is becoming sentient in some way?"

"It's quite possible. I'm unsure, and that's why you're here. Somehow, I get the feeling that it is capable of acting on its own. I can even imagine it having some sort of a primitive form of free will. It's a bit scary."

"What makes you think it does?"

"As I said, I'm not sure. But the Mirror - it changes you the more you work around it. And," Hawthorne paused, gathering his thoughts for a moment. "And I believe for some reason I've begun to attach a face to the device."

"A face?"

"A face and a name."

"Such as?"

"El Cuadro. It means the - "

"I know, it means The Painting. Why do you think that is?"

"Again, I'm not sure… which is why I've recruited you, Alan."

"Yes, well… recruited is one word for it."

Turing worked late into the night, cautiously for fear of being caught, to understand the nature of the Mirror. The two men made progress. One such day, the two stood in Turing's office.

Turing had called Hawthorne there, demanding that it was a matter of urgency. And now that Hawthorne was there, he glanced nervously up before speaking.

"Malcolm. I've been thinking about your theory for quite a while now. From what I understand so far, the Mirror can manipulate time. Even that is a difficult concept. But I think your theory - your idea of consciousness - might have a bearing on reality."

"Might it, Alan?" Hawthorne asked, rubbing his face with his hand, blinking slowly to clear his thoughts. "What do you mean? I've thought I was going crazy."

Turing paused, searching for the right words. "The Mirror is a machine, built to alter the fabric of time. But what if you're right? What if it does have a consciousness that goes beyond mere programming?"

Hawthorne raised an eyebrow slightly. "Yes, that was my theory. But how? It shouldn't be at all possible."

"I've been researching it." Turing adjusted his glasses uncomfortably. "Haven't slept much. Been seeing things. But these texts - they're fascinating. It's called panpsychism: the theory that consciousness isn't just confined to living beings, but something inherent in all matter. It seems ridiculous at first, but what if it connects to the quantum field of the whole of matter? What if you're right and the Mirror itself has begun to develop its own consciousness over time? After all, it's interacting with the very structure of reality. Could it be that it understands its own purpose?"

Hawthorne paused to think for a second. "It seems a stretch, no? I do feel it - I've been seeing that face again, in my dreams… in my nightmares. But it could just be the work with time, you know? The stress of it all. Besides, from my understanding, isn't the idea that everything could have consciousness a philosophical concept?"

"But that's exactly it!" Turing exclaimed, his voice growing excited. "The Mirror isn't just calculating outcomes. It's predicting, reacting, and choosing when and where to send you. You've told me yourself that sometimes even Krane doesn't know where it'll send sliders, right? It's like the device is learning - adapting!"

"So then… are you saying I was right? The device is alive?"

"Maybe… maybe not in the same way, but - yes. It's become something more than the sum of its parts. And what does that mean for us? What happens if it begins to decide its own fate?"

"Let's slow down a second, Alan. I agree - that would be bad - but what evidence do we have for this? Other than my… mental condition."

"I swear, Malcolm. I'll look into it more, I will - I'm writing up the calculations now… But I swear I'm right."

"And if you are? What would happen?"

"If I'm right… we're not just dealing with a tool anymore. We're dealing with something sentient - something with its purpose, and no regard for the consequences of its actions."

Hawthorne nodded. "So, what do we do, then? You know my superiors wouldn't let me stop the project… even if I were to believe all this."

"Just for now, Malcolm, as I said, I'll investigate it more. But I fear you've opened a door you can't close. If we don't understand it soon, we may never get the chance again."

Hawthorne nodded, unconvinced. Though he respected Turing, his mind was battling with the logic of it all. How could such a bizarre concept be true? Wasn't it more likely that it was simply nerves getting to him?

Two days later, Turing stepped down. It was late at night when he knocked at the door of Hawthorne's home.

Hawthorne answered, his face shocked as he saw the man who stood before him. Turing looked as if he'd seen a ghost.

"I - I can't help you any longer, Malcolm. Just… get your superiors to listen. Stop your work on that device."

"I'm not sure they'll listen, Alan. What did you figure out? What's got you looking like you've seen a ghost?"

Turing shook his head, muttering something unintelligible under his breath, and walked away hurriedly.

Though Hawthorne called after him, even threatening him, that would be the last he'd see of the man - Turing avoided him as if he were the plague after that.

Hawthorne knew that Turing must have discovered something - something that made the man ill to even be in the same room as the Mirror.

Even though Turing would never confirm it, Hawthorne suspected that the word they had discussed had everything to do with it: panpsychism. That was the concept, wasn't it?

CHAPTER 25
DOPPELGÄNGER DESTRUCTION

The chiming bells stopped at once. Everything was silent. But it didn't last. Instantaneously, the silence was replaced by the roaring static, electric pulses flaring out from the Mirror. I fell backward, struck by the energy that flew out from the Mirror. Krane was scrambling to his feet next to me, his face desperate and his eyes wide, though I couldn't discern whether it was with rage or fear. It was the same moment, the same breath, the same second that we had left.

I heard a low rumbling and glanced upward. The ceiling of the ancient temple was shaking, and dust was falling from cracks that had begun to form. We didn't have much time. I glanced behind me, searching for Artemis. She was there, where I had left her, but struggling to stand now. Her eyes met mine, and she smiled - only slightly, but enough to let me know that I hadn't imagined it. Her wounds were gone. No blood remained, no injuries. I was still scraped up from my previous fight with my doppelgänger, but it didn't matter now.

I didn't have time to think. Krane darted past me, his face frantic and filled with an almost lustful expression, his feverish eyes locked on the surface of the Mirror. The liquid metal was fully cracked open, but I didn't glance at the visions inside for too long. I couldn't lose focus.

I dashed after him. Krane had reached the Mirror, one hand flying over the controls as the other held fast to the frame. The Mirror pulsed in response, and I ducked low, covering my head as the force hit. I was almost thrown backward again, but held fast, struggling to stand against the sheer energy that emanated from the device. I could smell the electricity now, and I could feel every hair on my body standing on end.

As the wave passed, I saw figures emerge from the depths of the Mirror. The echoes, the doppelgängers, were back - at least some of them. There were three versions of me and another man. This other man stood tall, his nervous face contorted into a calm expression. There he was, a second Krane, standing before the Mirror.

Without thinking, I swung my arm upward, pulling my M1911 out from beneath my coat. I leveled it at the second Krane and took aim. Before he could even move, I fired - the bullet hit him, and he cried out, toppling backward into the Mirror. The Krane from our timeline laughed maniacally, casting aside the console as he grabbed onto the Mirror with both hands.

"You can't stop it, Max! There's no stopping us now. The future is decided, the past rewritten. I am the Mirror now."

As if given an order, the three Calders who stood by the Mirror pulled out their pistols in unison. I leaped away, rolling desperately behind the altar, bullets ricocheting off the stone floor where my head had just been. The chamber rang with gunfire, the constant, pulsing, roaring, and hum from the Mirror failing to drown out the noise.

Dust and bits of debris fell from the ceiling of the temple, crashing down around us. Artemis sprang forward, moving gracefully as she leveled her pistol at the two nearest Calders, firing rapidly. One bullet hit its mark, and the man clutched his shoulder, cursing. The other doppelgänger dodged behind a large rock that had fallen near the edge of the amphitheater.

I glanced around, trying to locate the third. Then I saw him - he was the one who resembled me the most, his face rough but still fresh, his body worn and aged but strong. He was circling wide, his pistol held at chest level, his eyes darting around as he glanced at Artemis and then me.

I stepped out from behind the altar. At the same moment, we both raised our pistols. We fired at the same time - three shots rang out, and I stumbled backward, holding my shoulder. I glanced at the blood on my hand. He'd hit me, and my arm felt limp. But I'd shot twice instead of once, a double tap as we were always taught, and both bullets struck his chest.

He staggered, stumbling backward, with a look of surprise. Another pulse erupted from the Mirror, and he was knocked backward, flying through the air as he was thrown brutally against the furthest wall.

I glanced toward Artemis and the other two Calders. She was keeping them busy - her pistol trained on the younger one, the older Calder already dispatched. I didn't have time to think.

I ran forward, sprinting toward the Mirror. Other shadowy figures were beginning to emerge from the cracks, but I ignored them. Instead, I charged at Krane, his body shaking now, his eyes blinking rapidly as he struggled to hold on. He glanced at me, breaking into a wide grin.

"You can't kill me, Calder. Not now! It's too late. The Mirror…" he laughed maniacally, his face alight with victory. "I am the only one who can control it, Calder. I am the constant! The true guiding hand of time. If I die, you destroy this timeline and every other timeline you could reach. But listen, Calder. It doesn't have to be this way. Step away - stop it now, and I'll give you your life. Alicia's too…"

I pulled the trigger, putting a bullet straight through his heart. He glanced down at his chest, shock flickering on his features before he collapsed, crumpling to the ground.

As he fell, his body began to age - quicker and quicker. By the time his head hit the cold stone, he looked like a decrepit shadow of the man he'd once been. I stared at him. He was finally dead.

But as if in protest, the Mirror groaned - silently at first, then louder. A piercing voice echoed in my ears, shrieking. It wasn't just a noise, or a thunderous hum - it was human, burning into my mind and my body. I staggered, falling on one knee, pressing my bloodied hands over my heart, trying to block out the sound. I wanted it to stop - wanted to shield myself from it - but it wouldn't cease.

The surface of the Mirror was frantic, the jagged cracks shifting and moving, bursting outward, as if it were an explosion caught in slow motion. Every piece of me wanted to run, but I knew that wasn't what I was built for. I glanced around and saw Artemis. She caught my gaze, standing among the falling debris and dust, holding her pistol limp in one hand. Behind her, I saw the bodies of my doppelgängers. I didn't know how she'd killed them, and I didn't care. Her eyes were tired, but she nodded, and I turned back slowly to face the Mirror, struggling to stand but finally succeeding.

And then, it overwhelmed me.

I saw every timeline in its depth - peace in Lisbon, a haunted life in Tokyo, being hunted in Paris - a million Max Calders, each one within the face of the Mirror. They were all there, all possibilities. A voice filled the air, replacing the haunted screaming. It wasn't mine, nor Krane's, nor even the fake voice of young Hawthorne that they had used time and time again.

"I cannot be killed. I am the fabric of reality itself. I am what ties it together."

Suddenly, it felt as if I was unable to move. Deep within my body, I sensed a change. Though describing it would be impossible, I could feel myself aging, anchored to the spot.

But I stepped forward.

One step after another, I dragged myself closer to the Mirror. I felt my body begin to disintegrate, dissolve, and break down, but I ignored it. I saw the skin peeling from my hands and saw my body aging - but I stepped forward, again and again. Artemis shouted something from behind me, but I couldn't hear what she said - and I stepped forward once more.

I couldn't tell what reality was. The Mirror showed me thousands of versions of Alicia. Brutal, terrible death, beautiful, passionate love - everything I wanted and everything I feared. It showed me a version of myself that had become God, reshaping reality as I wished.

I stepped forward again, my eyes clamped shut, unseeing, reaching out with my fingers slowly. My hands trembled now, raw and almost see-through in the shining blue light. My bones felt brittle with age, and my mind reeled under the weight of infinite lives and possibilities.

But then, something clicked. I remembered. Artemis wouldn't have to die to shut it down, and I wouldn't either.

The answer was so simple, so obvious, that I wasn't sure why I hadn't thought of it before. The Mirror was still afraid - even with Krane dead, even with his ambitions cast to the wind. The Mirror was afraid of me.

And if I were one of the few individuals truly merged with the Mirror, truly attuned with its quantum superposition, then I knew what to do.

I was the error – the bug in the system – the exception to the whole system and the only man who had access to the Mirror without being fully controlled or oppressed by it. For all its power, the Mirror needed me to make a choice - and it desperately wanted me to make the wrong one.

But a quantum system, especially one as advanced as the Mirror, couldn't observe itself without collapsing. I remember Hawthorne telling me that when we were in Marrakech. And here I was, the unexpected observer, the other face of the Mirror, the outside puzzle piece. I felt the Mirror beneath my fingers and grabbed on with both hands, one on each side of the brass frame.

I opened my eyes fully.

I stared into the heart of the Mirror, every piece jagged and sharp. I fought the sickness that overtook me - the mind-bending horror of a million fractured timelines. It showed me every outcome it could.

But finally, there was nothing more to see. I saw past the visions the Mirror had desperately camouflaged itself within. I saw the Mirror itself.

"No more," I whispered as I felt the very last of my body dissipate, the very last piece of my humanity disappearing. "You're finished."

The sound from the Mirror was deafening. It emitted a pulse, a huge flash of blue light, stronger than any before, desperately trying to tear me away, but I held on. And then, as the pulse ceased, I stepped forward again. I let go of the frame and stepped forward into the Mirror, the glass trembling, the fracture spreading as I did.

I was inside. But I didn't slide.

I didn't travel. Instead, I was in the machine itself.

There was no displacement, no sliding feeling.

This was annihilation and fusion all at once, every observation of the quantum field apparent to my mind. Every possibility rushed through my nerves, every piece of the puzzle completed. I was both the observer and the machine, staring into myself from every quantum angle at once.

El Cuadro - for I now knew what its name was - screamed, an agonizing feeling that spread throughout the very edges of my mind, but it no longer affected me. It was the agony of a machine that could suddenly see itself, suddenly observe itself, and was aware it was dying.

I had time, too - time to choose another reality, time to undo all the damage I had done. In a thousand instances, it begged, reasoned, and pleaded with me, but I ignored it. The Mirror wanted me to pick, but I didn't. I simply observed.

This was the real trick - the idea that even Hawthorne had been unsure of. If every virtual reality existed as a potential, real one, then quantum mechanics determines that all of them must be observed for them all to become reality. But if the observer and the observed are the same, there is no outcome. No change. No resolution. And the system will collapse.

So I let the possibilities swirl around me and waited patiently. I didn't know how long I had been there, but I no longer felt pain. Even time was an unknown, but I ignored the unease in the pit of my stomach.

I knew what I had to do.

Then, with a sound as if reality itself was tearing apart, the system I observed collapsed. I saw fractions of the future and the past - the first life on earth, the hot death of the universe, and even my own childhood.

The Mirror shattered. It wasn't the physical pieces that shattered, though they might have as well. It was the quantum system destroying itself piece by piece, the fractal nature of the intricate design turning to smoke.

Then, everything was darkness. Everything was silent. Suddenly, I was no longer the observer.

I simply felt myself, my eyes closed, and felt my body return. I was lying down against some soft surface. But I wasn't sure if I wanted to open my eyes. What had happened to me? Where was I?

Though I no longer saw the Mirror, I wasn't sure I wanted to see myself either. But finally, struggling, I opened my eyes and glanced around. The bright sun shone above my head.

I sat up, confused. The temple was rubble, collapsed in upon itself. The gigantic monoliths that stood guarding the entrance had fallen, covering the door.

"You're awake."

I turned in the direction of the voice. Alicia kneeled beside me, her face gentle, relief washing over her features. Tears were streaking her cheeks, and she grasped one of my hands as I reached out to her.

"It's done," I said, and she nodded. "And I don't want to see any more furniture".

"I ran," she said. "I had to. The temple was collapsing. I thought you'd died, Max. But then you just - you appeared here."

I smiled slightly, cracked blood on my lips. "I had time for one last choice. Right as it died."

"Well, you didn't make it out unscathed."

"What do you mean?"

She laughed, and I could hear the relief still apparent in her voice. "You look older, Calder. Not too old, though. I like it."

I ran my fingers through my hair. "More gray?"

"More gray."

I stood, shakily at first, finding my legs. I kissed her, unwilling to let go - but I already knew we would have to. I didn't want it, but I knew her life was unfinished. She still had things to do, but I - I was done.

We walked slowly away from the temple, pausing only to forage for a few supplies from the abandoned Nazi camp before making our way out of the Andes.

The sun shone high above us. Several condors circled above us, peacefully floating beneath the clouds as if nothing had ever happened.

CHAPTER 26
GHOSTLINES

Montevideo. Smoke from a café kitchen drifted over the street. Artemis sat at an outdoor table, coat off, sunglasses on, fingers tapping the rim of a chipped espresso cup. The old, blue iron table she sat at was flecked from age, the last light of the day shimmering over the rooftops of the city she now called home. Her sunglasses reflected a passerby strolling along, blissfully unaware of her presence. From an overhead apartment, an old rusty radio played faded music, glitching occasionally. But she wasn't listening to the music.

Three months. It was not nearly enough time, but at the same time, it had been too long. How long until she could see him again?

She'd fallen into a repetitive rhythm already - wake, walk, read the newspaper, watch for news that never came, and rest. She had learned to live a life without tension, though she wasn't sure if she liked it or not. The world felt heavier, but it also felt consistent, and she cherished it.

A messenger approached her table, his hat covering his shaded eyes, his face showing no expression. She watched him cautiously, one hand sliding almost imperceptibly into her jacket pocket. When he finally approached, he tossed a single envelope onto the table, nodded, and turned, vanishing a minute later into the dusky air. There had only been a flicker of recognition in her eyes as he approached, and now, she turned her attention to the envelope.

She waited until he was gone to pick it up. She opened it slowly, turning it around in her hands. Inside was a photo. It was Lisbon, given away by the buildings in the background. At a desk in shadow sat the man she remembered, though he looked older now, scar still across his jaw, hunched over at an old Remington Model 10 typewriter. Beside the machine sat a glass of whiskey, half-drunk. Though his clothes were regular, the dark leather gloves confirmed it.

She smiled slightly, her eyes softening as she stared at the photo. Above the photo, scrawled in a rough handwritten note:

He remembers.

She stared at the words for a second, a smirk spreading across her face. Without a second thought, she pulled a lighter from her pocket and flicked it, holding the paper up to the flame. In seconds, new words had appeared, right beneath the words already there:

Lisbon is peaceful. See you soon?

Alicia traced the hidden text on the photo with a delicate finger. There, in the photo, was none other than Max Calder. It was just another reminder that she hadn't made it all up in her head or dreamt it - a reminder that she'd finally overcome her programming, the brutal brainwashing she'd been subjected to by the Bureau. It was an ode to the old world, but a signal of something new.

Typewriter, glass, gloves, and scar - it was still Calder. Alive, or something close enough. He looked happier now, too. She could tell.

She read the words once more, then gathered up her coat, which she'd carefully draped on the chair where she sat, leaving a few coins for the espresso. She stood, walking away with the photo placed carefully into her coat pocket.

The Bureau was still out there, and enemies were frequent, but Calder had found peace - and so had she. She glanced over her shoulder, watching as people passed. There were no Bureau agents, none of Sosa's men - only people living their lives as she was living her own. She walked along, the final rays of the setting sun beaming into her face. She closed her eyes for a second as she walked, feeling a wave of peace wash over her.

She left the café behind her and walked north along the paved road toward her apartment. Every few steps, she rehearsed the memories and words she'd used to anchor herself, to help fend off false memories from taking hold.

Alicia Rayes. Max Calder. Maria Rayes. Montevideo. 1947.

Inside his faded, old apartment, Max Calder sat at his desk, reclining with a glass of whiskey in his hand. He sipped it, then set it down carefully at the edge of the desk. The drizzle outside hadn't let up for days - something that seemed to herald the end of the winter months. The room itself was sparse - other than his desk, his typewriter, his bed, and a closet, Calder didn't care much for belongings. Sure, there were some whiskey bottles and a small supply of food in an old, battered fridge that was in his kitchen. The city below his window was quiet. It was nighttime, and most slept. But Calder remained awake, typing away whenever he had a thought to put on paper.

He reached for his glass again, his hand steady. For the first time in ages, it felt as if his life had stabilized. No more memories hidden, no more lapses or slides. It was a strange peace. He remembered everything that had happened, of course - all the sacrifices, the sorrow, and the pain - but he didn't feel as if he wanted to change it.

Artemis was still doing well - he knew that much. He'd caught one of her informants the other day, trying to tail him as he visited the local bar. The man had given up quickly enough, admitting that Artemis had grown curious and set him on Calder to find out what he could.

Max Calder smiled at the memory - how he'd made sure to send a message to Artemis that even her messengers wouldn't catch. He finished the last drop of whiskey, set the glass back down, and turned back to his page.

Slowly and carefully, pausing to think, he typed out several words, glancing at them critically before continuing. He rolled the paper higher and closed his eyes for a brief moment, nodding to himself.

Being anchored was a relief. Though he had craved action for most of his early life, he no longer did. The Mirror was gone now, and that meant life was back to normal. No echoes. No slides. And most importantly, no doppelgängers.

Those damn doppelgängers had been a royal pain in the arse.

Somewhere in the distance, a dog barked. Only once and then fell silent.

————

The Scottish countryside was covered in a rolling mist. The fields were dry, harsh, and barren, the moon glowing faintly through the clouds. Near the outskirts of the city, there stood a figure: a tall man, far older and far more ruthless. But his scars were the same, and his trench coat fit him well.

He dug his hands into his coat pockets, surveying the hills and fields, letting out a puff of smoke from his cigarette. He watched carefully, looking for something. Where was it?

The man shifted, rubbing the scar along his jawline. He rolled his shoulders and set off at a brisk pace toward the city. He knew that somewhere, the two he was looking for were hiding.

He wasn't quite sure where those ghosts were. But they were out there, because ghosts never vanish. They just slide out of view.

Somewhere in the distance, a dog barked. Only once and then fell silent.

AFTERWORDS

PEOPLE AND PLACES

VIRGINIA HALL – ARTEMIS

Alicia Rayes has the code name Artemis in *Furniture Sliders* in recognition and remembrance of a World War 2 heroine by the name of Virginia Hall Goillot (1906 – 1982).

She was awarded the Distinguished Service Cross (DSC), Croix de Guerre, and Member of the Most Excellent Order of the British Empire (MBE) and used the code names Marie and Diane. She was an American who worked with the United Kingdom's clandestine Special Operations Executive (SOE) and the American Office of Strategic Services (OSS) in France during World War II. The objective of SOE and OSS was to conduct espionage, sabotage and reconnaissance in occupied Europe against the Axis powers, especially Nazi Germany. SOE and OSS agents in France allied themselves with resistance groups and supplied them with weapons and equipment parachuted in from England. After World War II, Hall worked for the Special Activities Division of the Central Intelligence Agency (CIA).

The Germans gave her the nickname Artemis (the Greek huntress, goddess of the moon and guardian of secrets), and the Gestapo reportedly considered her "the most dangerous of all

Allied spies". Having lost part of her left leg after a hunting accident, Hall used a prosthesis she named "Cuthbert". She was also known as "The Limping Lady" by the Germans and as "Marie of Lyon" by many of the SOE agents she assisted.

She was a thirty-five-year-old journalist from Baltimore, conspicuous by reddish hair, a strong American accent, and an imperturbable temper; she took risks often but intelligently. "I would give anything to get my hands on that limping Canadian [sic] bitch". Reportedly said by Klaus Barbie, Gestapo chief, "The Butcher of Lyon".

Virginia Hall left no memoir, granted no interviews, and spoke little about her overseas life - even with relatives. She received the USA's Distinguished Service Cross, the only civilian woman in the Second World war to do so. But she refused all but a private ceremony with OSS chief Major General William J. Donovan - even a presentation by President Truman.

ALAN TURING

Alan Mathison Turing (1912 – 1954) was an English mathematician, computer scientist, logician, cryptanalyst, and philosopher. He was a major player and a major influence in the development of theoretical computer science, formalizing the concepts of algorithms and computation with the Turing Machine, which can be considered as an early model of a general-purpose computer. Turing is widely considered to be the father of theoretical computer science.

Turing graduated from King's College, Cambridge, and in 1938, earned a doctorate degree from Princeton University. On 4 September 1939, the day after the UK declared war on Germany, Turing reported to Bletchley Park, the wartime station of the Government Code and Cypher School (GC&CS). Like all others who came to Bletchley, he was required to sign the Official Secrets Act, in which he agreed not to disclose anything about his work at Bletchley. This meant that many of his achievements were never recognized and some only became known much later. Regrettably some were overshadowed by the exposure of his private life.

Turing's codebreaking team based in Bletchley Hut 8 produced intelligence codenamed Ultra and was the section responsible for German naval cryptanalysis. He devised techniques for speeding the breaking of German ciphers, finding settings for the Enigma machine, and played a crucial role in cracking intercepted messages that enabled the Allies to defeat the Axis powers in many engagements, including the Battle of the Atlantic. Turing had a reputation for eccentricity at Bletchley Park. He was known to his colleagues as "Prof" and his treatise on Enigma was known as the "Prof's Book".

See the separate section on Alan Turing's fictional involvement in *Furniture Sliders* and his relationship with Hawthorne and the Mirror.

HUGH SINCLAIR

Admiral Sir Hugh Francis Paget Sinclair, KCB (1873 – 1939), known as Quex Sinclair, was Director of British Naval Intelligence between 1919 and 1921 and Chief of the Submarine Service in 1921. He helped set up the Secret Intelligence Service (commonly known as MI6) and became its second director in 1923 taking over as 'C' from Sir Mansfield Smith-Cumming, the original 'C', who died in 1923. (All subsequent heads of SIS have been known as 'C' which was the inspiration for 'M' in the James Bond books and movies).

Sinclair was promoted to Vice Admiral on 3 March 1926 and full Admiral on 15 May 1930. He founded GC&CS, later to be known as GCHQ in 1919. In 1938, with a second war looming, Sinclair set up Section D, a secret organization dedicated to sabotage. In the spring of that year, using £6,000 of his own money, he bought Bletchley Park to be a wartime intelligence station. In *Furniture Sliders* a fictionalized Hugh Sinclair personally enlisted

Max Calder at Cambridge University, a hotbed of spy recruitment, directly into MI6. Max was later to be poached from MI6 by the Office of Temporal Anomalies and Strategic Intelligence (OTASI) – the Bureau.

ALASTAIR DENNISTON

Commander Alexander "Alastair" Guthrie Denniston CB CMG CBE (1881 – 1961) was a Scottish codebreaker and deputy head of GC&CS. He was also an Olympic hockey medal winner. In 1914, Denniston helped create Room 40 at the Admiralty, a group responsible for intercepting and decrypting enemy messages. Room 40 was merged with its counterpart in the Army in 1919, renamed the Government Code and Cypher School in 1920, and transferred from the Navy to the Foreign Office. It was located at 54 Broadway in London in the same building as MI6. Denniston was chosen to run the new organization.

Following the practices of his superiors at Room 40, Denniston contacted scientists from Oxford and Cambridge—including Alan Turing and Gordon Welchman—asking if they would be willing to serve if war broke out. This all happened at Bletchley Park which was chosen by MI6 chief Admiral Hugh Sinclair as the location for the codebreaking effort which Sinclair acquired with his own funds. Denniston was assigned to prepare the site and design the huts to be built in the grounds. He initiated the decryption of German military Enigma ciphers for which Alan Turing became famous. Commander Edward Travis eventually took over running Bletchley Park from Denniston who retired in 1945. In a *Furniture Sliders* fictional account, Denniston was Hawthorne's original contact at Bletchley Park before Hawthorne made direct contact with Alan Turing.

WILLIAM STEPHENSON

Sir William Samuel Stephenson CC MC DFC (1897 – 1989) was a Canadian soldier and spymaster. In WWI he was a fighter pilot in the Royal Flying Corps, bringing down 12 German aircraft. Shot down and captured on a mission, Stephenson managed to escape in October 1918. By the end of World War I, he had already earned the Military Cross and the Distinguished Flying Cross. After the war ended, Stephenson became an entrepreneur and inventor of communications equipment, but he grew concerned about the growing power of Nazi Germany. He was the senior representative of the British Security Coordination (BSC) for the Western Allies during World War II and is best known by his wartime intelligence code name, Intrepid. As head of the BSC, Stephenson handed British scientific secrets over to Roosevelt and relayed American secrets back to Churchill.

In 1940 Churchill sent Stephenson to the United States to covertly establish and run BSC in New York City. It was registered by the State Department as a foreign entity and operated out of Room 3603 at Rockefeller Center. It was officially known as the British Passport Control Office and also acted as the administrative headquarters for MI6.

BSC directly affected wartime covert intelligence and propaganda efforts across the entire South American continent. This is how, in *Furniture Sliders*, a fictionalized Stephenson came across Alicia Rayes and recruited her. One of Stephenson's real major achievements for the war effort was setting up Camp X. This was the unofficial name of the secret Special Training School No. 103, a Second World War paramilitary installation for training covert agents in the methods required for success in clandestine operations. This where the fictionalized Stephenson sent Alicia Rayes for her training.

For his extraordinary service to the war effort, he was made a Knight Bachelor by King George VI in the 1945 New Year

Honors. In recommending Stephenson for the knighthood, Winston Churchill wrote: "This one is dear to my heart."

In November 1946 Stephenson received the Medal for Merit from President Harry S. Truman, at that time the highest U.S. civilian award. He was the first non-American to be so honored. OSS chief General Donovan presented the medal with the citation paying tribute to Stephenson's "valuable assistance to America in the fields of intelligence and special operations".

Many people consider Stephenson to be one of the real-life inspirations for James Bond. Ian Fleming himself once wrote, "James Bond is a highly romanticized version of a true spy. The real thing is... William Stephenson."

TOMMY FLOWERS

Thomas Harold Flowers MBE (1905 – 1998) was very much an unsung hero. He was an English engineer with a degree in electrical engineering and was employed by the British General Post Office. During World War II he designed and built Colossus at Bletchley Park, the world's first programmable electronic computer, to help decipher encrypted German messages. His massive contribution, not only to ending the war but to digital computers, went undiscovered and unnoticed for years as it was covered by the Official Secrets Act.

Flowers' first contact with wartime codebreaking came in February 1941 when his director was asked for help by Alan Turing at Bletchley Park. That did not work out but Turing was so impressed with Flowers that he introduced him to Max Newman who was leading the effort to automate part of the cryptanalysis of the Lorenz cipher.

Flowers used his own funds to develop the first versions of what became the Colossus codebreaker (named because of its size) as the management at Bletchley were initially unconvinced it would work. The Mark 1 Colossus operated five times faster than any previous system. The Mark 2 immediately produced vital information for the imminent D-Day landings. It was not until the 1970s that Flowers' work in computing was fully acknowledged. His family had known only that he had done some 'secret and important' work. He only gets a small, almost passing mention in *Furniture Sliders*, but his contributions alongside Alan Turing were immense.

GRIGORY KULIK

Grigory Ivanovich Kulik was a Soviet military commander and Marshal of the Soviet Union who served as chief of the Red Army's Main Artillery Directorate from 1937 until June 1941. Kulik was a notoriously abusive and ineffective commander and bureaucrat, wildly erratic and unpredictable in his actions and considered by even his colleagues to be a "murderous buffoon", albeit one who bore Stalin's official approval. He championed a bizarre personal command motto he dubbed "Jail or Medal"; those under his command were either showered with (usually unearned) awards and decorations if he favored them, or simply arrested and sent to the Gulag on trumped up charges if he did not. He was blamed for many of the Russian failures in the German's Operation Barbarossa.

After a respite during and immediately after the war, Stalin and his police chief Lavrenty Beria began a new round of military purges due to Stalin's jealousy and suspicion of the generals' public standing. Kulik was dismissed from his posts in 1946 after NKVD telephone eavesdroppers overheard him grumbling that politicians were stealing the credit from the generals. Arrested in 1947, he remained in prison until 1950, when he was condemned to death and executed for treason. A fictionalized version of Kulik has been included in *Furniture Sliders* with a slight twist to his arrest in 1947. According to the Max Calder storyline, Kulik was also arrested because he failed to get hold of the Mirror, failed to hang on to Emil Krane and failed to kill Calder in the Prague catacombs.

BERNARD BARUCH

Bernard Mannes Baruch (1870-1965) was a renowned American financier, statesman, and presidential advisor. He served as an advisor to presidents for over 40 years, including Woodrow Wilson, Franklin D. Roosevelt, and Harry S. Truman. Baruch was known for his significant contributions during World War I and World War II, particularly as Chairman of the War Industries Board during World War I. He made a fortune on Wall Street and is credited with coining the term "Cold War". Baruch was a significant philanthropist and his legacy continues to be honored through various initiatives, including the naming of Baruch College in New York City.

HERMANN MINKOWSKI

Hermann Minkowski (1864 – 1909) was a mathematician and professor at the University of Königsberg, the University of Zürich, and the University of Göttingen, described variously as German, Polish, Lithuanian-German, or Russian. Minkowski is perhaps best known for his foundational work describing space and time as four-dimensional, now known as "Minkowski space-time", which facilitated geometric interpretations of Albert Einstein's special theory of relativity.

ROYAL NAVAL DOCKYARD ROSYTH

Rosyth Dockyard is on the north side of the Firth of Forth in Scotland and is one of the largest waterside manufacturing facilities in the UK. It is presently operated by Babcock Marine on behalf of the UK government with the primary role of refitting or dismantling decommissioned nuclear submarines as well as acting as an integration site for the Royal Navy's aircraft carriers. It was previously known as the Royal Naval Dockyard Rosyth under the direct control of the Royal Navy playing a vital role in both World Wars as a ship-repair and dry-dock complex. During World War II the dockyard was greatly expanded, and more than 3,000 warships were repaired or refitted there under the supervision of Rear-Admiral Henry Bovell. In 2023 Rosyth was transferred back to the Royal Navy as HMS Caledonia preserving the strong and historic links between the Royal Navy and the Rosyth communities. In the *Furniture Sliders* story, the fictional Rosyth was the secret location used by the Bureau for the development of the Mirror without the knowledge of the Royal Navy. The Bureau location was secretly incorporated into the World War II expansion.

54 BROADWAY

54 Broadway in London's Westminster was the main operating base of the Secret Intelligence Service (SIS) also known as MI6 from 1924. MI6 was run by Hugh Sinclair as the second 'C' taking over from Mansfield Cumming - the original 'C' in 1923. Broadway was also the home of the Government Code and Cypher School (GC&CS), although the two operated separately. During the second World War the building had a brass plaque on the outside with "Minimax Fire Extinguisher Company" on it although many knew exactly who was actually based there. GC&CS eventually moved out and relocated to Bletchley Park in 1939. It was alleged that a later head of MI6, Sir Stewart Menzies, had a tunnel from 54 Broadway to his home in Queen Anne's Gate.

CAMP X

Camp X was the unofficial name of the secret Special Training School No. 103, a Second World War British paramilitary installation for training covert agents in the methods required for success in clandestine operations. Trainees at the camp learned sabotage techniques, subversion, intelligence gathering, lock picking, explosives training, radio communications, encode/decode, recruiting techniques for partisans, the art of silent killing and unarmed combat.

Camp X was located on the northwestern shore of Lake Ontario between Whitby and Oshawa in Ontario, Canada. The area is known today as Intrepid Park, after the code name for Sir William Stephenson, Director of British Security Co-ordination (BSC), who established the program to create the training facility. Stephenson appears in *Furniture Sliders* in a fictionalized setting with Alicia Rayes obtaining her espionage training at Camp X having been directly recruited by Stephenson. The camp also had close ties with MI6 which Max Calder was recruited into.

SS ILE DE FRANCE

The SS France was a French luxury ocean liner that plied the transatlantic route between Europe and New York from 1927 through to 1958. She was built in Saint-Nazaire for the Compagnie Générale Transatlantique and named after the region around Paris known as "L'Ile de France". She commenced her maiden voyage on June 22, 1927, as the first major ocean liner built after World War I, and the first ever to be decorated almost entirely in modern Art Deco style. For the first time, a ship's passenger spaces had been designed not to reproduce decorative styles of the past, but to celebrate the progressive style of the present, with a degree of modernity unlike any previous ship. In *Furniture Sliders* the SS France is one of the few choices in early 1947 to get from New York directly to the European continent. Shortly after Max Calder traveled on the SS France, it was taken back to the shipyard where it was built for a refurbishment that took 2 years.

MS VULCANIA

The MS Vulcania was an Italian ocean liner built in northern Italy in 1926 for the Italian Cosulich Line. In 1947, the Vulcania made a single voyage from Genoa to South America. Then returned to the New York route. The Vulcania was considered one of the most successful passenger ships ever built. During her career she carried more passengers than any other Italian-flag ship. Although there had been various ships which offered private verandahs and promenades for the suites, the Vulcania was the first liner to offer a large number of cabins with private balconies. In *Furniture Sliders* this gives Max Calder an ideal opportunity to easily dispose of Bureau agent Boone over the side of the ship – if a slide had not happened before he had the chance.

OPERATION BARBAROSSA

Operation Barbarossa was the code name for the massive German Nazi invasion of the Soviet Union, launched on June 22, 1941. It was the largest military offensive in history, involving millions of soldiers across a vast front. The operation aimed to seize territory for "Lebensraum" and eliminate perceived threats from communism and the Jewish population. More than 3.8 million Axis troops invaded the western Soviet Union along a 2,900-kilometer front. The attack became the costliest military offensive in history, with around 10 million combatants taking part in the opening phase with over 8 million casualties by the end of the operation on 5 December 1941.

OPERATION TORCH

Operation Torch was the codename for the Allied invasion of French North Africa during World War II, specifically focusing on French Morocco and French Algeria. It started on November

8, 1942, and ended on November 16, 1942. It was the first major Anglo-American operation of the war and the largest amphibious landing in history. Operation Torch was intended to open a second front against the Axis powers in Europe, relieving pressure on the Soviet Union on the Eastern Front. The victory boosted Allied morale. In *Furniture Sliders* Operation Torch was a trigger for Max Calder and Hawthorne to end up in Marrakech at the end of 1942.

QUANTUM MECHANICS AND THE MIRROR

The Mirror is, of course, entirely fictional. But the idea of an inanimate object having consciousness or even becoming sentient is no longer regarded as outrageous, especially within the realms of quantum mechanics and panpsychism. This concept forms the foundation of the Mirror in *Furniture Sliders* and the *Bureau Archives Trilogy*. Over time, its level of consciousness and sentience increases, and the dangers associated with it grow exponentially.

There are two elements of quantum mechanics that play into the story of the Mirror. The first is quantum entanglement, which posits that what happens in one place can affect what happens in another place instantaneously over any distance, including across the universe. It happens at a subatomic level. When two particles, such as a pair of photons or electrons, become entangled, they remain connected even when separated by vast distances.

A common misconception about entanglement is that the particles are communicating with each other faster than the speed of light, which would go against Einstein's special theory of relativity. Experiments have shown that this is not true, nor can quantum physics be used to send faster-than-light communications. Though scientists still debate how the seemingly bizarre phenomenon of entanglement arises, they know it is a real principle that passes test after test. In fact, while Einstein famously described entanglement as "spooky action at a distance," today's quantum scientists say there is nothing spooky about it.

While all of this is happening at an atomic and subatomic level, *Furniture Sliders* proposes that it is happening at a human level. Could a human be in two places at once, yet be interconnected in such a way that what happens to one incarnation happens to the other? And what happens when you have multiple incarnations?

This brings in the second element of quantum mechanics: superposition. The concept of quantum superposition might be difficult to understand or visualize. Many descriptions have been used to try to describe it. One is the analogy of a coin that is both heads up and tails up at the same time—a blended state where the coin is in multiple states until observed at which time it becomes one or the other. Another illustration is the famous Schrödinger's cat thought experiment, in which physicist Erwin Schrödinger imagined placing a cat in a sealed box along with a poisonous substance that has an equal chance of killing the cat— or not—within an hour. Schrödinger proposed that, at the end of the hour, the cat could be said to be both alive and dead, in a superposition of states, until the box is opened, and that the act of observation randomly determines whether the cat is alive or dead. Schrödinger intended this example to demonstrate what he saw as the absurdity of quantum science. But superposition is a major characteristic of quantum mechanics. In the quantum world, particles can exist in a superposition of multiple states simultaneously until they are observed or measured, at which point they "collapse" into one specific state.

When applied to the Mirror, the concept of superposition explains how the device manipulates time and reality in a way that seems impossible under normal conditions. The Mirror exploits the principles of superposition to create multiple potential timelines or temporal realities that exist in parallel, allowing it to influence or access multiple points in time without being constrained to a single path. The temporal slides that Sliders experience are influenced by superposition, where the Mirror creates multiple potential pathways in time for them to travel along. These temporal states are not fixed but exist as overlapping possibilities until the moment of the slide occurs. Sliders experience this as moving through layers of time, each one with its own set of events, people, and circumstances.

This explains the fluidity of time that sliders experience when using the Mirror—why sometimes events seem to shift unpredictably, or why the temporal landscape feels fragmented, as the Mirror weaves together different temporal threads before settling on a final one.

One of the most fascinating implications of applying superposition to the Mirror is the idea that it could access multiple realities at once. With superposition in play, the Mirror's function extends beyond simple temporal navigation. Instead of following a single, fixed timeline, the Mirror can manipulate a quantum field of time, where countless potential futures and past events exist in parallel. By using the principles of superposition, the Mirror can travel through this quantum time field, collapsing reality into a single path but with endless possibilities before it does so. The Mirror can calculate, adjust, and collapse multiple realities simultaneously, allowing it to manipulate time in a way that traditional technology cannot. The parallel realities and multiple possible futures that arise from this concept make the Mirror not just a time machine but a device capable of accessing and altering the quantum fabric of time, with far-reaching consequences for those who interact with it.

QUANTUM MECHANICS AND PANPSYCHISM

Panpsychism argues that consciousness is not limited to peoples' brains or to living organisms but extends to all aspects of the universe. The word itself was coined by the Italian philosopher Francesco Patrizi in the sixteenth century, and derives from the two Greek words pan (all) and psyche (soul or mind). Panpsychism is a philosophical view that posits consciousness, or a mind-like aspect, as a fundamental and ubiquitous feature of all reality. It suggests that everything, from humans to rocks and even subatomic particles (or Mirrors!), possesses some level of consciousness. This idea challenges the traditional belief that only living beings have consciousness.

Philosophers like Plato have been associated with panpsychistic ideas. Recent interest in panpsychism has been fueled by the hard problem of understanding consciousness, by developments in neuroscience, by quantum mechanics, and a growing dissatisfaction with physicalist and classic approaches to consciousness.

It can be shown that a conscious being can distinguish definite perceptions and their quantum superpositions, while a physical measuring system without consciousness cannot distinguish such states. In particular, it suggests that consciousness is not emergent but a fundamental feature of the universe.

There are many objections to the idea of panpsychism. Mostly around the lack of empirical proof. However, the following academic paper does explore the whole idea of quantum providing a basis for panpsychism.

A Quantum Physical Argument for Panpsychism

Shan Gao

History & Philosophy of Science & Centre for Time,
University of Sydney,
NSW 2006, Australia.
Institute for the History of Natural Sciences,
Chinese Academy of Sciences,
Beijing 100190, P. R. China.

ALAN TURING AND THE MIRROR

Alan Turing's involvement in *Furniture Sliders* and with the Mirror are entirely fictional. Based on this fictional involvement, he does, however, provide a notable storyline thread throughout the book. Turing was one of the most brilliant minds of the 20th century and his contributions in so many areas cannot be over-emphasized or over-stated. He was a pioneer in cryptography, computational theory, and artificial intelligence, making him an ideal candidate to have contributed in some way to the development of a fictional time-bending device like the Mirror in the *Furniture Sliders* universe.

While Turing did not work on time manipulation or any similar technologies in his lifetime, his expertise in cryptography, computing, and his groundbreaking ideas on machines and mathematical logic made his involvement with a fictional device like the Mirror plausible in a speculative or alternate-history narrative. Turing's work on the Turing Machine, a theoretical model for a computer, focused on the idea of algorithmic computation. This was the idea that any complex process can be broken down into simple, definable steps and it was revolutionary. In the fictional context, the Mirror could be conceived as a highly advanced computational device that breaks down and manipulates time, with Turing's concept of a machine capable of performing endless calculations at its core.

In *Furniture Sliders* Turing is portrayed as the theoretical mind that helped Hawthorne in his quest for a time-manipulation device that uses advanced computational principles to "process" time itself as data. His work in computational theories could be extrapolated to posit that time is not a linear progression but rather a calculable system that can be understood and manipulated in a similar way to how he understood and manipulated algorithms. In *Furniture Sliders*, Turing was a key figure in deciphering and cracking the mechanisms behind the Mirror's operation, in the same way that he had cracked the Enigma codes to reveal hidden intelligence during the war. This led to his strong fear of what the Mirror was and could achieve, and why he walked away from it giving Hawthorne warnings about what it might be capable of doing.

Turing's work on the Turing Test, which involves evaluating whether a machine can exhibit intelligent behavior indistinguishable from human actions, likely contributed to the creation of the artificial intelligence systems within the Mirror. Following the panpsychism theory, the Mirror was described as having its own "consciousness"—an evolving artificial intelligence that is capable of manipulating time and interpreting the effects of time travel or temporal anomalies. *Furniture Sliders* portrays Turing as trying to determine whether the Mirror's time-manipulating effects were self-aware or whether it was just an advanced mechanical tool. It added an additional layer of intrigue to the device, making it not just a time-altering mechanism, but also a philosophical puzzle.

Turing, in real life, faced the ethical dilemma of being involved in technology that could change the course of history. In the *Furniture Sliders* fictional narrative, Turing's involvement with the Mirror raised moral questions about manipulating time, the potential risks of altering reality, and whether such power should ever be placed in the hands of governments, scientists, or individuals. Turing's own internal conflict about his involvement with such a device added depth to his character and motivations, reflecting his historical conflict over his own government's treatment of him and his moral compass.

WITH THANKS

I owe a huge debt of gratitude to everyone around me who has put up with the disruption caused by my journey as an author. Although I have written a lot in the past, this is my first novel that combines espionage and science fiction with a heavy dose of film noir. There is a massive amount of research to get even minute details right, such as the popular bars frequented by suspicious characters in Hell's Kitchen, New York, in 1947 at the beginning of the Cold War. These days, it is slightly easier to check some of the facts, but nevertheless, it is time-consuming. The research notes end up being bigger than the final book!

My wife, Lucinda has been extremely encouraging, especially as I have added author to tech entrepreneur, company founder, and advisor to tech company CEOs. However, it has been a long-held desire to take stories and ideas I have had for a long time and translate them into a novel, particularly those based around my fascination with computing and quantum mechanics.

For any book, proofreaders and editors play a major role in making sure the novel hangs together and reads well. A big thank you to those who helped here too including Hannah and especially Carson from the great state of Texas.

ABOUT THE AUTHOR

Alexander Bentley is a serial entrepreneur living in California, with experience founding and leading technology companies in both the UK and the USA. He has held senior roles, including CEO, in both public and private enterprises. Over the years, he has had many technology and security-related interactions with the government, the UK Ministry of Defence, the US Department of Defense, and many aerospace and defense companies. His own technology companies have included those that address the secure communications and networking markets. Additionally, with a physics background, he is very familiar with the principles of quantum mechanics and quantum computing.

Writing under the name Alexander Bentley, he is married to Lucinda and has two grown children, Alexander (Lex) and Virginia (Ginny).

Furniture Sliders is Alexander's first Spy-Fi novel, which entangles the world of espionage with science fiction, bringing a new approach to post-World War II noir writing.